DEVIL OF THE HIGH SEAS

PIRATES OF KING'S LANDING

BOOK III

LAUREN SMITH

This book is a work of fiction. Names, characters, places, and incidents are the product of the author's imagination or are used fictitiously. Any resemblance to actual events, locales, or persons, living or dead, is coincidental.

ISBN: 978-1-958196-13-7 (e-book edition)

ISBN: 978-1-958196-14-4 (trade paperback edition)

PROLOGUE

1735 Cornwall, England

GAVIN CASTLETON ADJUSTED HIS BOTTLE-GREEN FROCK coat and glanced about the crowded ballroom. His parents were occupied with guests and would not look for him for a little while. He quickly escaped the crush of dancers currently swirling around the floor and slipped out a back door into the gardens of his family's grand manor house, Castleton Hall.

Strains of music drifted through the perfumed gardens, lending the spring night an air of magic and romance that even he, a young man of nineteen, could appreciate. His eyes searched the twilight and caught a glimpse of shimmery silken skirts vanishing around a tall row of hedges.

She was here. She had come as he had asked. His heart leapt with joy. Tonight . . . tonight he would ask her the question that would change both their lives forever.

Gavin's heart pounded with excitement as he pursued the woman who had owned his soul for the last two years.

"Charity," he whispered as he stalked his love. This was a game they had played many times since they were seventeen. Chases and kisses in the garden. He heard a soft giggle as he rounded yet another hedge, glimpsing her skirts disappearing once more around a corner of the elaborate hedgerows. The long, flowing train of her sack-back gown was tempting him. He wanted to catch her, to get his hands under those skirts, just as he had done so many times before.

"Got you!" he gasped in delight as he caught her from behind. Charity chuckled and then moaned as he placed soft kisses upon her neck.

"Oh yes . . . please . . . yes," she encouraged as he began to pull up her voluminous skirts. "Please, take me here, Griffin."

Gavin froze, his hands falling from her skirts. "*Griffin?*" His head began to fill with an odd buzzing sound.

Charity spun in his arms, her lovely face a mask of confusion and then shame. "Gavin? I didn't—I thought you were . . ."

"I know who you thought I was," he said softly, as his heart fractured in half. "How long have you preferred my brother to me?"

Her brows arched up in confusion. "How long?"

"How long has Griffin been courting you?"

"Almost the same length of time that you've been courting me. You and I never agreed to be—"

"To be true to one another?" Gavin finished, his tone icy now as he felt like a stranger in his own skin.

"You never asked me to be, Gavin. You haven't even proposed yet." Charity frowned at him. "I will not let you make me feel guilty. I have a right to be courted by anyone until I accept a proposal."

Gavin had been planning to ask her to marry him tonight, but he wasn't going to tell her that. Not now.

"And my brother? Has he asked you to marry him?" Gavin demanded.

"I was going to this evening." Griffin's voice came from behind them. Gavin's twin brother was younger than him by a mere six minutes, and they were all but identical in appearance. Only someone who knew them well could see the minute differences in their features.

"So, what's it to be, my lady?" Gavin asked Charity, unable to keep the contempt from his voice. He loved his brother fiercely, but this . . . this felt like a betrayal. He had been the first to meet Charity two years ago when her family had moved here from London. It had been love, wild love. She wasn't simply beautiful. She was bold, carefree, intelligent. She'd made him want to be a better man, someone worthy of marrying her. He had told Griffin the day he'd met her that he would marry her someday. He'd always known Charity was going to be his. But oh, how wrong he had been.

"I . . ." She looked between them, her eyes pooling with tears. He knew her well enough to know that those tears were genuine. He could see in her face that now she realized her actions had torn apart the bond of brothers, and she regretted it.

"Oh, Gavin," she whispered, and he knew then that *he*

was not the one she would choose. *He* was not the one she would spend her life with.

Gavin shifted his gaze from her face to his brother's. Griffin looked stricken, as if he could feel the pain tearing through Gavin's soul. As twins, they had shared a thousand secrets between them and had always been able to sense each other's feelings.

"Brother, wait—" Griffin began.

"No," Gavin snapped. "No, Griffin. No." He turned and fled. He could not stay and see them together without his heart shattering any further. It felt as though a cannonball had blasted through his chest. His very soul was obliterated. He staggered back toward the house. He avoided the ballroom and the merry guests as he rushed up to his bedchamber. He slammed the door and leaned back against it, trying to control the horrible realization that now presented itself to him.

Charity would marry Griffin, and they would live here . . . or perhaps at Meadow Cross Cottage, but they would be here all the same. Gavin would someday take his father's title as the Earl of Castleton, but that title and its privileges were nothing in the face of living without the woman he loved.

Leave . . . The single word whispered dangerously in the back of his mind.

Leave . . . Never look back . . .

Could he do that? Could he abandon his parents and his twin? If it meant escaping the pain in his chest now, what choice did he have?

Without another thought, he fetched a traveling case

and began to fill it with clothing before he emptied a box of coins into a leather pouch and tied it to his belt.

When he opened his bedchamber door, he found his brother standing there, his hand raised as if to knock.

Griffin halted at the sight of him clutching the travel case of belongings. "You're leaving?"

"Yes." It was the only word he could manage.

"I didn't want to love her," Griffin said, equally at a loss for words.

"But you love her anyway," Gavin said.

"At first, I think I loved her because *you* loved her. I suppose that's because we're twins. But then I began to love her because of my own heart's desires. I told her tonight that she should choose you, take the title of countess, and live here. It is what she deserves."

"And did she agree?" Gavin knew the answer when Griffin's face fell.

"She still chose me."

"Then take her and the bloody title," Gavin said, his tone sharp. "Take it all. I am dead to you, brother. Take everything, because I have nothing left."

"Gavin, please. That is ridiculous. I cannot take the title even if I wished to, which I don't," he shot back.

"If I'm considered dead, Father will still have his heir to the title. You will never see me again." He pushed past his twin to leave the room, but then paused, his voice softening. "Tell Mother I love her, and Father too. Tell them I'm sorry and that the better son will stay here and be the heir they need."

Griffin caught his arm when he tried to leave again.

"Gavin, no matter what happens between us, this will always be your home. Always."

I love you too, brother. Always. But I cannot stay with a broken heart.

This time Griffin didn't stop him as Gavin slipped away. Soon he was gone from his home and headed toward the sea and the uncertain future that awaited him. Thunder rumbled in the distance, signaling an approaching storm.

CHAPTER 1

1742 – Seven years later
Cornwall, England

There was nothing worse than being the little sister of a notorious pirate.

Josephine Greyville hid in the shadows of the ballroom, watching her brother, Dominic, and his bride, Roberta, as they danced. Envy and longing struck her like a bolt fired by a powerful crossbow.

Josephine wanted to have a life of adventure like Dominic. He had gone to sea for fourteen years and had seen the world, and according to their mother, he'd caused a fair bit of trouble too . . . being a notorious pirate, after all. Adventure was all Josephine had ever wanted . . . and something she could never have. Gentleborn ladies could not run away to sea and become *pirates*.

At eighteen, she was more than old enough to marry and yet too young to experience life the way she wished. And she was a woman. Her twin brother, Adrian, had far more opportunities than she ever would because she had to wear skirts and play the part fate had assigned to her as an earl's daughter.

Not that she minded a lovely dress, like the green silk ballgown she wore now. The cream panels of her underskirt and the gold bodice embroidered with swirling patterns were exquisite. She felt beautiful when she wore such gowns, but what did beauty matter when life was without excitement and joy? Men simply didn't understand how trapped a woman could feel in a life restricted to domestic activities with no chance to do anything else.

Already her life felt as though it was ending. Tonight she was at the fine estate of the handsome Earl of Castleton, where she was to be presented to him as his future bride.

"There you are, my little love." Her mother, Lucia, had discovered Josephine's hiding place behind a Grecian statue. Lucia was a wonderful mother, a fiery Spanish beauty who held her own against her dashing husband, Aaron, Josephine's father, the Earl of Camden.

"Hello, Mother," Josephine sighed.

Her mother caught her chin and turned Josephine to face her. "What is it? You look like you've been crying."

She had, but she didn't want to admit it. She gently pulled away from her. "I'm all right."

"Your father has spoken to Lord Castleton, and the engagement has been settled. Your dowry has also been agreed upon. I thought you might like to dance with Lord Castleton now that the papers have been signed."

"Must I go through with this?" she asked in a desperate whisper.

Her mother's brown eyes softened. "Lord Castleton is young and handsome, but he is also a good man, my little love. He has been a good neighbor to us for many years, and he is lonely. This is a *good* match, better than anyone you would find in London. When you marry him, you'll live here, just beside our home, so Father and I will be close by, and you will be free to visit us and bring the grandchildren as well."

Children? She was too young to think of children and settling down.

"Come and dance with your betrothed." Lucia gently extricated Josephine from her hiding place and escorted her to a tall man in a fine burgundy frock coat who was watching his guests dance.

Lord Castleton was undoubtedly a handsome man. At twenty-six, he was the master of one of the wealthiest estates along the coast of Cornwall. His family and hers had shared a border for more than a century. With warm brown eyes and rich brown hair pulled back into a queue and tied with a burgundy ribbon, Castleton was the sort of man every woman would dream of marrying. His features had been perfectly carved by envious angels, but a hint of a tragic air hung about him. She knew he had been married as a younger man to a woman he had loved. She had perished in childbirth, along with the son she'd been carrying, and he had not married again. It moved her heart in his direction, even though this life was not the one she wanted.

"Lord Castleton, I have found her," Lucia said with a warm chuckle. "She was hiding behind a statue in the corner."

"Mother!" Josephine hissed.

Lord Castleton had a bemused smile on his lips as he bowed over Josephine's hand.

"I hope that I'm not so frightening as all that?" There was a teasing in his eyes that eased the flutter of nerves inside Josephine. His lips were warm on her knuckles, and she wished she could fall in love with him, live in this beautiful house and raise beautiful children with him.

But no matter how hard she wished for it, it didn't come true.

"Would you like to dance?" he asked.

Josephine nodded. One could not refuse a gentleman a dance, certainly not one she was soon to marry.

Lord Castleton tucked her arm in his and escorted her to the center of the ballroom. The quartet of musicians had just finished a song and were whispering, their powdered wigs bent as they spoke to one another. Then, as if deciding upon the next song, they raised their bows and began to play a lovely tune. Castleton spun her in his arms as the dance began, and she found she was able, briefly, to forget her fate. She passed by Dominic and Roberta as she twirled in Castleton's arms, and her older brother winked at her.

She adored Dominic and was so glad he was finally home. She and Adrian had been mere babes when Dominic had run away to sea. They had been too young to truly remember him, but they'd grown up with stories of him their entire lives. He had only been fourteen when he'd left, and he'd become one of the fiercest pirates of this new age. Not that Josephine or her family had known that about him until last year. To the rest of the world, he had been missing for almost fifteen years. Her parents had been brokenhearted every one of those years during his absence.

She would never forget that fine spring day last year when he'd come through the front door of their home. She'd taken one look at the darkly handsome man and had seen her long-lost brother. She'd flung herself into his arms, so glad to have him home. Her father had shared Dominic's tale with her, but Josephine knew that he had left many of the details out because of her supposedly delicate ears. Adrian knew more than she did about Dominic's life as a pirate, and it was the first time in their shared lives as twins that he had refused to tell her everything he knew.

Josephine had always been interested in pirates. As a daughter of Cornwall, she had the sea in her blood. She knew all about Blackbeard, Kidd, Bonnet, and other infamous pirates of the golden age, perhaps even more than Adrian did, but discussing pirates with other young ladies over tea was frowned upon, to say the least.

Castleton's voice intruded upon her straying thoughts. "What are you thinking about?"

"Pirates," she replied before she'd given her response proper thought.

She bravely met his gaze, expecting some kind of reproach, but his eyes only sharpened with curiosity.

"Indeed? And what about them holds your rapt attention?"

They continued to dance, and she bit her lip before responding. "They have grand adventures in faraway places." That was safe enough of an answer. She wasn't about to confess that what she truly envied was their freedom. Oh, to have the freedom to live outside the authority of others . . .

"You remind me of someone I loved long ago. They were fascinated with pirates and stories of buried treasure as well." Castleton smiled, the expression somehow enhanced by his sorrow.

"Was that your first wife?" she dared to ask.

"No, my brother."

The music ended, and she stumbled. "You have a brother?" Had she known that Castleton had a brother? She racked her memory but couldn't seem to recall having ever been told that. She had never met Castleton's brother, and no one had ever mentioned him to her. She was quite certain of that.

"I did. He's been gone for seven years now." Castleton's tone was heavy with old remembered pain. "Come, let me escort you to dinner."

And just like that, the discussion of his brother ended, and she didn't dare press him on it, though she did guess that if by "gone" he meant "dead."

The evening's festivities turned to the dining hall, which seated thirty guests at a large pair of tables. Wine flowed freely and everyone seemed to be enjoying themselves, everyone except Josephine. She had no appetite and quietly slipped away from the dining hall, making some excuse as to feeling a little ill.

She wandered through the candlelit corridor and

paused by a tall window that overlooked the drive leading up to the house.

Lightning suddenly illuminated the world outside, and she stepped back from the glass at the blinding flash. Her heart leapt into her throat at the violent crash of thunder that followed an instant later. It was only a storm. She liked storms, but that crash had been very close to the house.

When lightning flashed a second time, she gasped as a figure loomed out of the darkness behind her, briefly reflected in the window glass. She whirled around, but no one was there. The hall was empty, save for a painting that hung on the paneled wall opposite her and the window.

It was a large portrait, but despite its size, there was an intimacy to the subject and how he had been painted. She recognized the man immediately. It was her future husband.

Then Josephine silently corrected herself. No, that was not him. There were minute differences in the features. It would have been easy to assume the painter had simply failed to paint the subject exactly, but when she read the name beneath, she knew her suspicions were correct.

The small gold plaque under the portrait read: *Gavin Castleton, 1735*. Gavin, not Griffin. This was Castleton's brother. They must have been twins, just like her and Adrian, only Griffin and Gavin must be identical.

Gavin . . . The name caused the hairs on her arms to rise. This was Castleton's brother. Given the year on the plaque, she guessed he had to have been around nineteen when it was painted. A year older than she was now . . .

"He's a handsome fellow, isn't he?" a deep voice said, and Josephine jumped.

Her brother Dominic stood a few feet away, studying the portrait with her. "I knew Gavin when we were younger. He was a good sort of fellow, but a bit wild . . . like me." Dominic smiled at some old memory, and Josephine's heart ached. She hated being so young sometimes. Dominic had had an entire life while she'd been a child on leading strings. It was the same with Lord Castleton. He was twenty-six, though that wasn't terribly far from her in age given that many women her age married men in their forties. Yet when she was around Lord Castleton, there seemed to be an ancient pain inside him that put a century between him and her.

"What happened to him?" she asked.

"No one is quite sure. He and Griffin quarreled one night during a ball much like tonight, and Gavin left. He simply vanished."

She scowled at her older brother. "You're trying to frighten me." Dominic gave her a curious look that she couldn't quite read, and she had the strangest sense that he wasn't telling her everything.

"I would never want to frighten you, little butterfly," Dominic said quite seriously, using his brotherly pet name for her. "It's true. Gavin was never seen in this house again. Some think he drowned in floodwaters, others think he was murdered by footpads, but . . ."

"But what?" She took hold of her brother's arm. "What, Dom?"

"*I think* he went to the sea, like me," Dominic said quietly, as if thinking deeply on the matter. The way he said *I think* sounded strange, though, as if he was more certain than uncertain.

"But he never came back. He must be gone." She didn't say *dead*. Somehow she could not put that word to the man in the painting. Even the oil on the canvas seemed to breathe in that quiet candlelit corridor while the storm continued to rage outside.

"Not all men lost at sea are dead . . . some are simply lost," Dominic said. For the first time since her older brother had miraculously returned, she saw some of the darkness he must have faced in those fourteen years he'd been away from home.

"Then he might return someday?" she asked, her tone as quiet as her brother's now.

"That depends," Dominic said.

"On what?"

"Sometimes all a man needs is light to find his way to shore, but not everyone is looking for that light. Some men stay trapped in the dark."

She and Dominic stared up at Gavin Castleton's portrait until a crash of thunder shook the house.

Dominic put an arm around her shoulders. "Come, Josie, let's go return to dinner."

She let her brother lead her to the dining room, but she had the strangest feeling that the eyes in Gavin's portrait followed her. Her brother's words echoed over and over in her head.

Not all men lost at sea are dead . . . some are simply lost . . .

Off the coast of Cornwall

"*Cap'n!*" Ronald Phelps bellowed through the storm. "Look out!"

Gavin Castleton leapt out of the way as a member of his own crew tried to slice him with a scimitar. The quarterdeck of his ship, the *Lady Siren*, was overflowing with battling pirates. Gavin swung his own blade, catching the nearest man in the arm and slicing through his biceps. The man's howl of pain was swallowed by the raging sea and a clap of thunder overhead.

Beauchamp and his men had been fools to start their mutiny in the middle of a storm. Men were being tossed over the sides every few seconds as grayish-black waves of furious water surged over the decks. The *Lady Siren* was a strong ship, a fast ship, but in such a squall, unmanned like this, she would break her masts and founder on the distant rocks.

"Ronnie!" he bellowed at his quartermaster. The red-haired man waved a blade before stabbing a man in the stomach and kicking him over the side.

"Cap'n?" he called back.

"Abandon ship!" Gavin ordered.

The quartermaster took the order and began to cut a path to the small dinghy that a loyal few men were attempting to lower into the water. Gavin had one goal: save the *Siren*. The only way he could do that was to leave her. Beauchamp was a fair sailor and could right the ship before the storm capsized her, but that meant he would have to stop trying to kill Gavin, and the only way that would happen was if Gavin wasn't on board. The day was Beauchamp's, damn his eyes.

Someday he would find his way back to his ship, and when he did, he would kill every man who'd dared to take her from him. He was the bloody Admiral of the Black, leader of the pirate fleet in the Caribbean. There would be consequences with the Brethren of the Coast for such a mutiny.

"Castleton!" Beauchamp shouted in challenge as he started toward Gavin. The usurper was not as tall as Gavin, but he was built as thick as a bull. He held two blades and swung them effortlessly, even though the deck pitched beneath them. Gavin tightened his grip on his own blade.

"We offered to maroon you," Beauchamp called and flashed his yellow teeth in a grimace of a smile.

"And I politely *declined* that offer," he reminded his enemy. "Ronnie and I rather objected to being stranded together on an island with one pistol and one bullet between us."

Beauchamp lunged, both of his swords raised. Gavin braced himself and used his short sword at an angle to parry Beauchamp's blades in a mighty clash. All he had to do was survive long enough for Ronnie to get the dinghy in the water. Beauchamp caught him in the shoulder with the tip of one blade. It sank deep enough for a fiery pain to radiate through Gavin's body. But Gavin arced his blade in the air, nearly finding its mark and forcing the other pirate to step back, wrenching the blade from Gavin's shoulder.

Beauchamp advanced again, swinging fast at Gavin, who retreated a step. But as he did so, he caught a loose rope from the mainsail and hoisted himself into the air with his good arm and danced out of the other man's reach just as a wave rolled over the deck. Gavin escaped the dangerous wave, but Beauchamp was not so lucky. The black water knocked him onto the deck, and he slammed into several crates that were tied down against a railing. They were the only thing that kept the mutineer from washing over the side.

Some bastards have all the bloody luck.

Gavin dropped back onto the deck, noting that the fight had died down.

"Ronnie?". Ronnie was nowhere in sight, nor was the dinghy or the rest of his crew who'd defended him in the mutiny. Gavin could only pray that meant his quartermaster had gotten the boat into the water. The remaining mutineers now converged on Gavin in a semicircle, trapping him with his back to the railing on the waist deck of the ship.

"Kill him!" Beauchamp ordered as he climbed to his feet. "Send him to Davy Jones!"

Gavin couldn't stay on the *Siren*, but he wasn't a man to turn and run, especially not from something he loved. The *Lady Siren* was his mistress, his love, his very soul. She had been the thing to save him all those years ago when he had fled home with a broken heart. And now he was forced to leave her in the hands of his enemies.

"By all means, jump—the sea will kill you for me," Beauchamp sneered as he joined the circle of men who had Gavin surrounded.

Gavin glanced at the distant shore behind him, seeing a familiar cliff face and a distant house whose lights flickered through the storm.

"Oh, Beauchamp, that was always your problem. You

forget, I've been dead for seven years. You can't kill a ghost!"

With that, he dove over the side of the ship. The water rose up in a dark wall to meet him, and with his arms pointed above his head, he cut through it with the ease of a boy who had learned to swim and dive in fathomless stormy waters like these.

As the water swirled and crashed around him, he kicked and swam until he broke the surface. He glimpsed the outline of the dinghy rolling on the waves and started toward it. As expected, Beauchamp and his men now rushed to tack the sails and guide the *Lady Siren* away from the rocky coastline of Cornwall. When Gavin at last reached the dinghy, Ronnie helped pull him over the side.

"Christ, Cap'n, you're hurt." Ronnie reached for Gavin's shoulder, but Gavin held up his hand.

"Where are the others?" He'd expected to see at least a few of his loyal crew on the boat with Ronnie.

"Lost 'em. They helped me get the boat in the water, then turned to fight to give you time to escape. A wave took them overboard."

Gavin said a quiet prayer to the sea, asking for peace for the men who'd perished in his defense.

"Let's get to shore. Scavenger crews watch for ships to wreck on this stretch of beach. We could be killed if we're spotted on the shore for long, even if we have nothing worth stealing."

"You know this bit of land?"

"Aye, Ronnie, I do, it's . . . a place I've been to many times." The word *home* almost left his lips. But this hadn't been his home for a very long time.

They rowed the dinghy in the direction Gavin gave. Once they were just out of reach of the waves rolling in, Gavin urged Ronald to stop rowing.

"What do we do now, Cap'n?" Ronald asked. He wheezed a little as he breathed. As a man in his late forties, he'd seen and done much as a sailor, and Gavin was fortunate to call him a loyal friend.

"You must go to town and find a crew for me, and then a ship. Then we'll go after Beauchamp and get the *Siren* back."

"Right," Ronnie said. "What are my orders?"

"Row down the coast until you see a trail up the cliffs. It will take you into a village if you follow the path. There's an inn on the edge of town, the Stag Antlers. Tell Mary McGiver, the woman who runs it, that you're an old friend of mine. She'll know to take care of you. I'll be in touch with you soon. I have something to tend to first." Gavin stared at the cave entrance.

Ronnie followed his gaze. "What do you have to do, Cap'n?"

"I must see my brother. Then, when all is prepared, you and I will be off." He handed Ronnie a bag of coins that he always kept tied to his belt. "Be careful and wait for me in the village."

"Aye, aye, Cap'n," Ronnie said.

Gavin slipped off the side of the boat and rode the waves toward the shore so Ronnie could keep rowing away. Once he reached the cliff face and the hidden cave entrance, he stopped and touched his shoulder, his fingers coming away soaked in blood. There was a chance, he realized grimly, that he would not rendezvous with Ronnie in the village at all. And if that was the case, he wanted to see his brother one last time. There were things that lay heavy upon his heart, and he needed to unburden himself.

Whatever happened after that? Only fate and the sea could tell.

CHAPTER 2

Josephine lay in the large bed, a candle lit on her bedside table as she stared unseeing at the pages of a very dull book in front of her. She'd chosen the book to put her to sleep, and somehow it was so dull it failed even at that simple task. Outside the storm continued, but the wind had ceased to rattle the windows, at least. After a long moment, she gave up and blew out the candle.

She burrowed deeper into the blankets and thought of how tonight had not at all gone as she had expected. Dancing, dinner, and then the storm arriving, which had kept her at Lord Castleton's estate. Now she was in an unfamiliar bed in that home that would never feel like hers. Was this to be her future? To live in this house, sleep in a bed that didn't feel like hers, and pretend to be someone she wasn't?

That was nonsense, of course. The storm had forced all of Lord Castleton's guests to remain for the night.

Everyone was likely as uncomfortable as she was, being so far from their homes.

Yet she couldn't escape the reality of the one thought that was keeping her awake. When she married Lord Castleton, she would have to find a way to settle into his life here, wouldn't she? This would be her new home, her new life. Everything she was used to would no longer be hers.

She didn't blame Lord Castleton for her discomfort. How could she? He had been a consummate gentleman all evening. He'd even escorted her to her chambers, explaining that these had been his chambers as a lad before his father had died and he'd moved into the opposite wing of the house. He'd wished her a good night and pressed a kiss to her hand.

With a hiss of frustration, she flipped onto her back and stared up at the ceiling, trying to will herself to fall asleep.

A sudden thump against the door made her tense. Was someone attempting to barge into her room? Or was she imagining things? Old homes creaked and groaned often. Surely a thump or two during a storm was normal? The handle of the door suddenly turned with a soft squeak, and the door opened to the darkened corridor beyond.

Josephine lay motionless, terrified, as a dark figure lurched toward the bed. She must have fallen asleep, and now she was having a nightmare. She'd always been afraid of ghosts, and this must be a ghost.

A hand clamped hard on her shoulder, giving her a violent shake.

"Griffin . . . ," a deep voice groaned. "Griff . . . *help* . . ."

The figure slumped to the floor next to the four-poster bed.

This was no ghost. It was a man, a man seeking her future husband. Her fear vanished and she leapt into action. She located the flint box and managed to light a lamp rather than a candle so she could better see the unexpected visitor. She carried the light around to where the man sat up against the post of the bed frame .

"Who are you?" She bent forward, trying to peer at his face, and then gasped. It was Castleton . . . but not Castleton. In a flash, she realized it must be Lord Castleton's long-lost brother. *Gavin*.

"Where's . . . Griffin?" She could barely hear the man's breathless words.

"Griffin? You mean Lord Castleton?"

The man winced. "Aye, bloody Lord Castleton." He then collapsed onto his back on the floor. It was then she saw the blood soaking his left shoulder.

"Oh heavens! You're injured." She set the lamp on the table by the bed and touched her hand to his forehead and cheek, trying to see if he was fevered. His eyes were half fogged with pain as he stared up at her. Eyes that matched Lord Castleton's. Yet when she looked into those eyes, Josephine felt like she was falling from the cliffside. She sucked in a breath as something deep within her shifted. She knew in that moment she would do anything to save him.

She laid him flat on his back and brought the lamp down on the floor next to him. He was pale, and blood soaked his shoulder. Josephine thankfully had a strong stomach, so she peeled back his torn shirt to better see the wound. It was a fairly deep gash, as though someone had stabbed him with a blade. How had he gotten such an injury? She needed to wake Griffin and have him send for a doctor.

Gavin moaned and his lashes fluttered weakly. Somehow, she felt his pain deep within herself.

"Please hold on. I will wake your brother and summon a doctor." She brushed her fingertips over his brow in an attempt to comfort him. His hand shot up, catching her arm before she could leave. His long, strong fingers curled around her wrist in a shockingly tight hold, given his wounded state. He stared at her more clear-eyed than he had been moments before.

"No doctor—no one must know. *Please* . . ." The first part of his words were a clear command, but the way he said *please* was a plea she could not ignore.

"Why?" Josephine asked. She was not nor would she ever be a person who just did something she was told to without knowing why.

Gavin's eyes seemed to stay on her for a long time as he replied in a quiet tone, "Because everyone here believes me dead, and it needs to stay that way."

Josephine thought of what Dominic had said about Gavin going to sea and being lost. If he'd pretended to die, or let that rumor spread, it would have given him a relative amount of freedom to live his life the way he wished, just like Dominic had.

"Are you a pirate?" she asked.

His lips twitched in a weary hint of a smile. "Aye, that I am. A feared, lawless pirate. It's best if you stay away from me. Once I'm better, I'll be gone."

She tried to hide the flicker of excitement that gave her. "Well, that is ridiculous. I'm not the least bit afraid of pirates. I know quite a few."

Gavin arched a brow. "Do you now, lass?"

"Yes," Josephine replied primly. "Now, if you don't want a doctor, someone still has to tend to your wound. Why don't you sit on the bed?"

"No, I cannot be seen here. There is a room . . . back the way I came. It has a bed. I can rest there without anyone discovering I'm here." He finally released her wrist.

"All right, but you'll have to show me." She grasped his hand on his uninjured side and helped him to his feet. "Put your arm around my shoulder."

He did so, and she felt the cold seawater on his skin and the briny roughness of drying salt on his clothing. She would need to get him out of those wet clothes before they stiffened, and she didn't want anything rubbing against his wound that might aggravate it.

They moved out of her bedchamber and through the corridor. Gavin pointed to something ahead of them.

"There . . . behind the tapestry, there's a door in the paneling." Gavin told her where to press against the wood, and a hidden door swung open. They ducked under the tapestry and walked through a tunnel until they reached a darkened room. A distant light came from somewhere on the opposite side from the way they'd entered. It looked like the entrance to another tunnel that led downward.

"Here. The bed should be . . . here." Gavin sank down, dragging her with him as he collapsed onto something she couldn't see in the dark. A cloud of dust billowed up, sending Josephine into a coughing fit. She fought to stifle the sound, lest anyone outside this room hear her.

She felt her way around the room. She thought she glimpsed a table with an oil lamp in the dim light. Stumbling over the rocky floor in her bare feet, she stubbed her toe and cursed up a storm at the flash of unexpected pain.

Gavin's rusty chuckle came from behind her in the dark. "Where did a lady like you learn such words?"

"My brothers," she replied. "Now where *exactly* are we?"

"In a secret chamber at the top of the cave entrance."

"Cave? That must be why I can smell the sea. Is that where the light is coming from? I assume it leads to the beach?" One could always smell the sea when one lived on the coast, but it was more powerful here, as if she stood just inches from the water.

"Yes, there is a cave at the base of the cliffs below that leads up here."

"Is your ship outside in the storm?" She bumped into the table and felt around for the lamp and match, along with a flint and steel striker. She lit the brimstone-coated match with the striker and set the lamp.

"No . . . my ship is gone." Gavin's tone warned her not to inquire further.

When she turned to face him with the lamp in her hand, she saw that he now sat on an old bed that was low to the floor and covered with dusty sheets.

"You can't sleep on that!"

"Why not? It's a bed like any other." He seemed completely unbothered by the condition of the bed and the old sheets.

"Stay here." She left the lamp on the table and exited

the secret chamber. The house was so quiet, despite the distant rumbling of the passing storm. It felt as though everyone else in the grand estate had vanished and only she and Gavin were here. It was . . . intimate, but in a way she'd never felt before, and it sent a shiver of excitement through her. But she tamped down her excitement quickly and focused on the task at hand. She had a wounded man to help and couldn't let her foolish fancies take control.

She retrieved a spare set of bed linens from the wardrobe in her bedchamber and quickly returned. She ordered him off the bed and then stripped it down before putting the clean sheets on.

"We need to get you out of these clothes," she said, eyeing the wet cloth seriously.

"I'm flattered, lass, and under other circumstances I'd be quite happy to topple you back on the bed and pleasure you until you screamed, but I fear I'm not quite up to it just now."

The effect of his arrogant teasing was lessened when she saw how weary he was. It was all male bravado to hide how much he was hurting. Something about that curled around her heart, smothering it with an unexpected heat and tenderness. She came toward him, forgetting she was still only in her nightrobe. She reached for his shirt, ripping it down the side.

He shrugged out of the torn shirt. "Easy, lass! You're a strong one, aren't you?"

Josephine shrugged. She wasn't petite, nor was she particularly tall, but if she was one thing, she was strong. Her father had taught her years of swordplay alongside her brother, and her mother had encouraged her to take long walks, where she'd ended up running more often than not because of her boundless energy. It left her stronger than most women her age. She knelt at his feet and pulled his boots off while he steadied himself against the table. Then she reached for his trousers.

"Best if I do this . . ." He pushed her away and with one hand unfastened his trousers and slid them down, until he was standing there only in his smallclothes. Despite his wound, the man was gloriously built, like a wall of muscles.

Josephine swallowed hard as her mouth was suddenly dry. She cleared her throat and gestured to the bed.

"Now you may sit," she ordered.

He sat, a soft and weary sound escaping him. She leaned in to examine his wound again. While she did, he seemed to examine her back.

"Who are you?" he asked.

"Josephine," she said.

She did her best not to look at his face. It was eerie how much he looked like Griffin. But where Griffin had a polished and powerful gentleness to him, Gavin had the same power but it seemed harsher. She had felt safe in Griffin's arms. But when *this* man touched her or looked at her the way he was doing now . . . it was like she was at the mercy of a raging storm. To touch this man was to risk the burn of lightning.

"Lie back. I'll fetch some hot water and some clean cloths. We'll need to clean your wound."

He obeyed and lay back, closing his eyes. But it didn't erase the sense of danger in him that filled the small room. But it wasn't a danger that made her fear for her safety . . . it was something else.

"Thank you, Josephine," he said.

"Josie—you may call me Josie," she found herself saying, even though it was scandalous to give him the use of her family's nickname for her.

"Josie," he breathed.

"I'll be back soon," she promised, and left to find something for his wounds.

GAVIN CLOSED HIS EYES, DRIFTING SOMEWHERE BETWEEN sleep and wakefulness, but even as he half slept, Josephine's bright gray eyes filled his mind. Who was she? Why had she been sleeping in his brother's bedchamber? He seemed to drift in a sea of unconsciousness for a long time before the pain in his shoulder pulled him back to the surface. He blinked against the flickering lamp that was too close to his face after so much darkness. He shifted, wrestling with the discomfort and pain.

"Hold still, blast you," a feminine voice uttered in frustration.

He realized Josephine was there, cleaning his wound. "It bloody hurts."

"I imagine it does." She held up a bottle of scotch for him to see. "I found this in a cabinet in the billiard room." She resumed dabbing the scotch-doused cloth against the wound in his shoulder.

Gavin stared at her while she worked. He was relieved to have such a beautiful creature to look at while in pain.

Josephine was an enchanting woman, with slightly olive skin and luscious dark-brown hair that tumbled over her shoulders in waves. She had classically elegant features that held a hint of mischief about them. She intrigued him more than he wished to admit. He reached up with his good arm and coiled a lock of her hair around his finger, marveling at its silkiness.

"I cleaned it as best I can, but I think I'll need to stitch it up." She lifted a small sewing needle up so that he could see it and produced a spool of sturdy-looking silk thread.

"Do you know how to stitch a wound?" he asked suspiciously.

She met his gaze evenly. "I do needlepoint quite well—I can't imagine this is much different."

"Needlepoint?" He barked out a laugh that hurt his shoulder. "Christ, lass, this is my skin, not a cushion." He didn't like the idea of her poking away at him with a needle and thread. Perhaps he should slip out of the house and head for town. If he could find Ronnie and a doctor, he might be better off.

"If I don't do this, the bleeding won't stop. Do you trust me?" she asked.

Gavin met her gaze in the candlelight and saw the serious focus in her gray eyes. A tiny wrinkle formed between her dark brows as if she was already envisioning the task of sewing his wound closed, and something about that, her focus and intensity, made him actually trust her. He nearly smiled at the stubborn tilt of her chin as she waited for his answer.

"I suppose I have to," he admitted.

It was that or let her find a doctor, and he could not

risk that. No one in Cornwall knew he was alive. If that changed and someone realized he wasn't dead, it would raise questions. He was wanted in the Caribbean and off the coast of the American colonies for piracy. If inquiries were made with the authorities here, the Royal Navy would know he was a pirate very soon. That meant anyone in this house who knew of his presence could be found guilty of harboring and aiding a pirate. He had only been back to this house and this room once in the past seven years when he'd thought he was ready to face the past. But he'd been wrong, so he'd stayed unseen by anyone who would have recognized him and left on the following tide, but he didn't want to take that risk now.

"Get on with it, then," he said. But when she reached toward him, he halted her hands. "A moment." He retrieved the scotch bottle from beside her and downed the contents in several deep gulps. Then he set the bottle back on the floor and gave Josephine a stiff nod for her to continue.

She set to work, stitching up the cut made by Beauchamp's blade. It hurt far worse to have it stitched than when Beauchamp had stabbed him.

The pain was sharp then dull, the thread moving through his skin, aching. He reached for that same coil of hair he'd played with earlier, and he rubbed it between his fingers, focusing on the silkiness of it, the softness, the way the dark color caught the lamplight. It soothed him while she worked and distracted him from the pain.

When Josephine was done, she once more dabbed at the wound with a clean cloth and cleared away any remaining blood.

"It appears to be clotting. I believe that's a good thing."

Gavin marveled at this woman's ability to handle the sight of blood and stitch up his wound without distress.

"How old are you, lass?" he asked.

She helped him back to the bed and he lay down, then she drew a warm woolen blanket up to his neck as though he were a child. Something about that made his heart twinge. He couldn't remember the last time anyone had taken care of him like that.

"I am eighteen," she said, her voice softening a little.

"Ah. So young," he sighed. She was young, but she had handled herself well in a crisis, better than most women twice her age.

"And you must be positively ancient, at what, twenty-six?" she asked archly.

"How did you know I was twenty-six?" His eyes drifted closed as his body finally began to surrender to the ordeal of the last few hours.

"Gavin . . ." She murmured his name. His eyes flew open at the single utterance.

"How did you know my name?" He stared at her, his eyes boring into her as he tried to figure out if her knowledge of his name was a danger he needed to prepare for.

She leaned away from him a little, as if fearing he'd grasp at her. The shadows played across her face as she swallowed hard. For an instant he regretted the sharp tone he'd used, but when she replied her tone was strong.

"I recognized you from the portrait I saw in the corridor. It wasn't hard to guess who you are."

Ah . . . the portrait his father had commissioned right before the ball. He and Griffin had both had portraits made that year. He ought to rip it from the wall and burn it. But perhaps the danger wasn't too great. She was one woman, alone on a stormy night. If she began to tell tales later . . . it was possible no one would believe her. Cornwall storms had a way of playing tricks upon one's mind.

"Josephine, you must tell no one I'm here," he insisted as he reached for one of her hands and closed his fingers around hers. "Swear it."

He had meant to speak to his brother, but now . . . now he wasn't sure he was ready to. Because once he did, if he was still alive, he'd have to leave shortly after, and he didn't want to give up these brief moments with Josephine. He was fast becoming attached to her kindness and her bravery and the peace her presence gave him as he endured the pain in his shoulder.

"I swear I won't tell anyone."

"Good . . ." He surrendered to exhaustion. As he fell into sleep, he dreamt of a pair of lovely gray eyes that saw clear through his very soul.

JOSEPHINE HELD ON TO GAVIN'S HAND UNTIL SHE WAS sure he was asleep. Then she went to her own bedchamber to collect another blanket and pillow and returned. After stitching up his wound, she was too afraid to leave him alone. It was a silly thought, but she somehow believed that if she stayed with him tonight, he would be all right. She briefly imagined telling Dominic about Gavin's presence, but if she did, her older brother would then keep her from seeing him again. The last thing Dominic would do would be to let her sleep beside a dangerous pirate and Josephine craved this time with Gavin. She craved the adventure and excitement that this secret rescue had given her.

She piled her blankets on the floor and shut her eyes, trying to catch some sleep. Sometime during the night after a violent crash of thunder, Gavin reached down over the edge of his bed, seeking her. His palm gently quested down her arm until he discovered her hand and then clasped it in his own, and she clung to it as though she was the one who needed soothing through the stormy night.

The wind was a distant, eerie howl from the tunnel that led to the beach. It made her dream of wolves howling in forbidden forests. Then she dreamt of a beautiful ship battling the elements toward smoother seas.

Later, she fell into dreams of a far different kind. Dreams of warm lips, hard, rough hands on her skin, and the heated passion of things she didn't fully understand but still yearned for. She whispered Gavin's name in the dark like a fervent prayer. The wounded pirate stole into her dreams and claimed her imagination.

There were no thoughts or dreams of the man she was supposed to marry or the quiet life she was supposed to surrender to. There were only dreams of pirates, heated kisses, open seas, and *freedom*.

CHAPTER 3

A light mist cloaked the rain-soaked graveyard. A recent storm had drifted in from the sea and now traveled away landward, leaving the grass damp and giving the air a chilly bite. From the edge of the woods, Gavin emerged, slowly treading to the stone markers contained within the hallowed grounds. His soul was set adrift as those stones beckoned him, stretching shadows within his heart, blocking out the light that used to burn so fiercely within him.

Dread draped over him like a shroud as he counted the stones that marked the plot belonging to the Castleton family. Three new stones rested among the group. He swallowed hard as he drew closer, afraid to see the names carved upon them. The first name he glimpsed was a blow to Gavin's heart . . . his father. Gavin had been gone from Cornwall for six years, and in that time he had unknowingly lost his beloved father.

But it was with a primal fear that he finally turned to the other two grave markers. The larger of the two had an angel carved into a bent position over the stone, her wings curved protec-

tively as she wept for the lost soul of the stone she clutched. He whispered the words carved on that stone aloud.

"Charity Castleton—All life is a wondrous but too brief dream." Gavin fell to his knees, his head bowed. She was gone, the light that he'd clung to in the darkest of nights. She had no longer been his to love when she had married his brother, but love was love, and it knew no boundaries. He had learned that long ago—when a person loved deeply and truly, it was as limitless as the sea.

"What would you have me do now, my love?" he asked the lifeless stone before him. "You have left me to grieve in my unwelcome solitude."

He summoned the last of his courage to see the smaller stone beside Charity's. A child. She lost a child. He noted the dates of death for Charity and the child were the same. She must have died bringing Griffin's child into the world, and the babe had perished with her.

Waxen green vines had grown over the child's tombstone, and Gavin cautiously pulled them away until he saw the name of the baby.

"Gavin Castleton—Named for his uncle, a grand adventurer who was lost at sea."

The culmination of that moment, of being with Charity and her child, along with the unbearable longing to have met this nephew who had been given his name, tore out Gavin's heart. Both Charity and Griffin had wanted him here, and knowing he could not stay, they had named their babe in his memory.

Gavin sucked in a breath as his chest tightened so harshly that his lungs were crushed just as if he'd dived too deep beneath the surface of the sea. The crushing darkness and the pressure of the water . . . He suddenly couldn't bear it and shouted, letting out all of his pain and rage until his face was streaked with tears and he had nothing left in him except the grief that had burrowed into his heart.

He pressed his forehead to Charity's headstone for a long moment in remembrance, then slowly stood and wiped his eyes.

"You were my dream," he whispered to her. "But I understand that Griffin was yours."

That was the way with twins—they shared everything most of their lives, but Charity could not be shared. She'd given her heart away to Griffin, and he knew why she had loved his brother, even if it had broken his heart.

He'd accepted her choice to marry Griffin, understood it as only a twin could. "I love him too, and I'm so very sorry I left you both. Forgive me."

What would it have been like if he'd stayed? He couldn't imagine it, but there was a huge part of him that wished he'd tried to stay. Perhaps then Charity might not have died . . .

It was vain and foolish to think he could have changed her fate. Love was never lost . . . it simply changed into grief for the person who was no longer there. And Gavin's grief ran deep, as deep as the sea that called to him.

The mist began to clear as a cool breeze brought whispers of the sea's endless secrets, made him turn toward the distant shore. The sea had always called to him, that desire to sail just a little farther, to see what lay beyond the horizon. He closed his eyes, swearing he could almost hear Charity whisper to him.

"Chase and find your future off the edge of the map . . ."

She had loved to talk about what adventures they could have in the exotic lands depicted in the maps and atlases they'd discovered in his family's vast library. They'd spent hours curled up on a couch together, the atlas spread out on his lap while she leaned against him, tracing the lines where the known world vanished.

She'd spun tales of imagined adventures that Gavin would never have dreamt up on his own. She'd been afraid of nothing—or so he'd thought.

Gavin's lips curved in a bittersweet smile as he remembered her talking about wanting to search for treasure and the glory of being a pirate roving the high seas. Charity had been his treasure. Now she was gone. The sparkle of her brilliance was left in shadow because the sun had set upon her life.

"Sleep well," he said softly and once more touched her tombstone. As much as he wished to lie down and die beside her, fate had other ideas.

Hoofbeats had him turning. A distant figure on horseback was trotting down the path toward the graveyard. Gavin left the stones and sprinted for the shelter of the woods. He wasn't sure why he turned back to look at the graveyard once more, but he did.

The rider halted at the edge of the sacred space and dismounted. A whisper of something came through along that invisible connection that had always existed between Gavin and his twin. Griffin was here.

Griffin made the same walk toward the three stones of their family plot that Gavin had visited just minutes before. His head turned in all directions, as if he was able to feel Gavin's presence. Or perhaps he had noticed that someone had recently cleared one of the stones.

"Gavin?" Griffin called out. Gavin almost made a sound, but he stopped himself at the last moment. Griffin's shoulders slumped and he faced the graves, leaving a bouquet of flowers on each one before mounting his horse and riding away.

"Griffin!"

Gavin bolted up, his brother's name escaping his lips, but he realized it had all been a dream . . . a dream of his last memory of when he had been here a year ago, long before he'd lost his ship in a mutiny. The injury throbbed in his shoulder, reminding him of what had driven him home again so soon.

"Gavin?" a feminine voice said drowsily. "Is your shoulder hurting?"

He drew in a steadying breath, getting his bearings. He was in the secret cave connected to his family's ancestral home, and not in the past. As his mind knitted together his memories from the last few days, he felt something squeeze his hand and that feminine voice spoke again, asking about his shoulder. He stared at the hand for a moment, then followed it down the arm and up toward the face that was illuminated only by a single oil lamp. The woman stared at him in return, openly concerned, but for a moment he couldn't find the words to speak.

Josephine.

Her name struck some deep chord within him, as though his heart was made of strings that could sing when touched. He drew in another breath, his chest tightening as he continued to look at her, then down at their joined hands.

Her palm was warm, and it fit perfectly against his, almost as though their hands had been formed to hold each other's. The thought caught him off guard, causing his heart to give a slow, painful beat against his ribs. He hadn't thought he could ever feel like that again, not after losing Charity. Yet this . . . connection, it was something he could neither explain nor defy.

"What's the matter?" she asked.

He stared at her, realizing she was lying on a pallet on the floor beside his bed.

"I . . ." He found himself unable to speak at first, then changed the subject. "Did you sleep here the entire night?" he asked as he reluctantly released his hold on her hand. A pale light was growing at the end of the tunnel that led down toward the beach, meaning dawn was approaching.

"I did. You needed someone to watch you through the night, lest you succumb to a fever." She sat up and ran her fingers through her tangled waves, combing out the wild dark strands before she gathered her hair at the nape of her neck and bound it with a bit of gold ribbon that she unwound from her wrist. For some reason, it amused him that she kept a ribbon around her wrist in case she needed it for just such a circumstance.

Gavin's eyes then strayed to the nightgown she wore. It was filmy, and he could almost see through it. The swell of her generous breasts and hips made him briefly remember that he had once been a gentleman, and he cleared his throat and looked away.

"You should return to your chambers before someone finds you missing. They will turn the house inside out looking for you, and it would doom me." He was being a tad dramatic, but he needed this tempting beauty to leave before he allowed his already spiraling emotions to make him do something rash and foolish, like seducing her.

"I should go . . . Vesper will certainly worry if she cannot find me."

He echoed the name. "Vesper?"

"My maid. If I can sneak some food up from the kitchens later, I shall bring it to you."

"Thank you." Gavin moved stiffly, careful not to put any pressure on his healing shoulder as he moved to the edge of the bed. His movements drew Josephine's eyes, and her gaze flashed with innocent desire. She glanced away from his bare upper body.

"And I will see about finding you some proper clothes to wear. Yours are quite ruined." She nodded at the tattered, bloody, and briny clothing left discarded on the floor.

Gavin gazed at her a long moment, enjoying her discomfort at his seminakedness, and when her oh-so-innocent eyes once more darted back to him, he gave her an arrogant grin.

"Best to stop blushing, lass. It gives a man a desire to make you blush more and in far more *interesting* places." He let his gaze slide down her body to her breasts before slowly rising back up to her face.

"Oh!" she gasped and suddenly seemed to realize she was still in a chemise that barely covered her legs. "You are far more wicked than your brother," she shot back.

"And what do you know of my brother?"

"I . . . well . . . He lives close to my family. That's why I'm here visiting. We were invited to a ball last night. But the weather turned, and he offered his home to all of the guests."

"He invited you to a ball?"

"Yes, my entire family. I . . . I should go . . ." She rushed from the room so quickly that he half wondered if she was merely another of his bittersweet dreams.

Gavin wished more than anything that he hadn't been injured. He wanted to leap up from the bed and grab her arm to stop her leaving. There was something she wasn't telling him. His Josie had secrets . . . But what secrets could this innocent young woman have? He stared at the low-burning oil lamp and, with a curse, climbed out of the narrow bed and crossed the room to the small cabinet in the corner. He knelt and opened the doors, to find an extra bottle of lamp oil. He did not want to spend the rest of the day in the dark. Had he frightened her off?

No, she would come back . . . she can't resist the temptation. She'd said she had known *many* pirates. She couldn't be too scandalized by him to stay away, could she?

Josephine, with those warm gray eyes and those lips begging for a man's kiss . . . she would come back to him. He could feel it in his bones.

"I've gone utterly mad," Josephine muttered as she hastily dropped the tapestry back into place and darted back to her own chamber. She had just stepped inside when she heard a shriek.

"My lady!" Vesper cried out. She threw down the ball gown she had been holding and rushed over, clasping Josephine in a fierce hug.

Vesper Lyndon, a girl in her early twenties, was an understated beauty with green eyes and gold hair. Josephine hugged her maid back, smiling at the relief she felt to have made it back to her room unseen by anyone but her maid.

"Where the devil have you been?" Vesper demanded like a mother hen.

"I . . ."

"Don't tell me any tales, my lady," Vesper warned. "Your chamber pot is empty, your pillow is gone, and you are covered in dust, and heavens . . . is that *blood*?" The word escaped Vesper in a much higher pitch than the rest of her words.

Josephine poked her head back into the corridor, checking to see if anyone else was outside. It was still empty. She shut the door and slid the latch into the lock position before facing her maid.

"Vesper," she began soothingly. "You mustn't tell anyone . . ."

"Tell anyone what? Oh, heavens . . . I'll get the boot for this. What have you been up to?"

Josephine clasped Vesper's hand in hers. "A man came into my chamber last night."

Vesper's eyes grew round. "A man?"

"He was injured, and he was looking for Lord Castleton. He found me instead."

"Where is the man now? Is he dead?" the maid inquired in a wary voice.

"No, he was injured in a fight. I cleaned the wound and stitched him up. He's resting in a secret chamber." She squeezed Vesper's hands. "Please tell no one. His life is in danger. Anyone who is found helping him will be in danger too."

"What sort of man is he? A thief? A murderer?"

"Neither. Well . . . perhaps both. I honestly do not know."

Her maid stared at her, waiting for an explanation.

"He's a pirate."

"A *pirate*!" Vesper shrieked.

She shushed her maid. "Keep your voice down."

"Lady Josephine, you *cannot* keep a pirate as a pet! Someone will discover him and that you've been helping him."

"No one will know if *you* help me," Josephine said with a hopeful look.

"Help you with your pirate? Certainly not! You have a marriage to think about. Lord Castleton . . ." Vesper's eyes softened in sorrow and longing before she banished those emotions from Josephine's view. "We all have our duties, my lady. And yours is to Lord Castleton."

"*Please*, Vesper. We must help him."

Her maid crossed her arms over her chest. "Why?" A stubborn Vesper was hard to motivate, in Josephine's experience.

"Because . . . because he's Lord Castleton's brother."

Vesper's eyes widened. "Surely you don't mean . . . ?"

"Gavin," Josephine confirmed.

"His lordship's twin . . ." Vesper suddenly sank down on the bed, her face pale. "Oh, my lady, we *must* tell him. He must know that his brother is alive."

"We will, but not yet. Gavin is still hurt. We need him to heal before we discuss his brother with him. If they fight and Griffin orders him to leave and he is not healed . . ."

Vesper stared at her, but the maid's gaze seemed miles away. "Oh, poor Lord Castleton. He doesn't even know his brother is alive."

Taking advantage of her maid's distraction, Josephine

retrieved a clean chemise and gown from the wardrobe to change into. Vesper always packed an extra gown in case they had to stay the night, even at a neighboring estate so close to home. Josephine had thought it so silly that her maid fussed over such details, but now she was grateful.

"Help me dress. I must have missed breakfast."

Half an hour later, Josephine was wearing a bright-pink and sky-blue gown with wide flowing skirts and a soft cream-colored underskirt trimmed with Belgian lace. Vesper had combed her hair into loose waves and pulled it back at her nape with a ribbon of pink satin. She no longer looked like a windswept creature who'd slept in a cave by the sea.

"I'll be back soon." She kissed her maid's cheek and rushed down to the dining room.

Half of the guests were eating when she arrived, including her parents and Lord Castleton. The moment Castleton spotted her, he rose and pulled back the chair beside him. She accepted the seat, and Castleton immediately offered to prepare a plate of food for her. She was about to politely decline, but her mother caught her eye and gave her an encouraging nod. Ah, so she was to accept Castleton's offer. That would be what a proper lady would do.

With a stifled sigh, she lowered her head demurely. "Thank you, I would appreciate that, my lord."

She survived the meal and the polite conversation of the other guests. When she was finished, she rose from her seat, but Castleton caught her hand.

"Would you do me the honor of walking with me in the

gardens? I have permission from your father to speak with you in private."

"Yes, of course," she agreed, and then let him escort her outside. The clouds were still thick in the sky and heavy with rain, even though the storm was long past. It enhanced the aroma of a dozen varities of roses blooming around them.

Josephine took Castleton's arm, resting her hand lightly on his forearm as they walked the garden path in silence. He presented such a striking, handsome figure, yet his countenance was tempered with solemnity.

"I want you to be happy, Josephine. I want you to be my wife. I know your parents wish for that too, but what is it that *you* want?"

Josephine couldn't believe someone was asking what she wanted. Then again, Castleton was a gentleman in every sense of the word. If anyone would think about others, it would be him.

"My lord—"

"Griffin, please," he corrected with an encouraging smile.

"Griffin . . . what I want is to be free. I want . . ." She swallowed the sudden lump in her throat. "I want a life I cannot have."

They paused in the center of the gardens, and Griffin gently turned her to face him. He tenderly brushed his fingers over her cheek.

"You remind me of my late wife. Charity was vibrant, so full of life and dreams. My world ended the night she and our child died. I understand more than you know what it means to lose one's freedom."

A flicker of shock must have shown on Josephine's face.

Griffin chuckled ruefully. "I've surprised you."

"Well, yes. I mean, you are a man. You can do whatever you wish in life. A woman cannot. She is bound by the rules of others."

"In some ways I can, but I am still bound to these lands and this house by my title. I was not supposed to be the earl, you know. Like you, I had a twin, Gavin. He was the firstborn, the one destined to live this life, but . . ." His gaze turned to the garden and the blooming roses.

"But what?"

"I made a grave mistake. We fell in love with the same woman. They were supposed to marry, but I stole her from him."

Josephine gasped, her heart aching for both men and the woman who had perished. "Gavin was in love with your wife?"

"Yes. She was his long before she was ever mine. I broke his heart when she was forced to choose between us and she chose to marry me. He left that night, and I haven't seen him since. Eventually our father died, and I was declared the earl because Gavin was presumed dead. But it was not the blessing one would assume. I was twice punished for displacing my brother. I was forced to take his place as the earl after our father died, and I lost Charity with our child." Griffin smiled sadly, and his distant gaze focused on her face again. "I believe love can grow between us, if we give it time. If we give it a chance."

Josephine's heart clenched. Griffin cupped her chin and slowly leaned down, giving her plenty of time to pull away, but she didn't. And then he kissed her. His lips were warm and soft, and she felt a stirring within her. The promise of a sweet life, a life of gentle love and tenderness and warmth. She knew she could be happy as his wife, happy enough, but the moment he deepened the kiss, Gavin's face flashed across her mind and she pulled away from Griffin.

"I'm sorry. I shouldn't have taken advantage," he apologized, a hint of color touching those aristocratic cheekbones of his.

"No, it isn't that," Josephine insisted. All she could think was how deeply she would be hurt if her brother left her for seven years and then secretly returned without telling her. It would be a pain she could never forgive, that awful not knowing.

Before she could consider the consequences, she blurted out, "Gavin's alive."

CHAPTER 4

Gavin examined his clothes from the previous evening where they lay in a shabby pile on the floor next to Josephine's abandoned pallet. Had she really spent the night beside him in case he should need her? Something in his chest shifted, like currents sliding deep beneath the waves. No one had worried about him like that in a very long time.

With a grunt, Gavin climbed out of bed and retrieved his trousers. It wasn't easy to pull them up, but he managed it without straining his stitches. The pants were stiff with dried seawater, but he was used to that. When one lived on a ship, one's clothes were often drenched with sea spray. He reached for his shirt, only to remember that it was badly torn. He fingered the frayed edge of the cloth, smiling a little at the memory of Josephine's hands digging into it. The lass was fierce indeed, ripping a shirt like that nearly clean in two. It made him want to return the favor and rip the laces of her bodice to get to her bare skin the next time he saw her. The thought of her stripped naked and at his tender mercy made his smile widen.

He turned toward the passageway leading back to the house when the scuffle of feet alerted him to Josephine's return. Perhaps he might just get his wish . . .

But it *wasn't* Josephine who came through the doorway. It was his brother.

Griffin stood there, his eyes adjusting to the dim light, his lips parted in shock. Just behind him hovered Josephine, her lovely features tight with worry. It was the first time he'd seen her in something other than a thin chemise. The pink-and-blue striped gown made her look like a sweet from a confectioner's shop in London. Yet no matter how much he wanted to look at her, his attention was riveted on his brother. They had not seen each other in seven years, and the room was thick with tension.

"You're . . . here." The way Griffin said *here*, like he couldn't believe Gavin was alive, opened up all of those old wounds he'd convinced himself had healed. For a second, he couldn't draw in a breath and his lungs burned. His chest ached with the pain of the years lost between them, and Gavin could feel the echoing pang within his brother at the same instant.

"Seven years. My God . . ." Griffin rubbed a hand along his jaw in disbelief. He still stood in the doorway, and Josephine remained at his side, glancing anxiously between them.

"Griffin." The name came out hoarse, as though he hadn't spoken in a century.

His brother drew a step closer. "Why now?"

When they were no more than a couple of feet apart, Gavin felt that old familiar tug at his heart. The connection that tied him to his twin was still there, even after all the time that had passed between them.

"My ship was . . . ," he started, but then swallowed the words that would have caused him shame to speak. "I needed a place to rest for a few days."

Griffin's eyes fell to Gavin's stitched shoulder. "What happened?"

"I fell on a sword." Gavin kept his answer simple. The less his brother knew of the matter, the better. "Josephine stitched it up."

Griffin's gaze darted between him and Josephine, his eyes narrowing.

"You should know better than to run with weapons. Father would have boxed your ears."

"Aye, that he would," Gavin agreed solemnly.

Josephine opened her mouth but then clamped it shut again, as if deciding not to interrupt their tense exchange. Griffin finally pulled his gaze away from Gavin and looked at the girl beside him.

"Thank you for telling me about my brother. Would you kindly leave us? I need a moment to speak to Gavin, and your father would be furious if he knew I let you stay in the presence of a half-dressed man."

Josephine looked reluctant to leave, but Gavin gave her a nod.

"Go on, lass. It will be all right."

Only then did she lift her skirts and quietly slip away

from the room. Gavin missed her the moment she departed. She'd been a brief ray of sunlight in this dark room, and yet she hadn't even said a word. Something about her silence bothered him. She hadn't been herself just now, he knew that much after being around her for such a short time. She'd seemed . . . closed off, more like a proper lady respecting the position and wishes of the master of the house, which in this case was Griffin. Whereas last night and this morning she'd been fiery and talkative—*alive*.

So lost was he in his thoughts about Josephine's behavior that he never saw Griffin's blow coming, which struck him hard in the face.

"Where the bloody hell have you been?" Griffin growled, fury lighting his eyes.

Gavin staggered back. The pain was unexpected, and he cursed as the stitches in his shoulder pulled tight. He touched his lip, which had split, and tasted blood upon his tongue.

"I've been dead," he shot back.

"No, Father is dead. *Charity* is dead. My . . ." His words broke with anguish, and he looked away, unable to continue.

"Your son is dead." Gavin finished Griffin's unspoken words with a heavy finality that held an echo of the grief that he knew Griffin must be feeling a thousand times over.

"I came back a year ago, hoping to make things up to you. I saw the tombstones in the churchyard."

Griffin finally looked his way again. "So you *were* there.

I thought myself mad for weeks, believing that I'd imagined feeling you'd come home." Tears glinted in Griffin's eyes. "You left me. You left *us* . . . I can't forgive you for that."

Invisible shards cut into Gavin's throat as he tried to speak. "I'm . . . I'm not asking you to." He felt like in that moment he was sailing his ship once more through a storm and praying to see light on a distant shore to guide him home. But all he saw in that moment were flashes, and then darkness fell again in his inner world.

A thousand words hung in the air between them, but neither brother dared to say them. They'd once shared everything, from the moment their lives sparked into being in their mother's womb. But after all that had happened, something had broken between them, and Gavin feared it could never heal.

"I'll see you well enough to leave," Griffin said at last. "I'll bring you some food and clothes. Do you need a doctor?"

Gavin studied his shoulder, intensely relieved at the change in subject. The skin wasn't inflamed around the wound. The lass had done a fine job of tending to him.

"No doctor, but I will take the clothes and food," he said quietly. He didn't like to fall upon anyone's mercy, not even his own brother's, but he'd given all of his extra coin to Ronnie.

Griffin stood there a moment, a silent war playing out on his face.

"She asked for you . . . in the end. She wished she could have seen you one last time."

Those words, no doubt kindly meant, were like a dagger to Gavin's heart. He sank onto the bed, still holding his ripped shirt in his hands. It seemed like a fitting metaphor for the state his heart was in.

"She regretted so much of what happened that night. We both did." Griffin took a seat on one of the chairs at the table. The waning light of the oil lamp fought the shadows on his face as he stared at the burning flame.

"You never remarried?" Gavin asked.

"Charity was the only woman who will ever hold my heart. But I am to be married again soon."

A sudden, terrible dread of that answer came rolling in around Gavin like fog.

"To whom?" he asked, his voice a little rough as he struggled not to betray any emotions.

"Josephine."

Once again, that knife slashed through him. He needed to lash out at something to take his mind away from the agony, and his brother was the only one there to take his pain.

"That woman is too wild for you, brother. Even Charity was more tame than she. You will only make her miserable, and she you." Josephine was not a woman who could be gentled. That much he knew, in just the short time he'd spent with her.

As if understanding Gavin's intentions, a frown tugged at Griffin's lips. "I'm well aware of Josephine's spirit. Her parents chose me because they hope I will settle her down. Sometimes a gentle hand will soothe even the wildest creature."

Gavin had a sudden flash of memory, of him and Griffin taming horses together. Griffin's gentle touch almost always won the wild horses over, but there had been one stallion that couldn't be tamed with gentleness. So Gavin had mounted up and let the horse loose on the land, and they rode together, wild and free, until the horse learned to trust him. That stallion had never been tamed, but Gavin had always been able to ride him. Not all creatures could be tamed, nor should they be. It would be a cruel thing to break the spirit of a woman like Josephine.

Gavin set aside his torn shirt. "When is the wedding?"

"Soon."

Soon. Gavin's jaw clenched.

"Don't worry. I shall be long gone before you take your new bride."

Griffin didn't argue, but he did square his shoulders. "What the devil happened, Gavin? Do not hide the truth. 'Tis only me here—you can tell me."

Gavin didn't want to tell him, but somehow the words tumbled free of his lips as he told his brother of Beauchamp's mutiny and his flight from his beloved ship.

"I will meet up with my shipmate soon and be gone once we find a vessel."

"By *find a vessel*, you mean . . . ?"

"'Tis better if you don't know," Gavin replied. He had no money to buy a ship, assuming he could even find one for sale, but stealing a ship, that was something he could manage.

"Don't be a fool, Gavin. The Royal Navy has vessels patrolling off the coast, and there are two docked in the nearest port. I hosted an admiral last week for dinner, along with several of his captains. They are hunting for *pirates*." He let the word hang in the air, heavy with meaning, as he met Gavin's eyes.

"You're warning is heeded, but I can't stay here." Gavin curled his hands into fists where they rested on his thighs as he weighed the danger of the navy prowling around the coastline.

"Where will you go?" Griffin asked.

"I'll go after my ship. I owe Beauchamp the taste of my steel. He'll be headed for the West Indies again. After that, well, I have a life elsewhere." He smiled a little as he thought of the tiny island off the coast of the Bahamas that he called home. The Isle of Song. It was the only place he felt was truly his anymore.

"I would give anything to have you stay . . . if things were different," Griffin whispered.

"Things are what they are . . . and I could not stay even if they were," Gavin replied just as quietly.

The two of them sat in long silence until Gavin dared to speak about their past again.

"Did Father ever forgive me for leaving?"

Griffin traced the edges of the handle of the oil lamp. "Of course he did. He loved you, and he understood that you couldn't stay."

Gavin's throat tightened. He had a terrible sense that he was running out of time, like the sand in the hourglass of his life was pouring far too quickly.

"I'm sorry, brother." He'd done it. He'd finally said the words that had driven him here in the storm.

"As am I," Griffin replied and then stood. "I'll be back

with clothes and food. You'll need more lamps to see properly until you leave. It's too bloody dark in here."

With one last look of bittersweet ache at his twin, Griffin left Gavin alone in the secret chamber. As he sat in silence, Gavin swore he could hear the pouring sand of that invisible hourglass growing louder and louder. What was he supposed to do before the sand ran out?

JOSEPHINE RELUCTANTLY RETURNED TO THE DINING room after Griffin effectively dismissed her from the secret passage. She hadn't really eaten much during breakfast, and now some of the guests were seated for an early lunch.

"Cheer up, Josie." Her twin, Adrian, set down a plate of food next to her at the table and joined her. "You look thoroughly put out, darling sister." His gray eyes twinkled with mischief, and his good mood almost managed to make her smile.

"You're not the one about to be married off to a stranger," she said, her tone more waspish than she'd intended. Adrian's brows rose at that. It wasn't often she and her brother quarreled, but her temper was up and her pride had been pricked by the events of this morning.

He reached over and covered one of her hands with his. "I tried to convince Father not to pursue this marriage, but he lectured me on my own duties regarding marriage." Adrian's tone hardened slightly. "It's as if the moment Dominic returned to England, they wanted us both gone."

"You know that isn't true. It's just . . . well, Dominic will be the Earl of Camden someday. He and Roberta will have a house full of children, and you and I will be in the way, won't we?" She and Adrian had given a lot of thought to the new dynamics of their household now that their elder brother, who'd been gone for fourteen years, had resumed his role in the family.

"Father suggested I join the navy. Can you believe that? Thank God Nicholas Flynn talked him out of such nonsense. I'd be lashed to death for rebellion within the first hour."

"You in the navy would be nonsense indeed," Josephine agreed. Many fraternal twins were opposites to each other, but she and Adrian were more like mirror images. Adrian would no sooner take orders than she would had she been in his position and facing life on a naval vessel. Life in the navy would be a disaster for him.

"I have been thinking, though. Dom said he will be needing masters to captain his new fleet of merchant vessels, and I thought I could join one of his crews and work my way up to captaincy in a few years. I wouldn't mind the work, knowing I could advance with hard work and not have to pay for a commission."

"I don't suppose I could go with you? Dress up like a lad, like in those stories Roberta told us about when she played Dom's cabin boy," she said, half teasing. Josephine briefly indulged in a fantasy of donning men's breeches and scaling the rigging of a ship with a knife between her teeth while the guns fired upon an enemy ship.

"Your husband might notice you missing," Adrian chuckled. At his comment, however, she flinched. "He seems like a good fellow, Josie," her brother quickly added.

"He is, and I suppose that's rather the problem. What sort of life would I have with a kind and gentle man?"

"A safe life?" Adrian countered. "Surely anyone would want that?" Yet even he didn't sound that certain. The siren's lure of adventure was irresistible to everyone in their family.

"I want to sail to the West Indies like Dominic. I wish —" She stopped herself before she voiced any more foolish wishes.

"What do you wish?" Her brother's gaze turned serious as he pushed away a plate of half-eaten food.

"It's silly . . ."

"Nothing you say is silly," Adrian replied. "Now, what's the matter? I've felt you've been different since last night. I saw you leave dinner, and Dominic went after you. Did he say something?"

Adrian had no idea how right he was. Dominic had said something . . . about lost men and the sea, and then Gavin had washed up on shore and found his way to her. And *everything* about her life felt changed on some elemental level that she couldn't quite explain, not even to her twin.

"I don't want a normal life."

"Does anyone?" Adrian's tone was teasing, but she shook her head at him.

"I am not meant to sit around and sew silly needlepoint until my fingers bleed and act as if I can't offer the world something more."

Her brother squeezed her hand again. "I rather doubt that will be your fate. You're a Greyville, Josie. Like me, like Dominic, like Mother and Father. We're bound for adventure. Give it time, and you'll see that the world is waiting for you."

"Promise me this marriage will be a good one..." she begged her brother.

Her brother's face was solemn. "I *promise*, Josie. You will marry Castleton and have a life you've always dreamed of. You'll sail the seas and have adventures and all the things you could ever dream of."

She wanted to believe him, but Adrian had always been such a positive believer in one's dreams. But as a woman, Josephine didn't have the same luxury to let her dreams be catch the wind and sail her away toward adventure.

She finished her small luncheon, and allowed her mind to wander back to the subject she had been carefully avoiding. Had it been a mistake to tell Griffin that his brother was alive? Surely Griffin wouldn't betray his brother to the authorities. She pushed her plate away and stood.

"Where are you off to?" Adrian asked her.

"Nowhere." When her brother raised a brow at her, she rolled her eyes. "*Nowhere*," she said again and left him to finish his meal.

She was halfway up the stairs when Griffin came flying down the steps. They met in the middle of the grand staircase.

"Ah, there you are, Josephine." He smoothly took one of her arms in his and escorted her back up the stairs the way he'd come. His sudden forwardness confused her. Mere hours before, his touch had been hesitant. Now there was an urgency to him that confused her. Had something happened to Gavin? Had his injury worsened? Josephine expected them to stop before the tapestry cloaking the secret passageway, but Griffin continued on to another room farther down the hall.

"My lord—"

"Griffin," he corrected automatically as he pulled her into an empty drawing room and closed the door.

"What's the matter?"

"Have you . . . ?" He cleared his throat. "Did my brother . . . ?"

"Did he what?"

"He didn't seduce you last night, did he?" Griffin finally asked, his back straight and stiff as he waited for an answer.

"*Seduce* me? Griffin, no, he was badly injured. I tended to his wounds and only stayed the night to make sure he was all right." She felt her anger coming out at Griffin's presumption. "Is that my only value to you? That my virtue remains intact?"

Griffin's cheeks turned red. "No," he said. "But my brother is more assertive in his desires than I am, and I know how charming he can be. I feared he might have taken advantage . . ."

"I am more than capable of handling an injured man's advances should he have made any, but he didn't." Josephine wanted to tell Griffin she also knew her way around rapiers and pistols and was perfectly capable of caring for herself, but she thought better of it.

"Good, good. I'm simply saying it's best you stay away from him." He took her hands in his and raised them to his lips for a kiss. "I also wanted to tell you that I shall be speaking to your parents today about the wedding. I believe we should wed sooner than planned."

"Sooner?" Her heart slammed against her ribs as dread settled over her.

"Yes. Two days from now."

Two days . . . and she would be married. Two days and the shackles of wifely enslavement would be around her wrists.

"Gavin will be gone by then, and you and I can resume our lives." He kissed her hands again, his eyes studying her face as she struggled not to let him see her terror at the thought.

She wanted to scream that she wasn't ready, that she needed a decade or more before she'd even consider marriage. But she held those protests in as she had been taught.

"You need not worry about my brother. He will be all right. I have seen that he has food and clothing, and I will continue to provide for his welfare until he leaves. Why don't you join the other ladies downstairs? I believe there was talk of a tour of the gardens before taking tea in the drawing room." He stroked a finger down her cheek and then bowed to her before he left her alone.

"A tour of the gardens?" She had no desire to walk around and gossip among the rosebushes with the other women. In that instant, she could see her life with Griffin playing out before her. Tours of gardens, gossiping behind fans with other ladies, hours of endless needlepoint, the occasional child born and taken away from her to be raised by nurses, and gentle kisses in the dark at night as Griffin made tender love to her. A dull ringing started in her ears as she felt that future rising toward her like an inescapable tide.

She closed her eyes, trying to breathe as her chest suddenly tightened. In a flash, Gavin filled her mind like a burning flame. She reached toward it, toward him in her mind, chasing that breathless joy of discovery and adventure. His kisses were a wild blaze that would set her soul on fire. He wouldn't cage her, wouldn't tame her. He'd simply chase her the way he chased each new horizon.

The tightness in her chest eased and a deep breath filled her lungs, clearing the blind panic from her mind as she left the drawing room and headed for the stairs. She stopped at the top of the stairs and glanced toward the tapestry that led to Gavin and the sea.

"You aren't my husband yet, Lord Castleton," she said under her breath as she headed straight for the secret passageway.

When she entered the hidden room, she saw three lit lamps on the table, giving the room a far brighter glow. Gavin was dressed in fresh trousers, a white shirt, and a leather waistcoat, which he'd left unbuttoned. He sat on the bed, pulling on the new leather boots Griffin must have provided for him. Upon her entrance, his eyes raked slowly up her body in a languid appraisal.

She suddenly felt how very small the room was with the two of them in it and blushed wildly. She turned her face away at the intimacy of knowing that he was dressing and tried to act calm by straightening the lamps on the table, quite unnecessarily. She did her best to ignore the feel of his gaze on her back.

"I suspect my brother likely forbade you from coming back here," he said.

She tried not to sound surprised at his correct assumption. "He did."

Gavin chuckled as he slowly stood. "And yet here you are . . ."

"Here I am." She stared at him as a wild and reckless thought caught hold of her. Griffin informing her that they would marry in two days had unleashed some sort of madness inside of her.

"He didn't seduce you last night, did he?" Griffin's words echoed in her mind. Perhaps she *had* been seduced . . . by the mere idea of an adventure with this man and the life he led. She wanted to know everything about him and his adventures, but she wanted other things too. Like the feminine knowledge of his kiss, his touch. The feverous need within her to know this man in all ways, to belong to him and claim him as her own, was so overpowering that it felt as if some spell had been cast. The hazy enchantment seemed to drape over her, whispering that she should go to him.

She walked toward Gavin as if in a dream. It was only the two of them in this room. No future lay ahead of either of them. There was the distant crash of the sea and the briny breeze that drifted up from the tunnel that led down to the shore. All that existed was them and the sea.

She stopped inches away from Gavin, and he gazed down at her, his rakish grin vanishing as he seemed to read what she hoped her eyes were telling him, *begging* him to do. He reached up with one hand and caressed her cheek, then curled his fingers around the back of her neck, holding her still as he lowered his head.

He claimed her mouth, his lips harsh at first, making

her gasp in surprise at the heat. His tongue plunged between her lips, assaulting her senses with a delicious sense of wonder and excitement. Her blood sang in endless arias the longer he kissed her.

Their mouths briefly parted, and he took a moment to stare at her. She blinked in a daze, then gripped his shirt, pulling him close again, taking him as he had taken her.

Gavin's eyes burned with harsh intensity, but his lips were soft as he made love to her mouth. Her womb clenched when he swept his palm over her backside and pulled her flush against him. Gavin made a soft sound at the back of his throat, and she trembled as a wave of dizziness swept through her. She couldn't get enough of the wonderful feel of his mouth, his body, all of it focused on her.

Why had no one told her a kiss could spin a thousand new dreams in one's mind and heart? Things she'd never noticed before seemed to sharpen, like the scent of Gavin's skin and the silken feel of his hair when she dug her fingers into it. The way his mouth tasted, sweet with a hint of wine and salt upon his skin from the sea.

She felt the hard, thick length of him pressed against the front of her, and for the first time she knew what it meant to create desire in another person. She felt a rush of power and passion at the thought of affecting Gavin in this way.

Josephine was only dimly aware of him backing her toward the nearest wall. Then she was pinned, helpless against the wicked pleasure of Gavin's sensual seduction. He angled his mouth over hers again and again, as if he could kiss her for a thousand years and never stop. She certainly didn't want him to.

When he finally tore himself away, he glared at her.

"You're playing with fire, child," he warned. They both caught their breath, panting hard in the golden room.

She raised her chin. "I'm not a child."

Gavin's gaze was purely piratical. "No, you aren't. It's just that I've lived in the world, and you haven't. You know nothing of the danger of passion...of being swept away."

She pushed away from the wall and he stepped back, just enough to let her pass by him to walk toward the door that led back to the house.

"I may not know...but I wish to," she said softly, her chest aching. So this was it. They would say and do nothing more despite what lay between them?

"He told me," Gavin said heavily.

She halted to look at him over her shoulder. "Told you what?"

Gavin's eyes were alight with a dangerous fire. "That you are *his*."

She let her own fire burn in her eyes. "I belong to no man, only to myself."

His eyes darkened at her response, as though he was excited by her defiant challenge.

"Be careful, Josie. Never tell a pirate he can't have something," Gavin warned. "He'll be tempted to steal it."

Her voice softened as she understood what he was saying. "I wish I could believe you . . ."

She wanted, no, she wished *desperately* that he *would* steal her away, but he wouldn't dare. Not from his brother. She was Griffin's future bride, and he would not take his brother's betrothed. She fled the room, needing to escape before she gave in to the need to lose herself in him again. She knew what she was missing now, the passion and fire that she so longed for . . . that she would not have with Griffin.

The terrible irony of her fate was not lost upon her. The one man she would have given her soul to . . . was a pirate.

CHAPTER 5

"Yes, that is lovely."

Josephine glanced at her mother's pleased face as Lucia smoothed out the exquisite skirts of what would be Josephine's wedding dress. It was a beautiful dress—ice-blue satin skirts and a cream bodice studded with pearls, swirls of gold embroidery decorating the flowing overskirt, shimmering in the light of the setting sun, as if fire danced along the threads. It was a gown fit for a princess, and any woman would be delighted to wear it. Josephine would be too—if it was actually marrying a man she truly loved.

She turned her face to the tall cheval glass in the corner of the bedchamber and studied her reflection in silent misery. Her head throbbed, and she desperately wanted to close her eyes and just escape this moment. And what was to come.

The two days since they had left Griffin's estate had flown by too quickly.

Josephine had but blinked and now she was on the eve of her marriage to Griffin.

She'd no sooner returned from that life-altering kiss with Gavin in the secret room than to find her parents preparing to return home. Her parents' announcement that she was to be wed in two days had stripped her of any chance of saying goodbye to Gavin. She'd been under the watchful eye of Vesper and her mother ever since, as if they'd suspected she'd take flight before the ceremony.

That was how she found herself two days later, wearing the most beautiful dress she'd ever seen and feeling like she was withering away inside like a rose planted in soil where no rain ever fell.

Adrian leaned on the doorjamb of her chamber, watching their mother and Vesper fuss over the gown. His gray eyes were dark as he met his sister's gaze.

Save me, she silently pleaded with her eyes to her twin.

His answering look told her that he wished he could.

"How does it feel, my love?" her mother asked her as she placed her hands on Josephine's shoulders. Lucia beamed at her, the brilliant smile digging an invisible blade deeper into her heart. She wanted to enjoy this moment, to make her mother happy and to feel as though this was the most wonderful thing in the world, but that would have been a lie.

It feels like a prison, she thought. "It's fine," she managed to say instead.

"Wonderful. You are ready for tomorrow morning." Her mother kissed her cheek. "Vesper, come with me. I want you to help me with something." Lucia gestured for the maid to follow her out of the room. Adrian stepped back, allowing the women to pass by before he joined Josephine in front of the mirror.

"*Lie* to me," she begged in a shaky whisper. "Tell me this marriage will be the start of an adventure."

Adrian smiled sadly, seeming to understand what she needed to hear. "This will be a *wonderful* journey. You and Castleton shall sail around the world and visit the places you've always wanted to. You'll find everything you've been searching for."

She was almost able to believe him. "Thank you."

Adrian embraced her, his arms tight around her. "Try to sleep."

"You'll stay with me tomorrow until we must part?" She couldn't imagine surviving her wedding day without him close by. They'd always been there for each other, a quiet support when needed.

"For as long as I can," he promised. Neither of them spoke of the day when he would have to leave to work on one of Dominic's ships. Now that he was a second son and not the heir he'd been raised since the age of two to be after Dominic left, he had a duty to make his own fortune, just as she had a duty to be married off.

She and Adrian had been together their entire lives, and tomorrow she would be separated from him forever, seeing each other for brief visits from that point forward. He was her best friend. What would her life be like without him as her constant counsel on all matters?

She clung to Adrian a moment longer before she let go.

"Sleep well. Try not to worry," he murmured before he quietly slipped out the door.

She stared around the room, wishing Vesper would

return to help her out of the gown so she could try to forget about the wedding, at least until morning. She sat down at the vanity table by the large bay window in her bedchamber and fingered the string of pearls her mother had laid out for her to wear tomorrow. The perfect white pearls gleamed with a soft luminescence against the velvet box they were nestled in. She touched each pearl, one by one, as her mind replayed that kiss she'd shared with Gavin. Nothing else felt real now, except that single memory. Was this the only thing she would have left of what had once been her life? That single moment where she'd finally, truly felt alive?

Distant thunder rumbled, and the falling night made her shiver a little. The storm wouldn't come this way, she could tell by the way the wind was moving, the sounds brought back such vivid memories of her first sight of Gavin's portrait, and his sudden appearance in her bedchamber, and the way she'd spent the night asleep beside him, their hands clasped together. They'd been complete strangers, yet that night, she had felt like she could breathe for the first time in her life and all the other moments she had simply been holding her breath.

Had he left that little cave yet? What if he was still there when she returned as Griffin's new bride? The memory of that exquisite, burning kiss was branded upon her soul, and she knew she would run to that chamber to seek him out, if only to say goodbye. She lifted the necklace from its velvet box, letting the soft pearls brush against her skin before she put the necklace around her neck.

Her eyes closed as she stroked her fingertips down the

column of her throat as she imagined that it was Gavin's hand that caressed her skin. The ache for him was so intense that her lips trembled and her eyes burned with tears at the deep, unfathomable longing for what she would never have. She wanted to feel like herself, feel the way she had when he'd kissed her. Anything had seemed possible at that moment when his mouth had touched hers, *anything*. For the first time, she'd felt as free as a falcon and not a caged songbird.

Josephine tilted her head back, still imagining Gavin's lips on her cheek, her neck, and how his fingers would fist in her hair, pulling on the strands just enough to keep her prisoner for his mouth's soft, heated exploration. He wouldn't hurt her, nor would he be gentle in his desire to kiss her. She liked that, the feeling of being so desired that he didn't treat her as a fragile, breakable creature, but rather as an equal. Her desire was just as strong as his.

The fantasy became so real that she could even imagine his scent, the smell of rain, forests and coastal shores. It enveloped her, adding to the daydream of Gavin's lips and hands upon her. She could even hear him speak in that low, slightly gruff voice that made her belly quiver.

"You're worth stealing," this imaginary Gavin murmured to her before he flicked his tongue into the delicate shell of her ear. A sharp pang of need clenched her womb, and she gasped, her eyes flying open at the unexpected intensity. Her flushed face shone in the mirror upon the table.

She *wasn't* alone. Another face above hers stared back at her in the mirror. Someone was standing behind Josephine.

Her lips parted, ready with a cry of shock, but a hand clamped down on her mouth as she gazed at the reflection of the tall figure who stood behind her. Gavin flashed her a wolfish smile.

This wasn't a daydream any longer. He was *here*. In *her* bedchamber. His hand was still clasped around her mouth to silence her. Her eyes widened as she saw a large jeweled cutlass tucked into his belt. In that moment, she really believed he was a fierce pirate and not the wounded man she'd cared for in the cave by the sea.

"I'll take my hand away so long as you promise not to scream," he whispered.

She wasn't afraid, so she nodded in agreement.

"Good." He let go of her mouth, and she turned around on the chair to face him.

"What are you doing here?" she asked in a frantic whisper. "Someone could see you!"

"Worried about me?" he teased.

"Of course I am! I didn't stitch up your shoulder just to watch you hang, you bloody fool!" She said this a little more loudly than was wise, given that she was trying not to let anyone know her "pet pirate" had snuck into her bedchamber. He merely smirked.

"What?" she demanded, not liking his expression at all. It seemed as though she had been left out of some joke.

"*You* . . . You have such fire when you're with me," he said. The way he said *with me* held a hint of possessiveness that sent a wild fluttering through her chest.

"Gavin, you must leave."

He braced one arm on the back of her chair and leaned down to cup her chin. "Is that what you want? For me to leave you to your fate?" It was as though he could read her mind.

What did she want her fate to be? Oh, that was a dangerous question. He had no idea how much she wanted to throw her arms around his neck and beg him to kiss her . . . to make her forget that her duty was to marry his brother.

"What I want doesn't matter," she said quietly, losing some of her fire.

Gavin's face darkened. "It *does* matter. Right now, it's the only thing that matters." His fingertips trailed down her throat, brushing along the line of the pearl necklace to the swell of her breasts. Her breathing hitched at his intimate caress, and her breasts rose in response.

"My God, you tempt me," he breathed. "I've never wanted to steal anything more in my life than I want to steal *you*."

His confession rolled over her in a slow, heated wave that made her belly quiver in heavy anticipation.

A hard shadow passed across Gavin's eyes. "Griffin had Charity . . . He had his chance for happiness. This is *mine*," Gavin murmured to himself before he pulled a strip of cloth from his trouser pocket.

Josephine was too lost with desire as he brushed his lips over hers to realize what he had planned until it was too late. He pulled her wrists together and the cloth was bound tight around them, trapping her hands together.

"Gavin—" She wanted to tell him that it wasn't necessary, that she'd go with him willingly.

"Hush, lass." He finished binding her hands, and pulled her up from her chair to stand.

He was *actually* going to steal her? The thought sent a riotous wave of excitement through her.

"Gav—" He silenced her this time with a second bit of cloth that he stretched between her parted lips and tied to the back of her head, effectively gagging her.

"In case anyone sees us. We haven't much time." He grasped her arm and guided her toward the bay window of the room, which overlooked the gardens. He forced the window open and then lifted her up by the waist and set her on the ledge. He climbed up beside her and dropped a few feet down to the ground before reaching up for her. Once she was on the ground beside him, he pointed to a horse that stood off in the distance, nickering softly at the edge of the trees fifty yards ahead of the house.

Gavin ran toward the horse, and she kept up with him as best she could.

"I'll lift you up first," he explained, and she reached for the pommel to steady herself while he hoisted her up. When she was firmly on the saddle, he mounted up behind her and wrapped one arm around her waist while the other gripped the reins. She braced her body against his to steady herself as the horse started to move.

Is this truly happening? Gavin had just kidnapped her the night before her marriage to his own brother. She wanted to ask where he was taking her, but the gag prevented any questions. As they rode, his cheek pressed against hers more than once as he leaned forward to guide the horse. The light stubble on his face scratched her skin, but she found she didn't mind the sensation. The wind whipped her cheeks and her heart pounded as she tried to come to grips with her situation.

They seemed to ride for ages before they came in sight of a little village that she recognized as a place called Jack's Cove, near St. Ives Bay. She was shivering with cold by the time they reached the small waterfront village. He removed a cloak from his saddlebags and wrapped it around Josephine. Her heart warmed with the thought that he'd taken such care to keep her warm. Until she glanced down and noticed that the way he'd tucked the cloak around her also conveniently hid her bound hands. He tugged the gag out of her mouth, and she licked her lips to wet them.

"Remember to keep quiet, lass. We don't want to raise any alarm," he warned.

She was tempted to tell him that she wouldn't scream, but she kept silent because it was too quiet on the street. She feared that even speaking other than in the lowest of tones would wake up the sleeping village.

It was dark, with the moon barely a sliver in the sky, lending enough shadows to conceal her and Gavin as he halted the horse by an inn.

He slid out of the saddle and helped her down. But he waited for a long moment, watching the darkness for something she couldn't see. He straightened his shoulders as a figure emerged from the darkness.

"Cap'n?"

"Here," Gavin replied quietly.

A red-haired man stepped out of the alley by the inn and looked at Josephine curiously before focusing back on Gavin.

"Where's the ship?" Gavin asked the man as he came toward them and shook Gavin's hand with a broad smile.

"There, out in the bay. We'll have to row out to it. It already has a crew in place."

"Good. See that this horse is returned to Castleton Hall, and then meet us on the dinghy."

The red-haired man grasped the reins of the horse and led it toward some stables farther down the street. Gavin escorted Josephine away from the inn and down a small dock to where a dinghy was tied up. He helped her climb down into the boat, and then he began to unwind the ropes that kept it tied to the dock. Gavin collected the oars just as the other man returned and leapt down into the boat with them. Josephine watched the two men take up the oars and row in perfect rhythm together as they headed toward the distant ship.

When they reached the ship, Gavin removed the binding from her hands.

"I don't think we'll need this anymore, will we?" he asked, a hint of a warning in his tone, but she knew it wasn't necessary. She wasn't going to call for help.

She nodded, her heart pounding hard as she stared up at the towering bulk of the ship. A long ladder was draped down the side toward them.

"Ladies first," Gavin said. "I'll be right behind you."

She grasped the rungs and lifted herself up onto the ladder. It wasn't easy keeping her skirts out of the way of her feet, but she managed to draw the fabric up to her knees with one hand and use the other to climb. It took far longer than anyone expected, and the red-haired man kept muttering about skirts and nonsense. But what was she to do? Gavin hadn't exactly given her an opportunity to change.

When she reached the waist deck, she leaned back against the ship's railing to catch her breath while the two men climbed aboard. Gavin and the other man dropped almost silently onto the deck beside her. Several of the crew of the ship stood there, watching them expectantly.

"I'll see my *prize* below, Ronnie. Have the crew make ready to sail at once. Tell them I'll make my introduction later."

"Aye, aye, Cap'n." The red-haired man headed in the opposite direction toward the waiting crew, while Gavin grasped Josephine's arm and led her belowdecks. She was familiar with ships and realized they were heading toward what was likely the captain's cabin at the stern.

"Gavin—"

"Hush, not yet." He opened the door to the cabin at the far end of the ship. It was a large room with tall glass windows facing the sea. A bed with a gilded headboard sat against one wall. A table was covered with sea charts, a compass and sextant, all neatly arranged. The ship felt *new*. Josephine noticed that every surface seemed polished and the wood positively gleamed. This couldn't be the ship that Gavin had lost.

Gavin closed the door and flipped the latch to lock it before he turned to face her. Was it finally safe for her to speak?

"Gavin, why did you take me?" she asked. Her blood was still rushing through her body too quickly from the excitement of the ride and the steep climb over the side of the ship. It made it hard for her to think as clearly as she wished to.

He came toward her and she held her ground as the

pirate gently grasped her chin, his smile rakish and almost hard as their gazes locked.

"Because I *wanted* you. We will enjoy each other's company while we sail the West Indies, and then once I've reclaimed my ship you will be free to do as you what you like and go where you wish." His brown-eyed gaze fell to her lips, and his intense focus made her tremble. He brushed the pad of his thumb over her bottom lip, and the feel of it was incredibly sensual. It didn't escape her notice that he made no mention of her returning to marry his brother.

"You would not let me go home now, even if I begged you?" she asked, but a dark voice whispered that wasn't what she wanted at all. Going home meant marrying Griffin. She had to know how much Gavin truly wanted to keep her.

Gavin's mouth twitched in another dark half smile. "No, not even if you begged sweetly enough to make the angels weep. My brother had his chance to seduce you and he did not." He smiled wider and leaned closer to her, a dangerous sensuality rolling off him that nearly made her knees buckle. "As for me, I *want* you, lass. And I shall have you."

His words sent her flying with hope and excitement.

"You won't ever want to think of Cornwall again." He leaned in to whisper, "Not when I can show you everything worth having in this life." He grasped her waist and turned her so she stared out at the dark sea through the windows. He pressed his body against hers from behind and reached around to grasp her neck, but the hold was gentle, soothing rather than restraining.

"No harm will come to you when you're with me. There will only be pleasure for you, sweet Josie."

No doubt he could feel the frantic beat of her pulse and could mistake her excitement for fear. She was strangely aroused by the thought of him taking control like this, making her gently bend to his will. Josephine couldn't help but press the boundaries of her situation. She wanted to be sure that he truly wanted her, not out of some need to take what was his brothers, but because he genuinely desired her.

"And if I say no to this grand offer of yours?"

His rumbling laughter was followed by soft kisses along her neck. She vibrated as the heat of his body and hers seemed ready to ignite some ancient fire within her.

"I'm a pirate, lass, and a pirate takes what he wants. And I want you." He bit the lobe of her ear, and the hint of pain made her moan and lean back against him, wanting more.

Gavin turned her head toward his with a hand upon her cheek and kissed her. The kiss was hard, ruthless, piratical to its very core. She groaned helplessly and melted. A proper lady would have been resisting him, fighting him like a wildcat and crying out for help, but Josephine was not a proper lady, no matter how hard her parents had tried. The truth was, she wanted this adventure and this man. She had been relieved to be willingly kidnapped but also excited beyond words. This was her chance to live, even though she knew that she would end up in Gavin's bed. Yes, she'd be ruined for marriage to any other man once she was no longer a virgin. But she believed all of that was such foolish nonsense.

Shouldn't a woman have the same freedoms as a man? It was what Roberta and Brianna, the former pirate that her brother's best friend Nicholas had married, always whispered about when the men were out of the room. They thought she didn't hear them, but she knew they were of the same mind. Women deserved freedom, especially freedom to enjoy their bodies and their lives as men did. So distracted in her thoughts, she suddenly realized he wasn't kissing her any longer. Instead, he was watching her eyes closely.

"What are you thinking about?" he asked. "You look so serious." He traced a fingertip over her brows as if to smooth away her concerns.

"Just that . . . I am free."

At that he grinned and tipped her chin up again. "You're still my captive," he reminded her seductively and bent his mouth to hers again. She couldn't help but smile as she thought, *And you're mine—you just don't know it yet.*

Gavin finally broke the kiss and held her a long moment, his breathing as hard as hers. He pressed his forehead to hers, eyes closed as he seemed to come back to himself. Then he stepped back.

"I have to see to our departure and speak with the crew." With one last scorching look at her, he departed the cabin.

She heard the door lock behind her, but it didn't matter. She was here, a willing captive, whether he believed her or not. She crossed the room to the bed and sank down on it as a tidal wave of relief swept through her. There would be no wedding tomorrow. She was safe. She was *free*. She lay back on the bed, exhaustion overtaking her, and let the waves and the rocking ship soothe her. She tried not to think of what her family or Griffin would do once they realized she was missing.

I'm free . . . Well, free enough. That's all that matters.

GAVIN CROSSED THE DECK TO JOIN RONNIE. THE CREW were gathered on the opposite end of the deck to meet him.

"What ship is this?" he asked Ronnie in a low voice so as not to be overheard.

"A good one, Cap'n, a *new* one." Ronnie beamed proudly at him as he patted the nearest railing. "Some rich fool just had it made for his new merchant fleet. He didn't have a master hired yet, just a waiting crew. I told the men you were their new cap'n."

"What?" Gavin couldn't believe his own luck. "What fool would leave a fully manned ship without a master in the harbor?"

"Some fool named Greyville," Ronnie chuckled.

Gavin's smile slipped. "Not *Dominic* Greyville?"

"Er . . . I don't rightly know. I only ever heard the name Greyville."

The name hit him like a smithy's hammer striking an anvil.

"Bloody hell, man! We've got to leave. *Now!*" Gavin raced toward the new crew, shouting orders and not bothering to introduce himself. They had to get the ship underway and out to sea as soon as possible.

Ronnie scrambled after him. "Why?"

"Why?" Gavin hissed as he whirled and grabbed his quartermaster by the shoulders. "Because I took another pirate's ship and kidnapped his younger sister to be my mistress. Greyville is *Dominic Grey's* true name." Gavin had known it was reckless enough to steal another pirate's little sister, but he'd been willing to bet that Dominic wouldn't guess that it was him. But a missing ship and a missing sister would be too much of a coincidence for Dominic to miss if Griffin told Dominic he'd returned. He would put the pieces together

Ronnie's face drained of color. "Not *the* Dom Grey . . . ?"

"The very one." Gavin and Dominic had been childhood friends, but as pirates they'd had mutual respect for one another. Ronnie had met Dominic in passing as their crews had met at the Black Isle for Brethren of the Coast gatherings. Dominic was a legend to all pirates in the West Indies. If he hadn't been caught up in marriage to an admiral's daughter, he likely would have become Admiral of the Black instead of Gavin.

Ronnie counted their sins numbly on his fingers. "We took his ship, his crew, and his sister . . . Oh, Cap'n., we're dead men."

"Only if we don't get out of this bloody harbor!"

The ship sparked to life as the crew dashed to their stations to carry out the orders Gavin had given them. No one questioned the mad escape from the harbor, but even as they sailed out into the open sea, Gavin kept glancing back, fearing he would see a second ship chasing them at any moment.

No one could outrun Dominic Grey once he had his sights set on them . . . except Gavin . . . if he had the right ship. Dominic had retired from piracy a short time ago, but that didn't change who he was. *Once a pirate, always a pirate*. Dominic would be furious enough to find Josephine gone, but at least he hadn't known Gavin was involved. But if Griffin told Dominic that Gavin had come home and then discovered his ship and sister were missing, the two men could put their heads together, and . . .

"Blast!" Gavin cursed into the wind as the sails unfurled and the ship began to glide away from the coast of Cornwall. He prayed this vessel could fly like the wind, or else the Royal Navy prowling the waters hunting for pirates would be the least of his worries.

Once he was certain the ship was safely out to sea, he would make proper introductions as the new master of the *Cornish Pixie*. He had to make sure the crew was satisfied that Dominic had hired him to be the master of this ship.

With Ronnie in charge of the ship, Gavin retired to the master's cabin and unlocked the door. He braced himself for a female in fine fury after being locked in the cabin. As he stepped inside the room, he was surprised to see that his fierce captive lay on the bed in the midst of a waterfall of pale-blue silk, fast asleep, as sweet as a kitten.

He hovered by the bedside, drinking in the sight of her. She wore what was no doubt supposed to be her wedding dress. It was too exquisite for a day gown. He could tell by the pearls embedded in the bodice and sleeves and the fine lace at the elbows that this was the gown that Griffin should have seen her wearing for their wedding. A stab of jealousy mixed with smug arrogance tumbled within his chest. His brother would not have this woman. He would not see her like this now. She was to be Gavin's and Gavin's alone.

"Sorry, brother, but you took my woman. It is only fair I take yours."

The pretty lass asleep in his bed did not stir, but he didn't mind that she slept tonight. They had a long voyage ahead of them to chase down the *Lady Siren*. There would be plenty of nights ahead to seduce his prize. With a wicked smile, Gavin sat on the edge of his bed and pulled off his boots. He stripped off his trousers and lay down beside Josephine, pulling her back against his body. He buried his face in her hair. She smelled like a garden just after a rainstorm. Her scent of roses and lavender filled his head as he breathed her in.

"Yes, I think I shall keep you, my darling Josie," he murmured in her ear.

Josephine let out a soft sigh, as though she'd heard him, and turned to burrow closer into him. Something tugged at his long-shattered heart, but he ignored it. He would never love anyone ever again. Not even this bewitching woman with fire upon her lips and her eyes full of dreams that sailed like ships in the clouds.

CHAPTER 6

"What do you mean, she's *gone?*" Griffin stood behind his desk in his study. The three men who faced him from the other side didn't flinch at his tone. Josephine's father, Lord Camden; her twin brother, Adrian; and her elder brother, Dominic, had arrived two hours before he'd planned to be at the church to marry Josephine.

He tried to calm the sudden fear in his chest for the woman he'd planned to tie his life to. "Where is she? Did she leave a letter?" After speaking with his brother, he could quite believe that Josephine might cry off and hide to avoid marrying him. While that stung his pride, he was more concerned that she was safe and unharmed than that she'd run out on him.

Lord Camden and his two sons exchanged worried glances before Camden spoke.

"I'm afraid we have no idea what's happened to her. My daughter was being fitted for her wedding gown last night when my wife last saw her. She and Josephine's lady's maid left to prepare her bridal presents, which would be a surprise for her today after the ceremony. When the maid returned to her chamber, she found it empty and the bay window open."

"Is the maid here? May I speak with her? Perhaps she witnessed something that can help us find Josephine," Griffin suggested.

"Yes, she's out in the corridor. Adrian, fetch her," Camden ordered.

Adrian returned a moment later with a young woman at his side, whom he introduced as Vesper Lyndon. The woman had her head down respectfully and was clearly too frightened to look at anyone. Griffin walked around his desk and approached her. She stiffened when he stopped just in front of her.

"Miss Lyndon?" He spoke the girl's name uncertainly.

"Yes, my lord?" Her voice was soft, but he heard a note of strength in it. She wasn't afraid of him—she feared for her lady's safety. She lifted her tearstained face to meet his gaze.

The sunlight touched upon her golden hair, and her green eyes struck him like a bolt of lightning. For a moment, he couldn't breathe. It felt like his head was spinning, and yet he was grounded at the same time, like an ancient tree stretching its roots deep into the soil and binding itself to the earth so that it might go on living forever. Was he *falling*?

Dear God, he thought with a warmth that seemed to cloud his head, and he nearly reached for something to steady himself.

Vesper stared at him expectantly, those green eyes

seeming to drink him in the way he had just done to her, as though she never wanted to look away, couldn't look away from him.

"I . . . er . . ." He struggled to regain his thoughts. "What I wish to ask you is . . . when you last saw Josephine, was she acting in any strange manner? Did she say or do anything that might give you any insight into what happened?"

Vesper licked her lips nervously and her gaze grew distant, as if she was replaying the last encounter she'd had with her mistress.

"She seemed . . . distracted during the gown fitting. She didn't seem overly anxious, but it was as if she was miles away. That is all I can think of," Vesper said.

"Thank you, Vesper," Griffin murmured as he released her chin. He hadn't realized he'd reached out and touched her. It had felt so natural that he'd not even noticed.

"I'm sorry I didn't notice more, my lord. Lady Camden and I were so very excited about your wedding presents. It was to be a surprise . . ." Her voice trailed off into a whisper.

"Please do not cry. I'm certain she is all right. Josephine is a brave lady."

"Yes, she is," Vesper agreed. "I should go. Lady Camden may need me." Vesper practically fled the room, and Griffin stared after her, his heart beating heavily at the loss of this woman he didn't even know.

"Well, that certainly didn't give us much," Dominic muttered. "All we know for certain, Castleton, is that she didn't leave on her own. I found footprints, hers and those of a man, leading into the woods. From there, I only found one set of hoofprints, so they rode off together on a horse."

"We must search the countryside," Griffin said. "We could divide up and ride to the nearest inns and taverns to look for her. She can't have gotten far."

At this Adrian snorted, causing everyone to look at him. Griffin had rarely spent time in the young man's company, but the boy was Josephine's twin and close to her the way he had once been close to Gavin.

"Did she run away?" Camden asked his younger son. "Tell us what you know, my son."

Adrian cleared his face of emotion. "Honestly, I don't know where she's gone. I only stayed a moment after Mother saw to her last night. But if I was her, I would have run." He gave a wry look at Griffin. "No offense meant, my lord."

"Why would she run?" Griffin asked the lad. "I would have given her anything she wanted." He had been committed to making his marriage to Josephine a sound one, with mutual affection and respect.

"Because even with your title and duties, there was one thing you could never give her, the one thing she needed." Adrian's face reddened a little.

"What?" Griffin asked warily.

"Adventure."

That single word reverberated through Griffin like the tolling of a great bell. *Adventure*. There was one person who lived only by his drive for adventure and passion. And he and Josephine had met.

"I've been a damned fool," Griffin muttered.

He strode quickly from his study, not caring that the

three Greyville men followed on his heels. He headed straight for the tapestry that held the entrance to the hidden chamber open. The passageway was cold and dark. No sounds came from within the room. Had Gavin already left? Griffin moved deeper into the chamber to see that it was empty. As he'd expected, Gavin was gone.

A single lamp was lit on the table, its light running low. Beside it was a piece of paper that had been pinned to the table with a jeweled dagger. Griffin gripped the blade and pulled it free of the paper and read the words written there.

"You took my prize, so now I've taken yours."

"What does that mean? Who wrote that?" Lord Camden demanded.

"My brother wrote this. It seems he has taken Josephine."

"Your brother?" Dominic growled, and his eyes narrowed. "Last I saw him was . . ." Dominic closed his mouth, realizing too late the mistake he'd made.

"What do you know of my brother, Dominic?" Griffin asked, his tone hard. As boys, the three of them had been friends. Not as close as Dominic had been to Nicholas Flynn, but they'd been close enough that they'd spent a great deal of time together.

Dominic exchanged a glance with his father before continuing. "I suppose you have a right to the truth . . . He was in the West Indies for many years. We met often. When I married Roberta and came home, he had just assumed the role of the Admiral of the Black."

"The Admiral of the *what?*" Griffin had never heard of such a thing.

Dominic's voice lowered to a whisper, even though no one but the four men could hear his words in that private room.

"The pirates in the West Indies are more organized than you might have heard. To keep them in line, one pirate is chosen to rule them. The Admiral of the Black. The previous admiral retired, and votes were taken to put a new man in his place. The last I had heard, that was Gavin. What was he doing here in Cornwall?"

Seeing that Dominic had been truthful with him, Griffin felt it necessary to be truthful with what he knew of Gavin's situation. "Apparently, my brother was off the coast of Cornwall when his ship suffered a mutiny. He barely escaped with his life. He was injured and came through this passageway into our home. He sought me out, only I wasn't in my old chambers. Josephine was."

Camden scowled at this, but Griffin continued. "Josephine tended to his injuries that night, then brought me to see him. He told me he would be gone in a few days. He planned to take his ship back somehow. Perhaps he's taken her with him."

Lord Camden let out an aggrieved sigh. "So my only daughter has been abducted by a pirate. And not just any pirate, but one intent on revenge who just so happens to be the current *king* of pirates of the West Indies?"

Dominic met Griffin's gaze, but the man's look was unreadable.

"Can *none* of my children stay away from trouble?" Camden snapped. He shot Adrian a glare, as if expecting him to confess he'd taken up with a pirate crew too. The lad raised his shoulders in an innocent shrug.

"They can't have gotten far if they have no ship," Dominic said. "Why don't we all sit down and craft a plan to bring Josie back?"

Camden gave his son a hard stare before he nodded at the jeweled dagger in Griffin's hand.

"Is my child safe with your brother?"

Griffin clenched his fingers around the hilt of his blade. "I honestly don't know. He wouldn't *harm* her, but from what I understand, there may be some passion between them."

"Passion?" Camden uttered the word in confusion.

"My brother is a charmer, Lord Camden. And your daughter spent the night in his company, tending to his wounds. I believe that it may have resulted in . . . feelings between them, however innocent for Josephine." Griffin had gleaned enough from his twin's reaction to Josephine and hers to him in that short time they'd all stood in this room to realize that Josephine was more than curious, if not attracted to Gavin in some way. Of course, she was far too innocent to realize her face and her words had betrayed as much to him.

"If he touches her . . . ," Camden began, his voice full of quiet fury.

"He will face the wrath of every man in this room," Griffin promised.

Gavin, you damned fool. What have you done?

As the four men exited the secret passageway, someone called for them in the corridor. A messenger had arrived from Camden's estate with a note for Dominic. Dominic rushed down to meet the young man holding the message at the bottom of the grand stairs. Dominic took the missive and read it, his face hardening as Griffin and the others joined him at the base of the stairs.

"It's from my wife. My new ship, the *Cornish Pixie*, which was anchored in St. Ives Bay, sailed out to sea last night." He crumpled the note in his palm. "The crew I hired *apparently* heard they'd been assigned a new master . . ."

"What was that you were saying about them not getting far without a ship?" Adrian asked, a hint of amusement in his eyes. "Castleton's brother will have a decent head start on us."

"This is no laughing matter, lad," Griffin said. "Gavin once loved a woman who chose to marry me instead. Now he's taken my intended bride, your sister. He'll likely seduce her before we ever catch up to them."

Adrian's humor vanished as he returned Griffin's look. "Yes, the bastard will likely try to seduce her, but he doesn't know Josie like I do. She's clever and stubborn. He'll not find her a rose so easily tamed. If she's there against her will, he will feel her thorns."

"I hope you are right," Griffin said. If anything happened to her because of Gavin, he would never forgive himself.

"So, what's our plan now that they have a ship?" Adrian asked.

"We must go after them," Dominic said darkly. "I once counted Gavin as a friend, but now he's taken my ship *and* my sister. He will pay for those transgressions."

"Agreed," Lord Camden said just as coldly. "No one takes my child without consequences."

Griffin would try to save his brother's life, if it came

to that, but he hoped these men would be in better spirits if Josie remained unharmed. If only it would be just an innocent adventure and Josephine would come home safe.

"We need a ship," Camden said.

"Nicholas and Brianna are here. Brianna's ship is in the bay. I imagine she would be happy to help us, given hers and Gavin's history," Dominic suggested.

"What history?" Griffin asked.

Dominic met his gaze reluctantly. "They are old friends . . . and occasionally they have been lovers."

"Ah . . ." So, his brother hadn't been a monk all these years. Griffin had been, though. Ever since Charity had died, he'd seen no other woman. Been tempted by no other. Until today . . .

He forced himself to shove aside his thoughts of the lady's maid or how his world had tilted on its axis when he'd laid eyes on her. He had a betrothed to worry about and a pirate to chase down.

"Let's make ready to leave at once," Griffin said to the others. He still held the jeweled dagger, vowing he'd return it to his brother in exchange for Josephine's freedom.

A prize for a prize indeed . . .

JOSEPHINE STRETCHED, THEN GROANED IN DISCOMFORT. Heavy blankets covered her legs, and something tightened around her chest as she tried to breathe. She kicked fussily, trying to dislodge whatever kept her legs unbearably warm and trapped.

"Ow!" a deep voice grunted close to her ear. Her eyes flew open, and she found herself staring at a man's jaw. A beautiful, chiseled jaw. Her eyes traced up the line of that jaw to the ear and nose and finally the eyes. Gavin was staring at her in amusement. As she got her bearings, she realized they were lying facing each other in a bed that rocked slightly.

Oh God . . . She hadn't dreamt last night, then? Gavin *had* kidnapped her on the eve of her wedding to Griffin and taken her out to sea? She glanced down the length of her body, seeing that she was still in the exquisite wedding gown she'd worn last night. It was her voluminous skirts tangled around her legs and her corset pulled tight around her chest that had caused her such discomfort. She raised her eyes back to Gavin's face, still in disbelief that she was *here* with him. She was supposed to be on the way to her wedding, not waking up in a pirate's bed.

"Did you sleep here too?" she blurted out.

"Yes, and you, darling creature, stretch out like a starfish in your sleep . . . and *kick too*," he said with a low chuckle. "I'll have bruises on my shins from your violence."

Josephine blushed in mortification. She knew she did stretch out a bit in her sleep, the evidence was in the state of her sheets each morning, but she'd never had anyone complain about it before because she'd always slept alone.

"Oh . . ." She inwardly cursed at the flood of heat in her face. She slowly sat up, and he rolled onto his back, folding his arms above his head, only to wince and put them back down. She glanced at his wound, but the stitched area looked clean.

She tried to comb her hands through her hair. "I see you're feeling better."

"Yes, I am." His eyes tracked the movement of her hands. "I rather like it when you do that," he mused softly.

"Do what?"

"Comb your hair with your fingers. It reminds me of a mermaid sunning upon the rocks." He settled his uninjured arm behind his head as he lay back again on the bed. She tried and failed to avoid looking at his chest. His skin was a light gold, and his pectoral muscles were well developed. The ropes of muscle in his abdomen made her throat strangely dry. *Lord . . .* He was a specimen of a man, wasn't he? Not that she'd seen many half-dressed men, but a woman knew deep in her womb what an attractive male looked like. Some things were too ingrained into the mind to be erased by the dictates of polite society.

"A mermaid?" she asked in an attempt to distract herself. "You've seen one?"

"Aye, of course. They are crafty creatures. They hide in the shallows at night and sing, but on fine sunny days when they expect no ships to come near them, they like to sun on the rocks within view of the beaches. I've hidden there and glimpsed them as they combed their hair."

He was teasing her. Mermaids didn't exist, nor did sea monsters. But she liked to imagine it all the same.

She climbed out of the bed and explored the cabin as he looked on in amusement. There was a chest full of fine gowns, as well as men's clothing. A large copper tub was in a corner of the room with a discreet sheet draped within the inside, which meant a lady could bathe in the tub and retain some of her modesty.

"This isn't your ship, is it?" she asked. He'd said he'd lost his ship, and she wondered if he'd managed to find it again. How did one lose a ship, anyway?

"It is now. I stole it," he said with a chuckle.

"You stole it?" Josephine bent over the trunk again as she examined some of the gowns more closely, then she froze. She *knew* these dresses. She'd seen them before . . . on her sister-in-law.

"What's the name of this ship?" she asked quietly.

"The *Cornish Pixie*."

She whirled to face him. "You stole *my brother's* ship?"

"Oh? Is this your brother's ship? How amusing. I imagine he will be quite furious once he finds out." Gavin yawned dramatically, as if he was not the least bit worried about an angry pirate coming after them.

"Oh dear . . ." She began to pace the cabin, her silky blue skirts whispering over the polished wooden deck. Dominic and Roberta had been planning to sail to the West Indies in a few weeks to check on his landholdings there. He'd planned to command the ship himself until he found a suitable captain.

Gavin finally stood and caught her arm as she paced about. He pulled her into his embrace, their gazes locking.

"We have a decent head start. Your brother won't be able to catch us." Griffin rubbed his hands slowly up and down her arms, making her shiver with an excitement she should not be feeling.

"You don't know him, Gavin. He's a . . ." She halted before she betrayed her brother.

"He's a what?" Gavin turned her face toward his when she tried to look away. "A pirate?" he supplied, his honey-brown eyes hot. "You need not keep that secret, not with me. I know your brother well."

"Yes, as boys you knew him—"

"No, as pirates. He and I often crossed paths upon the sea and shared ale and voted on matters together with the Brethren of the Coast. I know how dangerous he is, my darling."

Her eyes widened at Gavin's confession and the way he'd called her *darling*. He knew about Dominic? Then she realized how very silly she'd been. Of course they must've known each other. Pirates always seemed to know, or at least know *of*, each other. Then her mind caught upon his words.

"What's the Brethren of the Coast?"

"Think of it as a pirate parliament," Gavin explained, but he was still staring at her mouth, and she was finding it rather distracting herself to look at his lips.

"A pirate parliament?" she echoed. She started to lean into him, her eyes drifting closed as she waited for a kiss.

"I should go check on my men," he said reluctantly and stepped back. "Shall I bring you food when I return?"

She recovered herself quickly and smoothed her skirts in an attempt to regain her composure.

"What? Oh yes, please. I am rather famished." She watched him leave, and once she was alone, she examined the clothing in the sea chest again. One could not run about a pirate ship in a wedding gown. She needed to change her clothes. She suddenly wished Vesper was here. Her lady's maid was always prepared for such things. She would have had a light day gown and a clean chemise and stockings ready for her before she even woke.

"I shall have to make do without you, Vesper," she murmured to herself and began to dig through the gowns.

Roberta was a few inches shorter than her, but the gowns would still fit in all of the places that mattered. What did she care if she exposed an ankle every now and then? However, she didn't want to wear gowns, at least not right at the moment. If this was to be her adventure, she wanted more freedom to move about the ship.

She retrieved a pair of her brother's trousers and a shirt and waistcoat, much like what Gavin wore, and laid them upon the bed. The wedding gown did not come off without a fight, however. Thankfully, Vesper always tied her laces at the bottom of her dresses and tucked the loose laces into the skirts at the base of Josephine's spine. With some clever reaching from behind, she was able to free herself of the bodice and shimmy out of it before doing the same with her corset.

She probably ought to have kept the corset on, but once she was free of the undergarment, she didn't want to put it on again anytime soon. Instead, she donned the shirt and trousers and then buttoned up the burgundy waistcoat. Glancing at herself in the mirror, Josephine thought that she looked like a female pirate ready to storm a ship and seize treasure. She nearly giggled at the reckless daydream.

She pulled on a pair of her brother's boots next, only they were far too big for her, so she switched to Roberta's pair of black boots. Satisfied with her new clothing, she marched to the door and turned the handle. It didn't move. Gavin had locked her in. Why would he do such a foolish thing? It wasn't as if she could escape him or the ship, even if she wanted to.

Blast him! She kicked the door with one booted foot and marched angrily over to the bed and flung herself back down. When Gavin returned, they were going to discuss this foolish behavior.

GAVIN STOOD ON THE QUARTERDECK AND STARED AT THE row of sailors in front of him. Most looked to be hearty men of a young age. There were a few seasoned men among them. Ronnie coughed politely, catching his attention, and the quartermaster nodded at the men, indicating that Gavin should address them.

"Right," Gavin muttered to himself. He squared his shoulders and spoke to the crew. "My name is Gavin Castleton. The owner of this ship has hired me to sail you to the West Indies. This is Ronald Phelps, my, er . . . first mate. When I am otherwise engaged, you'll take your orders from him." On a pirate ship, a quartermaster was second in command beneath the master or captain, but he had to remind himself that on a merchant ship, Ronnie would be his first mate.

One of the older sailors in his early fifties politely stepped forward. "Cap'n?"

"Yes? Your name and position?" Gavin asked.

"Tom Greenwell, Cap'n. Boatswain," the sailor replied.

"What is it, Mr. Greenwell?" Gavin asked.

"We . . . that is, me and the others . . . we saw that you brought a lassie on the ship."

"Yes, what of her?" Gavin arched a brow.

"Well . . ." Greenwood exchanged glances with the other sailors again.

"Er . . ." The man's face reddened. "Is she with you? It's just that, well, 'tis bad luck to have a woman on board."

Gavin was surprised at the rather personal question, but Ronnie leapt in before he could answer.

"Aye, she is with the cap'n. She's his wife, an' she'll be treated with respect."

A few murmurs went up at this. Gavin inwardly groaned. This was not what he needed.

"Aye, his *wife*," Ronnie barked. "Any man who so much as looks at her funny will be thrown over the side."

Gavin barely stopped himself from rolling his eyes and smacking the back of Ronnie's head. The muttering about bad luck abruptly ceased, and the men straightened to attention once more.

"Besides, there's another woman on board. Mrs. O'Malley," Ronnie reminded the crew.

"Aye, but she's a cook," Greenwell added. "Cooks are *always* good luck, woman or no."

Ronnie looked like he was ready to argue on the matter of bad luck, but Gavin stopped him with a hand on his shoulder.

"Thank you, Mr. Phelps," he said, then spoke to the rest of the crew again. "Yes, my wife will journey with us to the West Indies. I expect you to be on your best behavior, as she is a gentleborn lady. I shall make it worth your while with extra rum rations once a week, and when we reach port, you shall have some time ashore to enjoy yourselves. Now, I assume we have a gunner and hopefully a surgeon on board?"

Two other men stepped forward beside Greenwell.

Greenwell nodded at the other two men. "This is Mr. Mefford, our gunner, and that is Dr. Gladstone."

"Right, you know your positions on this ship?" Gavin asked. Both men answered with a confident nod.

Good, Dominic had hired an able-bodied crew. One less thing to worry about. They had successfully gotten away from England last night with no trouble, but time would tell how tricky the crossing to the West Indies would be.

"I invite the three of you to dine with me and my wife this evening in my cabin at eight o'clock." He knew that on normal ships, those not captained by pirates, the occasional dinner with one's captain was expected for the higher-ranking crew.

Once everyone was back to work, Ronnie trailed after Gavin, who had stopped near the helm. A young man named Brandon gripped the wooden spindles of the wheel with confidence. He couldn't have been more than twenty-one or twenty-two, but he was a strong looking sort of fellow.

"Morning, Cap'n," the young man said cheerfully. He nodded rather than saluting him, that way he could keep hold of the wheel.

"Did Mr. Phelps give you our heading?"

"Aye, that he did."

"Excellent." Gavin then faced the rest of the decks, watching the men at work. There was a peace to sailing in good weather, when men could be on the decks, scaling the rigging and taking care of rope and other things. It was soothing work that he'd always enjoyed. The sails were full of wind and the skies were clear. He let out a breath, and the tension in his shoulders eased.

"Cap'n, what's our plan?" Ronnie whispered as they moved away from the helm. Gavin went over to the railing to lean against it. Ronnie joined him, his legs braced apart and his hands clasped behind his back in a posture to rival any admiral.

"Our plan?" Gavin replied.

"Aye, you have a ship and a wench . . . er, *wife*," Ronnie quickly corrected. "What's our plan? I thought we were to go after the *Siren*?"

"We are," he promised his friend. "Beauchamp must pay for what he's done." The faces of his loyal crew who'd died fighting in the mutiny hovered at the edge of his mind, haunting him. He had vowed he would avenge them, and that was a promise he would keep.

"Then why risk bringing a lassie aboard, Cap'n? She'll only be in the way."

"We will stop at my island first and leave her there. She'll be safe enough. Then we will go to Sugar Cove and recruit men for the recapturing of the *Siren*." He nodded at the crew around them. "These men did not sign on to be pirates, and I do not want to put them in danger, or risk another mutiny."

"We need cutthroats," Ronnie said sagely.

"Aye," Gavin agreed. "Now I'd better go and feed my *wife*." He emphasized the word to Ronnie with a mock scowl. "I must explain to her that we are to play the role of husband and wife before the crew."

"Sorry about that, Cap'n. I thought it best they didn't think you were the wenching sort. Might give 'em ideas."

Gavin chuckled at the words "wenching sort." He had never been the type to go wenching when in port. He had sampled the favors of a few women in his time, it was true, but he had never run to the brothels like most. He'd found he preferred the capable company of women like Brianna Holland. She had been both a pirate and a captain of her own ship. He had enjoyed the camaraderie of sharing a bed with someone who understood life at sea and knew her way around a ship. But alas, she had slipped from his grasp and married a naval officer.

He wished Brianna and her new husband well, but he was alone again. Perhaps that was what had sparked his mad scheme to take Josephine from his brother? He had suffered too many losses—his ship, his loyal crew—and now he needed something that he could claim for himself, even if it was only for a short while.

Gavin left Ronnie in charge and went down a few decks to the galley, where Mrs. O'Malley, the cook, was bustling about. She was a spry woman with dark hair streaked with hints of gray. Her strong hands gripped a rolling pin as she set about making bread. That surprised him. Most cooks couldn't handle any sort of bread while on board. She also had fresh lemons in a box, and it looked as though she'd been squeezing them into a glass bottle for juice. A chicken, freshly roasted, rested on a metal plate, the aroma making his stomach grumble. When the cook realized she was under observation, she set the rolling pin aside.

"You must be the master?" she said, sweeping a critical eye over him.

He couldn't resist flashing her a charming grin. "I am." A happy cook meant better food. "The name is Gavin Castleton. It's a pleasure to meet you."

"Well, aren't you a charmer," she chuckled. "I'm Olive O'Malley, then." She retrieved one of the lemons from the box, cut it, and gave him a slice.

"Is there a *Mr.* O'Malley?" Gavin teased before he savored the taste of the tart lemon. Some sailors believed that lemons helped keep scurvy at bay. He was glad to see the cook had the good sense to juice the fruit, since he was one of those who believed lemons helped a man's health while at sea.

"Oh, be away with you!" The woman waved a rag at him. "I'll have you know he's the ship's carpenter."

"He's a lucky man," Gavin said and then leaned over the chicken on the plate to inhale the scent, his stomach growling. "May I take this divine looking chicken for myself?"

"And share with your lady friend, I hope?" she asked, arching a brow in challenge.

"Aye, Josephine, my wife," he said, still silently cursing his quartermaster for the charade, even if it had been the wisest course of action.

"Yes, take it and share it with her. And take this." She gave him a bottle of red wine and two glasses. "I haven't had the chance to put them in your cabin yet, but I was told that you would want them there."

Gavin glanced at the bottle, noting it was a fine wine. He grinned. It was yet more evidence that Dominic had planned to captain the maiden voyage of this ship and take Roberta with him.

More's the pity for Dom to miss this, Gavin thought with a smug grin. He and Josephine would reap the benefits of Dominic's careful planning instead.

"Thank you, Mrs. O'Malley." He winked at her and collected the tray she prepared and headed toward the captain's cabin. As he returned to his cabin, thinking of Josephine waiting there for him, he had a sudden idea.

They were likely to be at sea for forty days or longer, and he didn't want to rush his seduction. He could easily have what he wanted. Josephine was wild and responsive to his kisses, but why rush the experience? He always enjoyed a challenge. So perhaps he would wait and slowly build Josephine's desires until she was begging for him to claim her. Their joining would be all the sweeter for the hunger having built up between them. Yes, that would give him something to amuse himself on this crossing. How long could a pirate go without taking that which he wanted?

With a grin, he unlocked the captain's cabin and stepped inside.

"I have food, my lady," he said as his gaze swept the room. The very *empty* room.

What the devil? He walked deeper into the room, trying to make sense of what he was seeing. Josephine wasn't there. Her silvery-blue dress lay on the bed, but she was no longer in it.

"Josie?"

He felt the caress of wind behind him, and he whirled around in time to see the cabin door slam shut and hear the lock click into place. Josephine had ducked past him, and he'd only glimpsed her out of the corner of his eye. Had that even been Josephine? He slammed the tray down on the table and stalked back toward the closed door.

"Let me out, *now*!"

"Rather a silly feeling to be locked in, isn't it?" Josephine shouted through the door, obviously trying to stifle a laugh.

"Open it *now*," Gavin growled.

"Or what, *Captain*?" she asked sweetly. "I think you should take some time to think about how to properly treat your guests, and I shall take a tour of the ship while you do so."

He rattled the door latch furiously, knowing it would not open.

"*Josie!*" he bellowed, but her steps faded away. He kicked the door with a growl, but the wood was sturdy. He let out another shout, but no one came to his aid.

When he got his hands on her, he was going to redden her backside. With a snarl, he stalked over to the table and flung himself into a chair and began to pick at the roasted chicken, planning a thousand wicked ways he was going to punish his "guest" once he got free.

CHAPTER 7

Immensely pleased with herself, Josephine removed the spare ribbon she kept on her wrist and bound her hair back at the nape of her neck. She walked away from the cabin, humming a jaunty tune, ignoring Gavin's cursing and pounding on the door.

She wondered why Dominic had a door on his ship that only locked from the outside. Then again, knowing Roberta and her temperament, if the ship was under attack, Dominic would quite literally have to lock his wife in their cabin to keep her safe. Josephine smirked at the thought that *she* had been the one to benefit from that unusually placed latch. Men were silly creatures, always locking women away and thinking it was the right thing to do.

She followed the aroma of food down the nearest gangway and stumbled into the galley almost by accident. A slender woman was tending a fire in what Josephine recognized was an iron galley stove. All around the woman were heating surfaces with pans and kettles surrounded by iron pipe railings. The stove and its equipment dwarfed the woman, but she worked her galley in a way that Josephine imagined a six-man crew would at their battle stations. She whirled about, checking pots full of boiling pork and beef, if the smells drifting beneath Josephine's nose were to be trusted. Then the woman removed bread from the oven and replaced it with small sliced potatoes that smelled richly of butter and garlic.

"What will you be wanting, lad?" the cook began before she glanced up and gasped. "Ho there, you're no lad!" the woman exclaimed.

"Yes, it is my one great failing to have the misfortune to be born female," Josephine said with a dramatic sigh as she took in the deep scents of the food, her stomach grumbling.

The cook recovered herself and dried her hands on a clean rag. "That's not what I meant. I was told the captain brought his wife aboard, but I was not told we had *other* ladies as well." She studied Josephine's clothing with a curious sweep of her eyes before she focused on her cooking again.

Gavin had told the crew she was his wife? Josephine blinked and tried to think quickly.

"Er . . . Yes, well. I am, in fact, the captain's wife," she admitted, deciding to play along. She could demand answers from Gavin later. It was only a matter of time before someone heard him fussing about in the locked cabin and set him free. Until then, she was not going to waste her chance at freedom before he locked her up again.

"*You* are the captain's wife?" The cook stared at her,

once more taking in the masculine clothing Josephine wore.

"Yes, my dress was . . . It was my wedding gown, and I didn't wish to ruin it by wearing it while I explored the ship."

"You're exploring the ship?" The cook mouthed the words in shock. "Does the your husband know?"

Josephine grinned, unable to help herself. "Why yes. He is still sleeping in our cabin. He's *exhausted*."

At this, the cook giggled. "Oh, I wager he is. That is one handsome man you have, lass. But even the best of them always tire out after lovemaking. My Davy does too. He'll be snoring away after a good tupping, and I have to get up and cook." She rolled her eyes.

Josephine, rather than being scandalized by the cook's frank words, was utterly delighted. She held out a hand to the cook.

"I'm Josephine."

"Olive O'Malley. My husband is the ship's carpenter."

"It's lovely to meet you, Mrs. O'Malley."

"Olive, please, my lady."

"Then you must call me Josie," Josephine replied with a grin.

The cook set out a plate on the counter and began putting bits of cooked beef on it. The beef fell apart at the slightest touch of the fork that Olive used to spear it and set it on the plate. The sight of the tender meat made Josephine's stomach grumble.

"I'm guessing the captain got your skirts up and got right to business and never gave you a chance to eat that chicken I sent with him?"

Blushing, Josephine nodded. She could certainly pretend to have been bedded by Gavin if it helped her win a friend . . . and some delicious cooking.

"I thought as much." Olive filled the plate with more food and fresh bread before handing Josephine a fork. Josephine dug in, barely remembering to eat like a lady.

"Olive, what can you tell me about the ship? All I know about it is that my brother owns it."

"Does he, now? Well, it's a brigantine, and I believe it's fitted with twelve guns and a crew of eighty or so men."

"Were those swivel guns mounted to the rails I saw when I first came aboard?"

"Aye, they are," Olive said. "You know your ships." The cook looked approving rather than upset. But then again, Josephine guessed that the cook was a rarity too.

"My brother was a sailor for many years. I learned as much as I could from him." That wasn't quite a lie. She had been reading about pirates and ships all of her life while Dominic was away and she couldn't help but learn something about ships. Her mother's father had been the captain of a Spanish ship, and her father had been to sea quite a bit when he was younger. Seafaring was in her blood on both sides.

"Well, your brother commissioned a fine ship. My husband said we're lucky to be working aboard her."

Josephine agreed. The ship was beautiful. The wood was clean and polished, the surfaces freshly painted. It was rather like a fine English country house that had been given sails and set out on the water. She felt quite at home on it.

She and Olive gossiped about the ship's crew while

Josephine ate. When she simply couldn't eat another bite, she thanked her new friend and resumed her exploration of the *Cornish Pixie*. When she reached the upper decks and felt the bracing wind race across the deck to fill the sails that billowed out above her, her breath caught in her throat. The sight of fresh white canvas against deep clear blue skies was *everything* she'd ever dreamed of, and yet somehow even more magical than she could have imagined.

"Nothing like seeing the wind in the sails, eh?" an old sailor near the railing said as he set to work repairing the loose ends of the thick rope that lay around him in messy coils. He appeared to be in his late sixties but was still lean with muscle. His skin was weathered beneath his white beard, and his blue eyes were bright with gentle mischief.

"Yes, it's the most beautiful thing I've ever seen." Josephine joined the man by the railing. She nodded at the ropes he was holding. "My name is Josephine. May I help you with that?"

"No, I've got it, but you can keep me company. An old man still likes to look at a pretty lass when he has the chance. My name's Bartholomew." He winked at her and grinned, which made her laugh.

"Oh all right, I can't refuse you. What shall we talk about?"

"Well, you can settle an old man's curiosity," he said as he continued his work on the ropes.

"Oh? How so?"

"Your husband, the captain."

It seemed everyone on board had guessed she was the

captain's wife. Josephine waited for the old sailor to ask his question.

"Yes, what about him?" When she'd come aboard last night, there had only been a handful of crew members who had seen her. Gavin had rushed her down belowdecks so hastily she'd barely seen any of them, yet they all knew she was supposedly Gavin's wife.

"What sort of man is he?"

She was confused by the question. "What do you mean, what sort of man?"

"Er, he looks . . . Well, let's just say I've seen men with his look before," the old sailor said seriously.

"I'm afraid I still don't understand what you mean."

The sailor sighed. "He attracts danger, that one. I'd bet my life on it."

Josephine couldn't disagree with that.

"Should we be worried, lassie?" the man asked in a softer voice. "Does he have a temper?"

"I . . . well, he doesn't . . . I don't think so."

"What I mean is, will he flog a man to death for disobeying orders?"

"Oh, heavens, no, I would hope not." Josephine couldn't picture Gavin whipping a man or even ordering that. But the truth was, she'd only known him a handful of days and she couldn't swear to anything when it came to his behavior. He was certainly mercurial in his moods, but that wasn't the same thing as having a temper.

Before she could speak further, her "husband" emerged from belowdecks, his gaze dark and foreboding. It seemed someone had finally freed him.

"I think we're about to find out about that temper," she muttered to herself.

The sailor looked between her and the captain and put two and two together. "Can you climb?"

"Yes," she replied at once.

"Then head for the lookout on the topsail. There's a large bucket of sorts at the middle of the crossbeams. He may not catch sight of you if you move fast."

Josephine ducked down behind the guns along the deck and headed straight for the mainmast while doing her best to keep out of sight. She gripped the ropes and darted up the rigging with a speed that surprised even herself. She passed a few men on the way up as they worked to adjust the sails. She nodded at them and continued up without stopping.

When she finally reached the lookout spot and climbed over the wooden sides, she kept out of sight. Her heart pounded as she waited a long while before chancing a peek over the side. Gavin was standing on the quarterdeck, talking to his first mate. She blew out a breath of relief. He didn't appear to be searching for her. They both knew she was on the ship and couldn't escape. Not that she wanted to.

Down below, the men began to sing sea shanties while they worked. Josephine smiled as she hummed along. The warmth of the sun soon put her to sleep, and as so often of late, she fell headlong into exciting dreams that made her smile.

"THERE'S NO SIGN OF HER ANYWHERE, CAP'N," RONNIE said in a low voice on the quarterdeck. Only fifteen minutes ago, Ronnie had released him from confinement in the captain's cabin. They had searched the ship discreetly, not wanting to alarm the crew. If the men on board discovered that Gavin was not in fact the man hired to captain the *Cornish Pixie*, he and Ronnie could be overpowered and manacled in the hold.

When they had no luck finding the girl belowdecks, they moved upward. The moment Gavin set foot on the deck, he took note of the men currently at work. One old sailor stood by the mainmast and was clearly avoiding making eye contact with him.

Gavin subtly roved his gaze up the mast and glimpsed a figure darting over the top of the wooden bucket built large enough to hold a man in a lookout position. She vanished from view. There was no mistaking that attractive backside.

"Don't worry, Ronnie. I've found my wayward captive." Gavin had to work hard to keep from grinning. "She's not going anywhere."

"Oh, aye? Where's the lassie got to?" his first mate asked.

He gave the faintest nod toward the lookout point.

"Will you be fetching her down, then?"

"Not yet. The important thing is she's out of everyone's

way. I'll let her have her fun." It wasn't as though the woman could escape the ship, or him.

Gavin stayed on deck for the next few hours with the men and took a turn at the helm before deciding to scale the rigging to see what Josephine was up to. Once up there, he peered over the top and found Josephine fast asleep beneath the partial shade of a billowing sail. The sun had passed its zenith a few hours previous, and now most of the lookout point was in a decent shade.

He took a moment to watch her sleep. She had donned Dominic's clothing and rolled the pant legs up to uncover her boots and strapped a belt around her waist to keep the large white shirt tucked into the trousers. The shirt cuffs had been rolled up to allow her hands to be unencumbered by the long sleeves. She'd pulled her hair back into glossy waves at the nape of her neck and secured it with a ribbon. Her long dark lashes lay across her cheeks, and her warm skin held a hint of her mother's Spanish heritage.

The girl was *exquisite*, whether she wore a satin wedding gown or sailor's togs. All the frustration he'd had at her childish antics earlier faded away. She was so innocent of the ways of the world, and yet her eagerness to live reminded him so much of Charity.

But he was not a fool. The two were far more different than they were alike. Charity had been raised in London and had seen the ways of the world there. She'd known things of life that this young lady had not. Charity hadn't been jaded, but she hadn't had the innocence of heart in her that Josephine did. Of course that innocence would fade as the years passed, but the curiosity, and courage, would remain within her. It was a part of her adventurous soul, and it called to his own.

"Where were you when I was seventeen?" he whispered to the sleeping woman. He knew she would have only been a child nine years ago, but he wished in that moment she was the same age as he was and that he had met her as a younger man. Had he met Josephine first instead of Charity, he knew he would have fallen in love with her. The thought bothered him more sharply than he expected. Charity could have married Griffin, and Gavin could have married Josephine. Then the break between him and his brother never would have happened and—

He stopped before his thoughts could deepen into melancholy. It was no good to dwell upon what might have been and to forget to live with the reality of the here and now.

"You weren't there then, but you're here *now*, and I shall cherish what time I have with you."

He was surprised at the wealth of tenderness he already felt for Josephine. His plan had been to take the woman who was to be his brother's, but deep down, he knew it was more than that. They were still strangers, yet his soul seemed somehow to call to hers as if they'd been seeking each other for centuries. He hadn't wanted to admit it before now, but there it was, like the tolling of church bells on a fine spring morning.

The wind changed slightly, and the ship angled a little in the water. Gavin held on to the mast, riding the waves with the ship as the air rippled against his clothing. This was the closest a person could come to flying, feeling like a storm petrel riding the air currents while the sun warmed his skin and the world before him seemed endless. For the first time in days, that dreadful feeling of the slipping sands in an hourglass ceased.

He watched Josephine, who slept on, and his wolfish smile softened. He would leave her to rest. However, just to keep her safe, he took one of the loose ropes that was partially tied to the crossbeams and wrapped it around her chest in a harness of sorts. That would keep her from rolling off the side of the lookout point. She'd been through much, and there was nothing like a true, deep rest when one found oneself at sea. And while she was *supposed* to be his captive, he had given her a freedom no one else ever would.

"Sleep on," he murmured. "And dream of me." He wondered if this wild creature would dream of him, if she would *want* him. It caused a deep and surprising ache in his chest, one that only deepened the longer he looked at her.

He knew what it meant to love someone with all of his soul only to be found wanting. He'd been turned away by Charity, then by Brianna. Would Josephine see nothing in him to crave other than a quick dalliance into danger and excitement?

It shouldn't matter. He didn't need to be loved. He'd learned long ago how to survive without it. But she hadn't simply fired a warning shot at his heart—she was unloading her guns on his broadside and preparing to board. What happened when she stormed his heart and claimed it?

A sudden shout of a sail being sighted jerked his attention back to the men on the deck below. Ronnie was on the forecastle, pointing portside. Gavin followed the man's direction and spotted the approaching ship. He studied the ship from his position on the crossbeams, noting it was a large ship and gaining on them. They could likely outrun it, but he sensed this was one ship they shouldn't flee. He quickly descended the rigging and joined Ronnie at the forecastle, who had a spyglass pressed to his eye.

"What do you see?" he asked.

"A naval frigate. It's gaining on us."

Gavin's attention turned to the Union Jack flag proudly flapping in the wind on the *Cornish Pixie*. They had no colors other than that, and for that he was grateful. The *Pixie* was not a pirate ship, and it should be safe for a naval frigate to sniff around. They wouldn't find anything wrong. Only he and Ronnie were outlaws. All they had to do was maintain course, do nothing suspicious, and they could fool the navy into believing all was well.

"What's our plan, Cap'n?" Ronnie asked as he handed Gavin the spyglass so he could get a look at the ship on their tail.

"We play our roles, keep sailing unless they stop us. Griffin said the navy was prowling the coast. Most likely, this is just another ship making its rounds."

"We barely made it a day away from the coast," Ronnie grumbled.

"We knew we'd be risking this," Gavin reminded his friend. "But at least this time we have a proper crew and a legal ship. They won't know what we're about—not even our own crew does."

"Aye. But it still makes me nervous."

"You'd be mad if it didn't," said Ronnie.

Gavin drew in a steadying breath and prayed the frigate would leave them be, but luck was not with him today.

Within the hour, the frigate caught up to them, and they were hailed to allow a group of men from the naval vessel to board for an inspection. Grim-faced, Gavin and Ronnie braced themselves for the meeting with the boarding crew. He'd kept watch on the lookout spot and still hadn't seen Josephine wake up. The woman could sleep through the excitement on the deck below, and that both worried and amused him at the same time. He'd learned long ago never to sleep too deeply. A man could get his throat slit on his own ship if he wasn't careful.

"Whatever you do, stick to the story," Gavin advised his friend. "We were hired by Dominic Greyville to sail this ship to the West Indies."

"Aye," Ronnie replied as they went to meet the officers approaching the ship.

GRIFFIN STARED AROUND THE CABIN HE HAD BEEN GIVEN aboard Brianna Flynn's ship, the *Sea Serpent*. She and her husband had graciously agreed to escort him, Lord Camden, Adrian, and Dominic to the West Indies in pursuit of his brother.

Lady Camden, Roberta, and the lovely maid Vesper had come along as well, assisting Brianna and Nicholas by helping take care of their son, Asa, who was but three months old.

Griffin had been stunned to see the baby being carried about by Brianna in a special wrapping that kept the child secure against her back. He'd only seen a woman do that a few times before with women who worked in fields near the crofters' cottages on his lands. Dominic had noticed Griffin's startled expression and explained that Brianna was more of a sailor than a lady at heart, and she refused to sail without her son at this tender age.

Griffin had raised the question of the possible dangers for the child, as well as the women aboard, but Dominic had shrugged and replied that no one had ever been able to tell his wife or his mother what to do. The maid Vesper was so anxious about Josephine that he simply couldn't refuse her when she'd begged to come along.

In just one day of sailing, Griffin had learned far more about his neighbors and their piratical connections than he had ever wished to know. Between his brother and his betrothed's family, it turned out he was *surrounded* by pirates.

"Have you settled in, Castleton?" Dominic asked from the doorway of Griffin's cabin. Griffin hadn't noticed him arrive.

"Yes. Are you certain Gavin is bound for the West Indies? I don't want to chase false trails halfway around the world."

Dominic stood with his arms crossed as he studied Griffin. "Quite certain. You said his own ship was taken, and I know what the *Siren* means to him. He'll go after her and the pirates who stole her. Those men will return to waters they know, which means the West Indies. Moreover, he has my hired crew, who in all likelihood do not know he is a pirate. If he's wise, he'll keep the crew loyal to him by sailing along the route I had originally planned, which will take him to my home at King's Landing."

"Ah, yes, that would make sense," Griffin replied. His brother was cunning and likely would keep the merchant crew on his side by playing the role of a hired captain. The question was, how would he explain Josephine's presence to those men?

"Dinner will be ready soon. Come to the captain's cabin in an hour."

"Thank you." Griffin nodded as Dominic left the room.

Griffin directed his energy toward putting away the last of his travel cases and setting up the desk in the corner of his cabin with a few books he'd brought. It was rather silly, he knew, to want to take a few books with him, but reading always settled him when he worried. And knowing his twin, this journey would cause a fair bit of worry. When he finally left his cabin and moved down the corridor, he heard a soft curse in the cabin beside his own. The door to the neighboring cabin was slightly ajar, and he saw Vesper fretfully examining the gowns she'd packed for when they rescued Josephine.

Vesper's blonde hair tumbled around her shoulders in gleaming waves, and her bottom swayed as she bent over the chest full of dresses.

A sudden, unexpected surge of lust hit Griffin out of nowhere. He hadn't felt like this since Charity had been alive. Vesper looked exquisite in a pale-green gown with cream underskirts and a gold bodice. It was far prettier than what a lady's maid would usually wear, but given what he had learned of her background and what Dominic had told him about Josephine treating her more like a companion than a maid, it was less than surprising to see her dressed like the lady she was rather than a maid.

He cleared his throat, causing Vesper to jump and twirl around.

She gasped, her green eyes flashing with surprise. "My lord! I'm sorry to have disturbed you. I didn't think anyone would hear me."

"You didn't, Vesper," he assured her. "You . . . you don't mind if I call you Vesper, do you?" He prayed she would agree to let him call her Vesper. He wanted so desperately to call her by her given name.

She hesitated, then shook her head. "No, my lord."

"Good, good. Have you settled into your quarters?"

She nodded, her face a little pale. "I'm afraid I've never been on a ship before. It's a little frightening to be surrounded by so much water. I'm trying to stay busy and not think about the fact that I don't know how to swim. My father thought it wasn't necessary for his daughter to learn such things, only his son."

"Your father? He was Squire Trenton, wasn't he?"

She blushed and stared down at her slippered feet. "Did you know him?"

"Not personally, no. But I heard about what happened."

Griffin had made discreet inquiries about Vesper's family shortly after first meeting her. He had learned that she was a country gentleman's daughter, and from what he'd gathered, her father had suffered some financial disgrace that had put the family in a dire situation, which was why Vesper had gone into service as a lady's maid.

None of this had deterred Griffin's interest. He felt strangely more comfortable around Vesper than he had

Josephine. It was in his nature to protect women, to care for them above his own needs, and something about Josephine warned him that he would never manage to give her what she needed to make her truly happy. He had a dreadful feeling that perhaps he would only ever make her content.

But Vesper . . . The way she looked at him when she thought he wasn't watching, he saw that she wanted him. It wasn't a simple desire of the flesh, although that was certainly there, but it was also something deeper, something that made him afraid and excited all at once. It had been too long since such feelings had flashed through his heart.

He shouldn't have any feelings toward his betrothed's maid, but he simply couldn't stay away from this woman. She pulled him in with a quiet but intense gravity that was unique to her, like the way the earth pulled at the moon.

"If you've heard what happened to my father, then you shouldn't be speaking to me, my lord." She suddenly sniffled and returned her focus to Josephine's gowns.

Unwilling to see Vesper upset because of something he had said, Griffin came over and gently placed a hand on her arm. The moment his fingers touched her, it seemed to send a whisper of lightning up his skin. She straightened and looked up into his eyes.

"Your father's actions hurt you, but they are not yours to carry. You must leave such burdens behind you," he said.

A flash of fury lit her green eyes, which startled him. "How can I leave them behind? He's forced my entire family to work, to be brought low among those we once called friends. I am not ashamed of working, but I am ashamed that others have judged me for it."

Griffin caught her chin, gently turning her face to look at him. "You will find no judgment here."

She bit her bottom lip in frustration, and that proved too much for him to resist. He leaned down, pressing his lips to hers. The kiss was soft and sweet, but an instant later, a fire sparked to life between them. He cupped the back of her neck and deepened the kiss, savoring her mouth as he plunged his tongue between her lips. For the first time since he'd lost his wife and son, he felt like he could breathe, and Vesper was the very air his lungs needed.

She moaned against his lips and her hand curled around his neck, and she kissed him back. His soul burst from his chest and seemed to soar above him until he grew almost dizzy with the delightful feel of it.

The ship pitched and rolled through a wave, causing them both to stumble. He caught hold of her by the waist, pulling her against his body as he braced himself against the wall of her cabin. They gazed at each other a long moment, their bodies pressed together.

"Oh dear," Vesper said, her eyes luminous.

"Bloody hell," he echoed in grim agreement.

CHAPTER 8

Josephine jolted awake to the sounds of men shouting. She blinked away the sleep from her eyes and peered over the edge of the lookout platform on the topmast. She expected to see Gavin having the *Cornish Pixie*'s crew scour the ship for her, but what she saw instead filled her with dread. A naval frigate floated about two hundred yards to the port side of the *Pixie*, and a crew in a small boat was rowing toward them.

She squinted at the boat and thought she glimpsed at least one officer in uniform aboard. On the *Pixie*'s decks, the crew stood at attention while Gavin and Ronnie leaned over the railing facing the frigate, watching the progress of the boat coming toward them.

Josephine had to act quickly. She started to move but found a rope had been tied around her chest, tethering her safely to the lookout spot. Had old Bartholomew come up here and secured her to the crossbeams? He must have, the old dear. She made a mental reminder to thank him later.

She abandoned her hiding spot from the lookout post on the topmast and hastily descended the rigging. She could hear the voices of the navy men growing louder as they climbed aboard.

Someone hissed, and Josephine glanced around. The older sailor stood at the back of the *Pixie*'s assembled crew and pointed to a spot beside him.

"Come here," the man whispered.

Understanding what he was about, she quickly crossed the deck and took her place next to him. She gave him a questioning look when she reached him. The old man looked down, and she followed his gaze to where he was waving a lowbrow brimmed hat at her.

She grabbed the hat he held out and promptly pulled it down on her head. The brim dipped, hiding her face. Though she was wearing her hair tied back in a queue, it was still too long for most men, but hopefully no one would look at her too closely right now.

"Good, lassie," the old man said. "Now don't move."

A British officer stepped over the side of the ship and onto the *Pixie*. Several other men followed suit, quickly getting into formation as they faced the *Pixie*'s crew.

"I am First Lieutenant Landers of the HMS *Torrington*. I wish to speak to the master of this ship." He was a tall fellow with a white wig and a fairly muscular body. He was clearly a seasoned officer, not a young midshipman.

"I am Gavin Castleton, master of the *Cornish Pixie*. We welcome you aboard, Lieutenant."

"Thank you, Captain Castleton." The lieutenant's cool gaze explored the ship, and Josephine stared down at her feet, praying he wouldn't look at her.

"Look up a little," the old sailor said in a harsh whisper. "Or else he'll suspect something is going on with you."

Josephine raised her head again, but now she was too afraid to breathe lest that action draw attention to her unbound breasts.

"You don't mind if we inspect your hold?" the lieutenant inquired of Gavin.

"Not at all. Please look wherever you wish, Lieutenant."

Gavin kept pace with the naval officer while the lieutenant strode about the deck with his hands clasped behind his back. Gavin casually conversed with the officer, and Josephine occasionally overheard bits of their discussion.

"My apologies. Must do this with every vessel, you understand," Landers explained.

"Of course," Gavin replied.

"Pirates about, you know. Trade routes. Have to keep watch . . ." The rest of his words were lost upon the breeze.

Twenty minutes passed in tense silence for Josephine and the crew of the *Pixie* until the officer and Gavin returned above deck.

"I imagine you are in a hurry to be off, but if you are interested, our captain would be delighted to have you and your wife dine with him."

Josephine flinched as she heard the word *wife*. Had Gavin told the man he had a woman on board?

"Er . . ." Gavin hesitated.

"Please accept.. It isn't often we find company while out at sea and less often that we have female company." The officer looked so earnest that it would have been poor form to refuse.

"Very well. How soon should we come to you?" Gavin asked.

"The sun will be setting in a few hours, but our captain dines early. Say, a half hour?"

"Thank you." Gavin shook the lieutenant's hand and helped the man over the side and down to his waiting boat.

The moment the naval officer was out of sight, the crew let out a breath of relief and returned to their stations. Josephine followed the older sailor across the deck, but Gavin passed by her as he headed in the opposite direction and grasped her arm, swiftly turning her around to escort her belowdecks with him.

"Wait, I can't move so fast!" she gasped as she stumbled down the gangway behind him. He was taking such long strides that she couldn't keep up.

Only when they were out of sight from the other ship did he let her go.

"How the devil did you know it was me?"

"I would know the curve of those breasts anywhere," Gavin cut in. "Lass, we have a dinner with those officers on the *Torrington*. You must dress quickly and come with me."

"As your wife?" she added dryly as she removed the floppy old hat she wore.

"Aye, my loving, devoted wife. This is our honeymoon voyage, and we are celebrating my new position as the master of the *Cornish Pixie*."

She tapped her chin thoughtfully. "So I shouldn't mention that you are a pirate who kidnapped me on the eve of my wedding?" She was teasing him, but he didn't seem to realize that.

He moved to press her against the nearest bulkhead

with his body, and he cupped her cheek. Their faces were close and his eyes dark as he gazed at her seriously.

"If you mention pirates, then Ronnie and I are dead men, and the crew would likely end up in prison and possibly hanged."

"Gavin, I was only teasing," she said more seriously.

"'Tis not something to joke about, lass. Do I have your word that you will keep silent?"

"Of course," she promised. "I won't breathe a word."

"Good." He relaxed and smiled at her. "We'll discuss your punishment for locking me in my cabin later tonight."

"Punishment?" she fired back, her temper flaring. "You locked me in there first."

Gavin dismissed the argument. "I think a spanking is what your bottom needs. After that, we'll see." He leaned down the last few inches and kissed her. It was raw and wicked. He cupped her buttocks with one hand and gave her a light smack. She jolted and then moaned as a flood of unexpected heat followed in its wake.

He stepped back. "Put on one of the gowns in that chest and I will join you shortly." He strode away and climbed back up the companionway, and soon she could hear him hollering orders to the men.

With a heavy sigh, she returned to the captain's cabin and abandoned her sailor's togs. From the chest, she selected a peach gown with blue underskirts. She managed to tighten her corset up nearly all the way, but cursed because she could not finish the rest without help. As if answering her silent prayer, the door opened. She was actually relieved to see Gavin enter.

"Do you require assistance?" he asked, his eyes skating over her dress.

"Unfortunately, yes."

He came up behind her, his hands settling lightly on her bare shoulders. His touch burned deliciously on her cool skin.

He chuckled. "I'd much rather remove your gown than help you into it." His hand slid down her back before he fastened the corset tight, though not too tight, then helped her with her skirts and laced up the back of her gown. She held a palm flat against the embroidered stomacher of the bodice.

"You barely fit this, but it'll do," Gavin mused. Neither of them could miss how the snug bodice pressed her breasts up high.

"This gown is my sister-in-law's. She is shorter than I am and her bosom is smaller, but thankfully not by much."

"Well, I shall never complain about a larger bosom." He playfully leered at her before cinching the last two laces up and tying them. He already knew to tuck the strings of the laces beneath her overskirt, and she wondered how many women he had undressed and dressed to be so familiar with such a small but necessary detail.

"Have you helped many women into and out of gowns?" Josephine asked.

"A few, though not as many as you imagine. I'm not a wenching man. At least, not according to my quartermaster."

"A wenching man?" Josephine wasn't sure whether to laugh or be insulted.

"Never you mind about wenches, lass." Gavin pinched

her bottom. "You are the only woman I'll be wenching anytime soon. Now hurry up and fix your hair."

He turned his attention to Dominic's sea chest, removing a fine pair of dark-buff breeches and a blue brocade frock coat. She borrowed Roberta's mother-of-pearl comb to tidy the wavy mane of her hair while Gavin changed his clothes. She peeped at him a few times from the corner of her eye as he changed. There was something intimate about being in the same room with a man as he dressed. Something a true husband and wife might do.

"How did I become your wife?" she asked, wondering how the rumor on the ship had gotten started.

"Oh . . . Yes, I suppose we shall need some kind of story for the officers, won't we?"

"Yes, I will need a story about how we met, but also why does the crew think I'm your wife?"

He pulled on the frock coat. The rich blue brocade accented the lighter tones in his brown hair, which he pulled into a queue and tied with a ribbon. In that moment, she saw how clearly he and Griffin were identical twins. He could have passed for Griffin to someone who didn't know either man closely.

"Ronnie told the crew you were my wife. Apparently, there was some concern and the usual superstitions among the crew about women on ships, so he reassured them you were a gentleborn lady and that we were married. Few crews want a lothario as their captain. It shows a lack of discipline, and they need to trust a man who can control himself."

"Really? I thought pirates liked—"

"These men aren't pirates, Josephine. Your brother

hired a crew of honest men. Still, even pirates have rules about women on board. It can be a cause for trouble to have females on ships. If there are too many men and only one woman . . . it leads to fights. And a ship on long or dangerous voyages cannot support having a dozen women on board to service the men's needs."

Gavin's brutal honesty about the use of women on ships filled Josephine's head with a faint buzzing sound and a ringing in her ears. Did he see women that way too? As objects to be used?

"You've nothing to fear, Josie. I won't let anyone hurt you." He placed a palm on her arm.

"That's not what concerns me. It's the idea of women being used for a singular purpose—to serve a man's pleasure—and being seen as nothing more. We are not puppets to use and discard. We have lives, we have souls and hearts . . . we aren't *things*."

Gavin's face tightened. "I agree with you. It happens, even though it shouldn't. Change is always slow in coming because change means conflict, and most so-called civilized nations try to avoid conflict, even if it means allowing bad behavior to continue unchallenged." He brushed his fingers along her jaw, his eyes soft and so full of compassion for a man who lived outside the bounds of the law. "Now, come along and let's pull the wool over these navy men's eyes."

Josephine followed him back up on deck, and with the aid of some sailors she was assisted over the side and down the ladder into a waiting boat. They were rowed a short distance to the looming frigate. Its bulky mass made her brother's ship look much like the fae creature of folklore it was named after. Still, she guessed if it came to a sprint on the open water, the *Pixie* could outrun the frigate if she needed to. But in a broadside battle, the *Torrington* would surely blow the smaller ship out of the water.

When she climbed aboard the *Torrington*, she was met by a line of officers ranging from very young midshipmen up to the captain, who was a fit but stocky man in his late forties. The captain bowed deeply as Gavin and Josephine stopped in front of him.

"My lady, please forgive me. I often forget the difficulties of having women transferred between ships. I admit, however, that I am delighted to have you for dinner this evening."

Josephine had never been a woman who craved the attentions of men, and having dozens of male eyes examining her bosom was unwelcome. She reminded herself she was the daughter of an earl and that this charade would save Gavin's life.

"Thank you so much, Captain. It will be a treat to dine with such handsome officers of His Majesty's navy."

The officers nearest them, most of them close to Josephine's age, turned ruddy at the compliment.

"I am Captain James Anderson."

"I am Gavin Castleton, master of the *Cornish Pixie*. I'm delighted to introduce my wife, Josephine, to you."

The captain claimed Josephine's hand and pressed a courtly kiss to the back of her fingers. Then he took her arm in his and escorted her to the captain's cabin, where a lavish feast had been laid out. He helped her into a chair, and only then did he and the other men take their seats.

"Would you care for a glass of Madeira?" the captain inquired of her.

"Yes, thank you." She accepted the glass but noted Gavin's polite refusal, using the excuse that he would be on duty that evening.

"Mrs. Castleton, I take it this is a honeymoon journey for you?" the third lieutenant inquired. He was a lad of no more than twenty or twenty-one, with a bashful demeanor.

"Yes, we've only been married about a week," she lied smoothly, and any heat in her face that might slip through would fit with the charade of a shy new bride.

Gavin tensed beside her, but she doubted anyone at the table was aware of it. For the moment, all eyes were on her.

"How do you like the sea?" Captain Anderson asked as everyone began to dine on a course of fresh fish.

"It's quite lovely," she replied.

Attention now turned to Gavin. "And where are you bound, Captain Castleton?" Captain Anderson asked.

"The West Indies," Gavin replied with a companionable smile. "My brother-in-law owns this vessel, and we are to sail to his estate holdings there."

"And who is your brother-in-law? I might know him," the captain inquired. Josephine realized too late that this was no simple dinner. It was an *interrogation*.

"The Earl of Camden's son." Gavin placed his hand on Josephine's knee underneath the table as if he sensed her rising tension. She drew in a deeper breath, trying to remain calm.

One of the lieutenants looked surprised. "Wasn't that the fellow who—" Captain Anderson shot the man a sharp look, and he quickly silenced himself.

"My brother was recently pardoned by the king." Josephine knew what those men were thinking. The story of her brother's rescue from the noose and the royal pardon their father had secured to save him had been spread far and wide.

"Yes," the captain said slowly. "The pirate."

"*Former* pirate," Josephine emphasized, and then she curled her arm around Gavin's in a display of what she hoped looked like wifely affection. "My husband only agreed to captain his current vessel when he had assurances from the necessary authorities that our voyage would be quite legal. My husband follows the law to the letter."

"I don't hold with piracy," Gavin agreed solemnly. "Rotten business. One cannot run an empire and conduct trade with those rebels roving the seas." He spoke with contempt so convincingly that Josephine would have believed him and his hatred for pirates had she not known better.

She attempted to change the subject. "Captain, have you been to the West Indies?"

"Oh yes, many times." The captain smiled at her almost dotingly, as though she were a child.

Josephine pressed her advantage. "I should like to spend time with my husband there before we make the voyage back to England. Would you recommend any places that would be suitable for us to visit?"

"I wish I could advise on that, but I urge caution instead. The Spanish are still giving us trouble, and it would be best to remain in English-controlled regions while you are in the islands."

"Oh, I see." Josephine pretended to be disappointed, but she did not fear the Spanish. She was half Spanish, after all. She doubted Gavin was afraid of them either.

As the meal concluded, Josephine managed to navigate the conversation into safer waters. Whenever the officers would bring up pirates or illegal activities, she would ask a silly question of the sort men would expect a woman who knew nothing about life at sea to ask.

"Well, thank you so much, Captain Anderson. We thoroughly enjoyed your company this evening, but I must return to my ship. We have a schedule to meet, and the winds are a fickle mistress."

Gavin's hand was back on Josephine's knee under the table, and he gave her what felt like a congratulatory squeeze.

"It was our pleasure." Captain Anderson and his officers stood the moment Josephine rose from her chair, and the captain once more claimed her hand with a kiss. "I imagine your husband will enjoy his honeymoon with you. You are the most delightful company."

Josephine blushed at the man's implications, which added to her delicate feminine façade.

"I certainly will." Gavin winked at her and then escorted her from the cabin before she could figure out how to respond to the captain's compliment.

Once they returned to the *Cornish Pixie*, Josephine's shoulders sagged as the coiled tension within her was finally let loose. Gavin spoke privately to Ronnie a moment and then returned for her, catching her lightly by the waist as they stood on the moonlit deck.

"You did very well, lass," he said. Before she could respond, he tilted her face up and kissed her. A warm buzzing like bees on a summer day filled her chest, and she leaned into him, savoring his strength as she surrendered to his kiss. He deepened it, gently parting her lips with his tongue to flick against her own, and she completely forgot she was on deck in full view of the crew.

She wasn't sure how long the kiss lasted. It could have been minutes or hours. She lost herself in his taste, the feel of his frock coat beneath her fingers, the silky strands of his hair as the wind tousled it, and the scrape of his stubble against her cheeks. Nothing she had imagined about kissing a man compared to what she felt now as she kissed Gavin.

It was the same way she'd felt when scaling the rigging while the ship sailed on a smooth sea with the wind behind them. It felt like *heaven*. This would be one of her fondest memories to take with her to the next life, the memory of Gavin's kiss and his praise in her ears.

When they finally broke apart, they both turned to watch the looming shadow of the *Torrington* grow smaller as the two ships parted ways. Then, without a word, Gavin led her down to his cabin and closed the door. He leaned back against the door, watching her with hooded eyes.

"Gavin?" She spoke his name as a question, even though she was not certain yet what she was actually asking.

"I truly am proud of your performance tonight." His compliment made her blush in pure delight. She thought she'd done rather well too, but it was nice to hear him agree.

He pushed away from the closed door and slowly came toward her from behind. When he reached her, he ran his palm up the side of her bodice, and even through the layers of cloth, she felt the heat of his palm, burning her like a brand. She watched his face as she gazed at him over her shoulder, drinking in the sight of him as though it was the first time she'd ever seen him. Her blood hummed with a new excitement. Was tonight the night he would claim her in the way she'd longed for him to since the moment she'd first touched him?

"Regardless of your brilliant performance, I believe I still owe you a punishment, lass," he said playfully, but his voice was soft, slightly rough with excitement. A frisson of awareness of his size and strength stole through her, sparking desire deep within her belly. He was still stroking his hand over her bodice, down to her hips and back up to her breasts before he moved that hand up to her throat and curled his fingers lightly around her neck as he pulled her body back against his. He didn't squeeze or even tighten his hold upon her neck, but she knew he could feel her wildly beating pulse beneath his fingertips. His brown eyes held a hint of danger that concerned her. She still didn't fully know him as a man or what he would deem an appropriate punishment.

"Frightened of me?" he whispered in her ear.

"Not exactly," she confessed. Her body was burning for him, but she was still a little afraid—not that he'd hurt her, only that she wasn't prepared for whatever he might do.

"Never fear me," he said before he gently nibbled on her earlobe. "But I will teach you to enjoy a light punishment when you need one."

"Surely I made up for any silly transgressions at dinner?" she asked. "And I only locked you in because *you* locked me in first," she reminded him as she fought off a moan when he licked the shell of her ear. It sent a wild heat throbbing between her legs, and she clenched her thighs together.

He lightly scowled at her. But she didn't see any real anger in his eyes, only teasing amusement.

"You fooled every one of those men and had them eating out of your palm like trained spaniels. I listened to all of those questions they asked you. Lord, you must have wanted to scream at them. You know more about sailing than those young midshipmen," he said. He sounded a little angry, but she knew it wasn't directed at her.

"Yes, it was frustrating," she agreed. "No one wants to be treated like they are a child."

"Well, I see you, Josie, I see your brilliant mind, your courage, your cunning. You must never hide that from me," he said.

She flushed again at his praise. "Then perhaps you don't need to punish me?" she suggested lightly.

His darkly playful grin returned. "Oh, I still plan to. You cannot be locking the captain of this vessel in his cabin." He caressed her throat with his fingers and nuzzled her neck as he held her pressed against him from behind.

"It's not as though I can escape the ship, and not once since you've taken me from my home have I protested. You didn't need to lock me in. I *want* to be here, Gavin . . . with you."

He slowly turned her to face him as he stared at her, and she saw a flash of something in his eyes, something too quick to understand fully, but it made her heart ache for what she thought she might have glimpsed in that brief glance into his soul.

"I locked you in for two reasons. I do not know the

men yet on the ship. There are nearly eighty souls on board. I know for certain of only one man who won't harm you, and that's Ronnie. I do not know where the rest of the crew's morals lie. I was trying to keep you safe."

"You said two reasons," she said. "What is the second?"

He released her waist and stepped back to remove his frock coat, tossing it on the table. Then he began to roll up his sleeves, exposing tanned muscled arms.

"The second is because the idea of you at my tender mercy sets fire to my blood. The thought of you tied to my bed to take what pleasure I give you, making you lose control at my whim . . . It's made me rather mad with desire for you."

He knelt by the trunk and began to dig through the contents until he found a long silk ribbon. Gavin wrapped the ribbon around his closed fist, testing its strength, but he lifted his head to grin at her.

Her heart was beating wildly. "You can't be serious . . ."

"Quite so, lassie." He took a step toward her.

Oh no, she was not about to allow this man to do whatever he planned to her.

"You'll have to catch me first," she argued and did the only thing she could do and bolted for the door.

He lunged, caught her by the waist, and with a deep, rumbling chuckle, he kissed the shell of her ear.

"This is going to be fun."

CHAPTER 9

Gavin pulled his captured prize close to him, and he could feel the frantic beat of her pulse as Josephine gazed up at him with a mixture of desire and apprehension. He didn't want to frighten her and he certainly wasn't going to hurt her, but she had to learn to trust him. He had meant what he said about the crew. They weren't pirates, but that didn't mean he could trust them, not with an exquisite beauty like Josephine. Not until he knew the men better. He wouldn't be able to watch her every minute of the day to make sure that she was safe.

She trembled in his hold as he kissed her neck and then gently fisted a hand in her hair and pulled her head back so she looked up at him. Lord, she was beautiful, but it wasn't simply her features that were stunning. It was the way she looked at him, the way she made him feel. He'd never been more aware of a female and all that she could be in one instant than he was as he held this trembling virgin with the heart of a warrior goddess in his arms. She was brave, and her trusting heart shone through from the depths of her silvery-gray eyes.

Gavin's next words were going to challenge her to trust him, but he had to push her to her limits, to see what she would accept from him.

He rubbed the back of her neck the way one might soothe a kitten. "You're going to take off your clothes and lie upon the bed."

Fire lit her eyes again as she jerked against his arm, proving she was no meek kitten. "And if I don't?"

"Then I will swat your bottom—your very *bare* bottom—after *I* remove your clothes myself." He emphasized his words with a wolfish grin. "But if you do what I ask . . . then I will be very pleased with you, lass."

"Oh, so this is a request, not a command?" Her rebellious tone made his body burn with heat. She raised her chin and added, "I didn't hear you say *please*." A hint of mischief twinkled in her eyes.

A youthful playfulness he hadn't felt in ages rippled through him, smoothing away the hard edges his soul had acquired over the last several years. Josephine made him feel like a nineteen-year-old lad all over again. He wasn't mad at her, didn't want to truly punish her, but he liked the rebellious side she showed him when she wanted to tussle. She was strong and playful too and liked to push him to show his own strength. He respected that.

With a chuckle, he released her and took an exaggerated step back. "*Please* would you remove your clothes and lie on the bed?"

Josephine combed her fingers through her hair in a way he was coming to recognize as a calming gesture she did without thinking. He made a note to himself to comb his fingers through her hair to put her at ease.

"Very well." She reached for the back of her skirts, but he shook his head.

"Remove your shoes first."

With a confused look, she raised her skirts and placed her foot on the sea chest, then delicately removed the blue satin mule slipper. Then she removed the second shoe. The sight of her slender feet covered in white stockings did something to him in the way nothing else had in a long time. He was so aroused he could barely breathe.

Gavin's voice deepened a little. "Now your stockings."

She tugged her voluminous skirts and petticoats up to her waist and peeled the stockings off her legs one by one. She bared her beautiful flesh, and he struggled not to make a sound that would most likely frighten her. But this act of disrobing was torturing him far more than her. His cock strained against the front of his trousers, and he was having to breathe slowly to steady his heart.

She removed the second stocking and flung it at him. He caught it with one hand. The filmy white silk was still warm from where it had touched her skin. He adjusted his trousers with one hand, fighting to hide his discomfort, and she watched him, a hint of a smile upon her lips as if the little minx knew exactly what she was doing to him. And he was glad—he wanted her to enjoy that feeling, to know she affected him that strongly.

"Now your skirts and petticoats."

She bent to remove the skirts, and her hair fell in a waterfall of dark umber waves. She shimmied out of the pannier hoops next and let them drop to the floor, then met his gaze, heat and a hint of fear still in her eyes. Without a word, she presented her back to him, and he came toward her. Gavin's hands shook now as he fought to control himself. He brushed her hair over her shoulder to see the laces of her bodice. He loosened them with slow and gentle tugs before she slipped out of the garment. Then he tended to the corset, which soon joined her bodice on the deck.

His breath was fast and shallow as he gently tickled her bare thighs while reaching for the bottom of her chemise. He lifted it off her body, baring her completely, finally, to his ravenous gaze. Her full breasts with her pale-pink nipples, pebbled from the chill air, made his mouth go dry. He wanted to kiss and lick a path along her lips, down to her mound, until he'd explored every hill and valley of her body.

"On the bed," he nearly growled. "Now."

She moved away from him and climbed onto the bed, giving him an all too perfect view of her heart-shaped bottom before she turned over and lay on her back. He came to her with the ribbons he'd retrieved from the trunk in his hands, grabbing her wrists and binding them together, making sure not to make them too tight.

"Keep them above your head," he warned, "or I shall tie them to the headboard."

Josephine settled more comfortably on the bed and raised her arms above her head. He sat down beside her, admiring her. Then with hesitant excitement, he stroked a finger down from the slope of her nose to her mouth. She parted her lips, and he pushed his finger between them and she sucked on it. The feel of her wet mouth sucking on his finger nearly made him come in his trousers like an untried youth. He tried to ignore the pain of his cock throbbing. Then she brushed her tongue against the pad of his fingertip, and he couldn't stop the moan that escaped him. He wanted to put something else between her lips, but that was not how her first time with him should be. This was about her, her pleasure and understanding. He wanted her to know that anything between them in the privacy of this cabin would always be for her or for their mutual pleasure.

Little tease, he thought with delight. She would indeed be a passionate lover, an adventurous lover, and he was the luckiest bastard in the world to have found her.

He slid his finger out of her mouth and drew patterns around each of her nipples before tracing down to her belly. Her muscles trembled beneath his slowly exploring fingertips before he teased the dark curls between her thighs as he reached her mound. She made a soft, startled sound and her legs clamped tight, trying to shut them out, not from pain or fear, but surprise.

"Open your legs," he said after a moment, and she obeyed. "Good lass." His praise made her face glow with happiness. He would remember that, that praising her filled her with joy.

He continued to explore her mound before lightly caressing the tiny pearl of sensations. Her hips bucked sharply in shock.

"Easy, Josie," he soothed. "'Tis the pearl that gives you pleasure," he said. "Let me stroke it."

"It's too much . . ." She struggled to put words together as he made tiny, delicate strokes over that bundle of nerves. The more he touched it, the more she reacted. First it was her hips wriggling, then her hands began to fist and uncurl above her head as she struggled to understand what he was doing to her. He kept his eyes on her face the entire time, studying every minute expression, watching for the places and the type of touch that caused her the most pleasure. When he could see she was close to climaxing, he moved his finger down to caress her folds. She whimpered in frustration and then gasped as he pressed his finger inside her. He didn't penetrate her deeply at first, but enough for her to realize that he was within her now. He withdrew and then pressed the finger back in, causing her to make a soft sound of curious pleasure.

"That's it, lass, feel me inside you. Now imagine 'tis my cock pushing deep into you." He painted a sensual picture for her as he pushed a second finger into her. Her hips bucked against his hand, and he urged her back down on the bed with a low chuckle.

She panted as he began to pleasure her more quickly, his hand moving faster and faster until he brushed his thumb over her clit. She exploded from pleasure with a soft cry, and he continued to draw out her climax until her thighs quivered and her breath was stuttering. Then he removed his finger from her and she lay still, her hands still bound above her head. He admired his prize with no small amount of satisfaction. Her lashes fluttered as she slowly descended from the peak he had raised her to.

There were so many things he wanted to do to her, but those things would wait for another time. He wanted to savor her, to take his time and challenge his self-control. The end result would be that much sweeter when he finally claimed her.

"Now, I want you to get into bed and go to sleep," he said.

"How can I possibly sleep after that?" she whispered shyly, and she sat up so he could unbind her hands.

"You'll find a way, lass." He leaned over and kissed her lips, tasting her sigh as she kissed him back. This was no burning, desperate kiss. It was soft and warm as the sun on a spring day. It made him think of those rare moments when he had no duties, no worries, and he would lie among the wildflowers and soak up the sunlight and imagine his soul growing with those flowers toward the heavens.

It also held a gentle yearning for love that made his chest ache. He pulled back, glancing away from her. It was too much, too soon. He was ashamed to think that he wasn't ready to feel this way again after Charity. Seven years was a long time and yet not long at all in some ways.

"Sleep now," he urged gently, then left the cabin. He didn't go far, but he needed to clear his head. He leaned back against the bulkhead and breathed deep several times. All around him, the *Cornish Pixie* rocked gently on the waves as she sailed through the moonlit waters toward the open Atlantic.

Remember what matters. Getting the Siren *back and killing Beauchamp and his traitorous crew.*

Knowing that Beauchamp and those who'd mutinied against him were still out there cooled the heat in his blood. He closed his eyes, remembering that moment he and Ronnie had rowed away from his beloved ship and the storm finally cloaked the *Siren* from view.

"Gavin . . ." The name wasn't spoken aloud but within his head. It felt like a distant echo. His brother's voice.

For the next six weeks sailing to the West Indies, he would be chasing his old ship while his brother would likely be chasing his new one. He wasn't sure how he knew Griffin was coming after him, but he was certain that he was. Griffin would want Josephine back. How could a man not want a woman like that back? But Gavin wasn't going to let that happen. Josephine was *his* treasure now.

IT WAS CLOSE TO DAWN WHEN GRIFFIN WAS ROUSED from sleep by someone pounding on his cabin door. He stumbled out of bed and pulled on his clothes before he called for whoever was at his door to enter. Dominic stepped inside the cabin and closed the door behind him.

"What is it? Have we found them?" Griffin asked.

Dominic shook his head. "No, but while everyone was sleeping, we crossed paths with HMS *Torrington*, which has orders to sail up and down the west coast of England. They saw the *Pixie* early last evening, even dined with the captain and his wife."

"*Wife?*" Griffin said. "Surely he didn't *marry* Josephine?"

"Knowing him, he would likely spin them a tale of marriage to throw any suspicion off him traveling with an unmarried woman. I have no idea if he did or not, but the *Torrington* officers were told that Josephine was his new bride."

"Did you tell the officers that Gavin kidnapped her?" Griffin asked.

At Griffin's question, Dominic's face darkened. "No, I didn't mention that."

Griffin was both relieved and confused. "I'm glad to hear it, but why not?"

"Because the men on my ship are former pirates or sailors who are down on their luck, looking for honest work. I promised them all a safe and legal way of earning their living aboard the *Cornish Pixie*. Anyone associated with Gavin, assuming he's captured for piracy, will most likely face piracy charges as well. If I told the officers on the *Torrington* that we were chasing a pirate, they would be obliged to run him down and condemn the crew right along with him. I think it's best if we keep His Majesty's navy unaware of our little rescue mission."

"I agree. I've no desire to see my brother hang. I only want to rescue Josephine and see your ship returned to you."

"I'm glad we agree," Dominic replied, his gaze solemn. "But I feel he may be heading into more danger than you originally expected."

"What do you mean?" If a former pirate was worried about danger, that didn't bode well for any one of them.

"Your brother was the Admiral of the Black, the ruler of the pirate court, the Brethren of the Coast."

"Yes, so you said," Griffin said, urging him to continue.

"This fellow Beauchamp who mutinied on Gavin and stole his vessel . . . Well, let's just say the other pirate captains will not approve of Beauchamp's actions. They do not hold with mutiny. Beauchamp must know this, which makes me believe Beauchamp has some trap laid that I cannot see yet. If he meets with any of the other captains, he may tell them Gavin and the rest of the crew were killed when they engaged another ship. He won't want Gavin alive to tell the tale of his mutiny, which means Josephine is in danger while she is with him. I want you on your guard." Dominic cleared his throat and glanced away. "If something happens and we end up in dire straits, my father, Nicholas, and I will attack. I want you and Adrian to take the ladies and Nicholas's son to safety."

"But—"

"I know you are no coward, Castleton, and that's why I am asking you. If we face true danger, I am trusting you with their lives. They'll need you."

Griffin knew from the look in Dominic's eyes that he understood the nature of what he was asking Griffin to do. That if it came down to it, he would give his life for the women and the babe. That he could do so without hesitation.

"I promise to do what is necessary," Griffin said.

"Good. I'm sorry I woke you, but I believed you would want to know the moment we had news."

"I'm glad you did," Griffin said. "But now that I'm awake, I should get some fresh air on deck."

The two of them went to face the dawn above deck. Griffin was surprised to see Vesper was already standing by the railing of the waist deck. The pink skies illuminated the bright—blue gown she wore. Griffin came toward her, pulled again by that invisible force that drew them together.

"I see you've lost your fear of the sea," he said as he leaned on the railing next to her.

Vesper shot him a shy look from beneath dark-gold lashes.

"The water still frightens me, my lord. But it's so beautiful, isn't it? I suppose that's human nature, to crave things that are beautiful and frightening."

"It is," he agreed. "The sea speaks to all of us in her own way. She gives life and in a temper, she can take it away. Nature is like that, both protector and destroyer all at once."

Vesper's hands tightened on the railing. He reached over, covering her left hand with his right.

"We haven't talked about it," she said softly.

"About what?" He tried to act oblivious, but he knew what she meant. *The kiss.* The one that had sent a surge of life back within his body.

"It cannot happen again," she said, her expression stoic.

Griffin watched the sunlight stretch across the water ahead of them with sparkling diamond glints.

"I suppose you're right, but not because I wouldn't claim you as my wife. I would if I could."

"But you can't. Because of my family, the disgrace . . ."

"That means nothing to me," he replied, squeezing her hand. She hadn't tried to pull away from him, and he clung to that sliver of hope. "But I asked Josephine to be my wife before I met you. If she still wishes to marry me when we rescue her, I am honor bound to see that obligation through."

Vesper was silent a long while. "And if she refuses you?"

"Then I shall be free to follow my heart . . ."

Her hand trembled beneath his as neither of them dared to look at each other.

"And would your heart lead to . . . me?" The hope in her voice sent him soaring.

"It would . . . if you would have me."

Vesper's joyful expression was all the answer he needed. Griffin's heart ached with a mix of joy and grief. True happiness, not mere contentment, was so close within his grasp. But he did not know which would be his fate until Josephine was safely returned to her family and he could see where her heart lay. If she wanted to be free of their engagement, he would give it to her. He wanted to assume she would refuse to marry him, but assumptions were a fool's game. He had to wait to see if fate believed in giving him a second chance at life.

JOSEPHINE WAS AWARE THE MOMENT GAVIN LEFT THE bed. He'd returned sometime in the night to lie beside her and after a few hours had pulled her against him. She'd been sleepily aware of his presence whenever she'd briefly awakened. Rather than feeling shy and uncertain, his body quietly claiming hers just by sleeping at her side had sent a thrill through her.

Now his absence caused her to roll over and stretch her hand along the cool sheets where he had lain. She placed her palm on the indent of his pillow and replayed every moment of last night as she ached with a longing for him to come back to bed.

She'd been frightened, excited, and finally brazen as

she had surrendered to the teasing removal of her clothing. And then . . . heavens . . . how it felt to let him touch her in so many wonderful ways and places. The sensations were familiar to her. She had explored her own body in the last few years, feeling things she'd been too shy to ask her mother about. What she had felt was nothing compared to how Gavin had brought her to those same peaks.

There was a purity in the pleasure she'd experienced at Gavin's hands. It was so clear, so perfect. She couldn't imagine any other man touching her like that and feeling the same euphoria. She rolled onto her back, giggling with the realization that she was completely naked in a bed that was rolling over the high seas. What would everyone think if they knew just how free she truly was now?

The warm sun bathed her skin, and she indulged in lying in bed another half hour before finally getting up and dressing in Dominic's clothes again. She walked up to the door and halted, her hands inches above the handle. What if Gavin had locked her in again? She would go mad if he kept her closeted away for a month and a half.

She touched the handle and it turned. With a sigh of relief, she exited the cabin and went in search of food in the galley. Olive was cooking up a stew and gave her a bowl to sample, as well as an apple.

"Best eat up while the fruit is still fresh," Olive said. "Now, while you eat, tell me all about that fancy dinner last night. What vittles did those fine navy men have?"

Josephine detailed her meal between spoonfuls of stew and discussed some of the conversation she'd had with the captain and his men.

"So they are hunting for pirates, are they?" Olive asked quietly.

"Yes, but they won't find any here," Josephine was quick to add.

Olive gave her a strange look before she masked it with a smile. "No, of course not. Run along now. You shouldn't be distracting me or the biscuits will burn. I refuse to make hardtack for the men at least for the first week while we're at sea. If I burn these, the lads will be in fits over it."

Having been politely dismissed, Josephine went above deck, still pondering the expression on Olive's face when she'd mentioned pirates.

The seasoned old sailor who had helped her was already on the deck, cleaning. "Back again, lassie?"

"I am." Josephine smiled at him.

Bartholomew returned her warm smile, and her heart swelled with affection for the salty old fellow.

"Have you seen . . . my husband?"

"Aye, he was running gun drills earlier this morning. They just stopped a few minutes ago. He's over there on the forecastle."

She looked over her shoulder at the ship's bow. The smallest and highest section of the deck at the front of the vessel, the forecastle, had but one lone figure standing atop it. The flying jib front sail billowed above and ahead of him, stretching out into the endless blue of the sea and sky. Gavin stood with his hands braced on the railing, his tall figure displaying his broad shoulders and narrow waist while showing off his powerful thighs. The glint of a short sword shimmered at his hip. Excitement flared within her again.

"My pirate," she whispered with a dreamy smile. *My lover,* she silently added with a blush.

She strode across the deck, dodging sailors who took a moment to glance at her before resuming their tasks. After the previous day of seeing her in men's clothing, they were growing accustomed to it. She had no desire to disrupt the crew as they saw to their duties. Gavin might use it against her as an excuse to keep her belowdecks in his cabin all day if he thought the men were distracted by the sight of her.

She climbed the steps to the forecastle, and Gavin turned his head at her approach.

"Am I to assume this will be a habit with you?" He nodded at her clothing.

She joined him at the rail. "Yes, at least during the day. I want to explore the ship and learn how to sail. Would you teach me?"

He was quiet a long while before he spoke. "To what end, might I ask? What will you do when we part ways, lass? You can't go to sea, you can't have this life. You'll have babies and the task of mothering them and running a grand estate. Why ask to learn about something that the world will deny you?" There was a hint of pain in his words, rather than judgment or censure.

She took her own time answering him and tried to ignore the stab of pain in her chest at the thought of them parting ways someday.

"I believe souls are neither male nor female—they are simply souls." She gestured to herself. "This body, simply because it's female, should not rob me of my dreams. I live and die like any man does. Why not let me hope for a future where my daughters aren't told their only value is in being wives and mothers? I don't want my identity erased. Motherhood and bearing children are important, but that isn't all that women are. We aren't *only* mothers. We are so much more, if only men would let us be so. Let me dream, Gavin, even if it's all I'll ever have. Sometimes holding on to the light of a dream is enough to survive a century in the dark."

Gavin placed a hand under her chin and turned her face toward his, his nose brushing hers as he leaned in.

"Very well, lass. I'll give you your dreams. But remember, the higher the climb, the farther the fall. I may not be there to catch you."

She kissed him. "Not all damsels need to be saved by heroes. Some save themselves."

He smiled as she kissed him again.

She shoved his shoulder with bold resolve. "Stop delaying. Show me how to be a pirate."

He threw his head back and laughed in pure delight. "So I'm to make a *pirate* of you now?"

"The fiercest one on the Atlantic," she said without any teasing now. "Give me a pirate's freedom."

He traced her lips with his thumb before he leaned down and delivered a most wicked kiss to her lips.

"Your first lesson is stealing a kiss from a pirate captain."

"Is that all? I will certainly get top marks," she promised as she threaded her fingers in his hair and pulled his lips back to hers. Then she showed him just how much of a pirate she could be.

CHAPTER 10

Pirating, it turned out, was not as easy as Josephine had imagined.

Despite the number of books she'd read on the subject, nothing had prepared her for the sheer intensity of work that went into being a sailor. There was no question that she loved the ocean and being on the ship, but she simply hadn't fathomed the sheer intensity of a sailor's duties. The first part of her morning had been a mental test in her ability to memorize and recite the names of the masts, yards, rigging, and sails, all while running up and down the ratlines to point at each one. There was the foremast, mainmast and mizzenmast. She'd been most familiar with those, but she had no idea that even the wooden spars affixed to the masts had names.

When the masts and spars were completed, a ship was considered "rigged," which meant all the ropes, cables, and chains used to support the masts and bars were set up. Gavin had drilled all of this information into her over and over with rigorous quizzing while she'd run about the ship like an excited young powder monkey, learning the work to be done on the deck level.

"Climb the shrouds," Gavin ordered for the second time that day as Josephine reached wearily for the rigging that ran from the ship's sides up to the masts. A ratline had been constructed on the ropes that formed a ladder for any sailors going aloft. After the second ascent and descent from the rigging, her lungs heaved and her arms and legs shook with the effort. Sweat dewed on her skin, and now that she was standing still, she shivered a little as she started to feel cold.

Gavin, hands clasped behind his back, watched her closely, his face a polite but cool mask. "Perhaps a third time will help you master the climb." The stern persona he assumed when he was playing the part of captain sent nervous flutters through her and made her heart pound from something other than excitement. It was so different from the man who'd been such a sweet lover the night before. With a shock, she realized she liked when he pretended to be stern with her. It made her more aware of him as a man, in a way a woman is when she can barely think of anything other than wanting to be in his bed and in his arms. In short . . . Gavin, the captain, aroused her.

"I think I've *mastered* scaling the shrouds." Josephine's hands rested on her hips as she took in a few deep breaths. Her heart was still pounding hard. Gavin arched a dark brow, his lips twitching as he seemed to fight off a smile. If she hadn't been so bloody tired, she would have smacked him for that.

"As a member of this crew, there are things you must

always be aware of . . ." He began to drone on about her duties, but she was more interested in the crew who'd been observing her as she learned her tasks. Bartholomew chuckled openly as he and two other sailors descended the rigging. They watched her and Gavin with no small amount of amusement. He'd teased her about it earlier when she'd passed him as she'd been climbing back down.

"The cap'n has an odd choice in foreplay," he'd said to her.

She had paused briefly on the ropes to speak to him. "Foreplay?"

"Aye, most men would have taken their wife to bed and . . ." He then seemed to remember he was talking to a lady and trailed off. Josephine guessed what he likely meant.

"I asked him to teach me all of this. I wish to learn what it means to be a sailor."

"Aye, I can see that you do, lassie, but I think the cap'n has other desires. He stares at you something fierce when you aren't looking at him, like he wants to tup you right there on the deck. So I ask myself, why does he look like a man who wants to but hasn't yet bedded his wife?" The older sailor's eyes sharpened with interest as he watched her face for any reaction to his words.

"I . . . Well . . ."

"So he *hasn't* bedded you yet," Bartholomew confirmed with surprise. "But it's clear he wants to."

"Move, Josie!" A blush had risen in Josephine's face when Gavin bellowed at her from below.

"Off you go, lassie!" Bartholomew had laughed again as she'd finished her climb down.

That was how she now found herself facing her stern pirate captain as he finally ended his pacing and lecturing. He then caught her chin in his hand.

"Tired already?" he asked, a teasing tone in his voice.

"I could climb the ratlines all day," she fired back, but her challenge was undercut by the shaking weariness in her limbs. They both knew she was exhausted, and she would be a fool to try to prove otherwise.

"Adventure sometimes comes at a cost," Gavin said softly.

"My mother said anything worth having isn't easy to claim," Josephine replied.

Gavin stroked her cheek with the back of his hand. "She's right. I suppose we could shift our focus to those duties that relate to the mind rather than the body. Mr. Phelps!" He called for his "first mate," as she had been instructed to call him. Apparently, pirates had *quartermasters*, but merchant ships had first mates. It was important she learned the differences so she didn't betray Gavin and Ronnie to the crew.

"Aye, Cap'n?"

"Man the ship. We are taking our studies below deck for the afternoon."

Ronnie snorted. "About bloody time. A good tupping—er, some *companionship* with your wife is a fine thing indeed."

Gavin cut his gaze to his friend. "Do not disturb us unless you absolutely have to."

"Understood, Cap'n." Ronnie prowled the length of the deck, issuing orders to adjust the sails as the wind moved across the ship's mast from a new angle.

"Come with me," Gavin said to Josephine as they descended the companionway to the decks below.

She followed him, but a little more slowly, her legs still weak from the activities of the morning.

When they reached the cabin, he pointed to a chair by the table in the middle of the room.

"Sit."

That was one command she was glad to obey. Perhaps now they would get to do the thing she'd been wanting to do from the moment she'd set foot on this ship. The excitement at the possibility had her spirits and energy rallying.

Gavin took a professorial stance as he stood in front of her. "Now, there are three sciences, or *arts* if you prefer, that define the core of a sailor's life—or a pirate's. They are seamanship, gunnery, and navigation. Each is a vital part of getting anywhere safely in a ship. Can you tell me what dead reckoning is?"

She nibbled her lip, thinking hard, but she was certain of her answer. Perhaps she could use her knowledge to her advantage somehow. As if he sensed her thoughts, Gavin spoke, his voice more seductive now than instructive.

"For every right answer you give me, *I* will remove one piece of my clothing," he said. "For each incorrect answer, I will remove one piece of *yours*," Gavin added with a rakish grin.

That was surprisingly motivational to Josephine. She liked the idea of seeing Gavin without his clothes, but if she lost hers she would end up tied to his bed again and something carnal would happen. While she liked that idea, she sensed that this was really about him maintaining his control somehow. He seemed to want to resist his feelings when it came to her, and she didn't want him to control himself. If this time with him on the *Pixie* was all she was to have, she didn't want either of them holding back. She needed him to lose his own control and be free with her.

"What if . . . the first one make the other lose all their clothing wins something," she suggested with a mischievous grin.

Gavin's eyes flared with interest. "Wins what?"

"Um . . ." She wished she knew more about lovemaking to know what would entice him. "Well . . . Whoever wins can kiss the other person wherever they want to."

At this, Gavin's eyes darkened. "An *intriguing* prize. I agree." He held out a hand and they shook on it. "Now, to the test. Dead reckoning. What is it?"

"It's a ship's position from its headings and the distance traveled. It's really a sort of educated guess that takes into account leeway and currents and other factors but is not as accurate as using a sextant or other navigational tools."

"Correct."

Grinning, she leaned back in her chair. Confident in herself, she pointed at his leather vest.

"Remove your waistcoat."

He held her gaze as he unbuttoned it and slid it off, letting it fall to the floor.

"How is the position and distance traveled calculated?"

She searched her memory for those moments when she'd pestered her father about sailing. "It's calculated by measuring the ship's speed and adding it to the time traveled at that recorded speed," she said hopefully.

Gavin gave a wolfish smile. "Close, but not quite. You

multiply, not add." He came toward her, his gaze sweeping over her from head to toe as if deciding which part of her body he wanted to bare first. "Your boots, if you please." He nodded at her feet. She pulled off her boots and stood barefoot before him.

"How do you use a ship's log?" he asked.

"It's a piece of wood . . . tied to a long strip of light cord. It's knotted at precise intervals and the cord is wrapped around a freely rotating reel. You toss the log over the side and watch it run out from the ship's wake. You count the number of knots that roll out from the reel against a log glass that drains sand in about twenty-eight seconds. If you count, say, six knots passing a particular spot in that amount of time for the log glass to run, you can estimate the ship at a speed of six nautical miles an hour."

Gavin's eyes widened. "Why . . . that's correct."

Josephine chuckled. "You seem surprised."

"I am, a little. How on earth—?"

"A pirate doesn't reveal her secrets," Josephine declared. Of course, the answer was obvious—she'd read it in a book—but where was the fun in that if she couldn't tease him?

He made a soft sound of disbelief in the back of his throat that sounded suspiciously like a chuckle.

"Very well. Let's make these questions harder."

"Not so fast, Captain. You owe me a piece of clothing. Hand over your shirt, if you please." She held out a palm and wiggled her fingers at him. He pulled the shirt over his head and handed it to her. She almost buried her face in the cloth to breathe in the scent of him, but she reminded herself to stay clearheaded if she wanted to win this game.

"How many points of sailing are on a compass?" he queried.

"Four," she answered confidently, but when she saw him smirk, her confidence faltered. "Blast. It's eight, isn't it?"

"Try thirty-two," he said. "There are four *cardinal* points, north, south, east, and west. Then there are cardinal half-points, northeast, northwest, southwest and southeast. The other twenty-four points are points in between, such as south-southeast or south-southwest."

Josephine scowled at him. "That was a trick question."

Gavin stroked his jaw, which made the muscles in his arms bulge. Lord, she liked his muscles. They made her delightfully dizzy when she looked at them.

"Pirates don't play fair, lass."

Then neither will I.

"Hmmm . . ." He studied her again, clearly enjoying making her restless as he pondered which bit of clothing to have her remove next. "Your trousers," he declared, a little too smugly.

"Oh, these?" She turned away from him as she unfastened the trousers and shimmied out of them. She wore no underthings and knew she was flashing the side of her bare bottom at him. When she had stepped out of the trousers, she turned to face him. The borrowed white shirt she wore now fell down to midthigh. The look on Gavin's face was worth the effort. His pupils nearly absorbed the brown of his eyes.

"Next question?" she prompted primly and flashed her thighs at him as she sat down upon the table.

"Minx," he muttered, then cleared his throat. "Very well. Celestial navigation. How do you accomplish it?"

"Hmm, it depends." She frowned, but when she saw the light of triumph in his eyes, she took a strand of her hair and began twisting it in her fingers, swaying slightly, drawing him into her.

"It depends on the measuring of the angle of the sun relative to the horizon. You use a sextant to take a sighting each day at noon when the sun is at its highest point. When you know the height of the sun above the horizon, your ship's latitude can be determined."

"Bloody hell," Gavin growled. "I didn't think you'd know that."

She walked up to him with a confident smirk and ran a hand down his chest to his belly. "I think I shall take *your* trousers."

He hissed softly, catching her hand before she could touch the bulge in his trousers. "I warned you, lass," Gavin said in a quiet, dangerous voice.

"About what?" But she knew exactly what. He'd warned her about playing with fire when they first met in Cornwall, and he was burning now. She could see it in his eyes, but he didn't speak, so she reminded him of her command.

"Your trousers, *Captain*," she said him as she leaned in, kissing him softly. He grabbed her forcefully, but without hurting her, taking control of her body. He spun her around and bent her face down over the table. He swiped a hand around her on the table, sending sea charts rolling onto the floor.

"I was winning—" she protested, but her words were silenced by the sound of his palm landing on her bare bottom.

Smack! She shrieked more from surprise than any sense

of pain. He delivered a few more light smacks before he leaned over, kissed the shell of her ear, and with his free hand parted the wet folds of her sex to stroke her with his fingers.

She whimpered, unable to think coherently enough to make a sound.

"I owed you that spanking, lass," he said as he continued to penetrate her with his fingers, moving them swiftly in and out of her. Her legs quaked as he drove her toward passion. She was both relieved and disappointed, however. She had wanted to tease *him*, not *be* teased, but he knew just how to touch her. She moaned as he stretched her with three fingers now. She was so close to—

Abruptly, he withdrew his hand and picked her up. She was turned around to face him as he set her back on the table. He cupped her face, then leaned in, kissing her leisurely for a long moment until she could only gaze up at him in wonder and desire.

"Lie back and let me show you the stars, Josie," he said, his voice as soft and dark as the scotch she'd once stolen from her father's liquor cabinet. It was forbidden, it burned and made her feel dizzy and wonderful. She knew in that moment that if she saw stars they would guide her back to him.

She lay back on the table, having only her shirt to cover her body.

He bent over her, spreading her thighs wide. But before she could close her legs and hide herself from his gaze, his mouth was between her legs, his lips and tongue conquering her. She had never experienced anything like this in her life. The way his tongue dragged against the most sensitive parts of her was a sensation beyond words. She closed her eyes, bathing in the glow that seemed to come from within her as she let him taste her. The pleasure built, like the growing waves of an incoming tide. And then she was flying, that exquisite pleasure a burst of stars behind her closed eyes.

She screamed as the climax hit her like a wave sweeping the decks during a squall. Gavin reached up, silencing her cry with a palm over her mouth. He licked and sucked and drew out that exquisite moment until she could take no more and lay quivering on the table beneath him.

Gavin licked his lips as he straightened. His body still leaned over hers, making her feel captive to him and the intimacy of what they'd just shared. He could do whatever he liked to her. He had full control of her body, and once again he had given her pleasure without taking any for himself. Why? Didn't he feel what she felt when they came together? What if she wasn't good enough, or too inexperienced for him? Perhaps he wanted a woman who knew what men liked in bed. Her lips trembled as she turned her face away and closed her legs against him out of shame and embarrassment.

"Josie?" He spoke her name with a hint of worry. "I didn't hurt you, did I?" She shook her head. "Did I frighten you?" Again, she shook her head and tried to pull away from him. If he touched her now, she would know it would be out of pity.

"What have I done, lass?" His voice was rough and low.

"I'm fine. Please, just give me some time alone."

He got up but didn't leave the room. "No you don't. You're not closing yourself off from me." He scooped her up and carried her to the bed, where he sat down with her in his lap.

"Talk to me, lass. Tell me what I've done." He gently stroked the shiny strands of her hair. "I know that having a man's mouth between your legs might be a bit shocking, especially when it's your first time . . ."

"It's not what you've done—it's what you *haven't* done."

He looked baffled. "What haven't I done?"

She buried her face against his neck, hiding from him. Her hopes of seducing him had come to a crashing end.

"Josie, love, what haven't I done?" He gently rocked her, yet his tenderness only made it worse somehow. She was no brave pirate—she was only playing one like she played at everything else in her life.

"You won't make love to me," she finally confessed.

"Oh . . . *that*." He breathed the words heavily against the crown of her hair, almost in relief.

"Am I undesirable?" she dared to ask. "Too inexperienced?"

His lips pressed soft kisses to her forehead.

"Quite the opposite. You're *too* desirable, Josie. 'Tis my fault. I wanted . . ."

He halted on whatever he'd been about to say, so she pressed a kiss to his chin to encourage him to continue.

"I wanted to take my time with you. The best things in life are not rushed. They are savored." He cleared his throat awkwardly. "Would you be patient with me?"

A watery laugh escaped her. "You wish for *me* to be patient while you take your time to seduce me?" she asked. "I thought pirates took what they wanted?"

"I am a pirate, through and through, but 'tis different

with you. You aren't like any woman I've ever met. Your first time in a man's bed should have meaning to you as well as the man. Call me a romantic fool, but with you, that matters. I do not want you to come to my bed out of a need to rebel at the restraints life has put upon you. Come to me because you want *me* and for no other reason."

Oh, but she *did* want him. If only he knew how much. She had wanted him from the moment he'd fallen beside her bed that stormy night. But she sensed he would not believe her if she told him.

"I'm not simply some prize you stole?" she asked, her cheek nuzzling his. She wanted to hear him say that he loved her madly, that he'd cross every ocean to be with her, but that was a dream likely out of her reach.

His wry chuckle made her burrow closer to him. "I think we both know that from the moment I saw you it was always *more* than that." He kissed her cheek. "When I stole you from your home, I wasn't quite prepared for what you make me feel. I don't wish to rush into this, not with you."

She stared up at him. His brown eyes were so warm, so soft with tenderness. Yet his face still held a hint of his piratical fierceness. He was looking at her the way she imagined a pirate would upon stumbling into a cave of golden jewels that had been hidden away from the rest of the world for more than a century. It was a look of wonder, obsession, and *longing*.

"How did you become a pirate, Gavin?"

He blinked at the change of topic. "Pardon?"

"I mean, I know you left home at nineteen, but how did you end up here?"

Gavin settled deeper on the bed, still holding her in his lap as he laid his head against the headboard.

"It is neither a short tale nor a happy one," he warned, his eyes darkening with an old pain.

She stroked his face with a fingertip, tracing his lips. "Sometimes those are the stories we need to hear the most."

He rubbed her back with his palm as if by soothing her he would soothe himself.

"When I was seventeen, I met Charity. She was the first woman I ever loved. But as you know, she choose to marry Griffin, when were nineteen and I decided to leave Cornwall. I took only a small bag of belongings to St. Ives Bay, where I booked passage on a merchant ship and sailed for the Carolinas. From there, I knew I needed work and was able to get hired aboard a private vessel. It wasn't until we were two weeks out to sea that I learned the captain and the crew were actually pirates."

"What? Why didn't they tell you? I thought pirates had codes they lived by?"

"They do, but needs must, as they say. Captain Harding had lost a third of his crew to malaria a month before he hired me and the newest sailors on board. He was in dire straits, needing to replace his crew quickly to man his vessel. Pirate ships carry fewer men than navy vessels, but even they cannot get by indefinitely with a skeleton crew. Each time a pirate ship takes a prize ship, they must send men from the original ship over to the captured vessel to crew it. Harding explained to me and the others that we were now pirates, and as such we might as well officially join the crew. We would be allowed to leave at the next port if we wished, but it would be a month before we would make berth in a pirate haven.

"I was reluctant at first, but I soon realized that Harding and his crew were good men who'd been driven to desperate measures to support their families and themselves. They chose to live outside the bounds of the law, but they didn't kill unless they had to when they captured prize ships. You have to understand, lass, pirates have more rights, more freedom, more money, and more food than most men who live on the sea. I took to pirating quite easily. Harding targeted heavily laden merchant ships that we oftentimes knew were headed our way, ships owned by wealthy merchants. He kept us clear of the Spanish and British navies. I lived that way for three years and worked my way up to being his quartermaster."

"And how did you become captain of your own ship?"

"We plundered many good prizes from the sea, and I saved my share. I was determined to claim my own vessel one day, but none of the prizes we'd taken felt right to me. They didn't feel like *my* ship. We paid a brief visit to the Carolinas in my fourth year at sea, and that's when I saw her, the *Lady Siren*—or rather, the ship that was to become her."

Josephine heard the joy in his voice, the love for the ship that would be his. She was envious. A captain's bond with his vessel was a sacred thing, and she wished she could have seen him on his beloved ship. She had secretly longed for a ship of her own. As a woman, everything she possessed belonged to a man. The clothes on her body, the food in her belly, even the bed she slept in. What would it be like to have something that was hers and hers alone?

"The *Siren* had never belonged to any man. She'd never even been sailed before. She was shiny and new. The colonists have a knack for building ships that are sleek and fast. They don't use English oak. Most are built from white oak of the north, but mine, she was made of North American live oak from the south. Few shipbuilders like to use it, but I knew the moment I stepped on her decks that her oak was superior to anything English oak could ever produce."

He smiled as fond memories softened his rugged features. "I could almost hear the shipyard echoes. The rhythmic thuds of the shipwrights' adzes, the clatter of hammers, and the hoarse grind of long ripsaws as they shaped the oak and spruce into frames and planking to build my beauty."

"How did she become yours?" Josephine asked.

"I paid all of what I'd saved over the years and bartered my soul for the rest." He stroked her cheek with the backs of his knuckles. It felt good to be held by him like this, to feel the warmth of his touch long after the heat of their passionate moment had cooled.

"And what of Captain Harding? Did he let you go?"

"He did, with the promise that I sail the *Lady Siren* alongside him for a few months. We worked together, taking prizes. We were off the coast of the Bahamas when a storm hit. Harding and his crew were forced to abandon their ship and head for land. We rescued them and salvaged some of the cargo. Harding was a broken man after that. He decided to retire, and gave me the mermaid figurehead we'd salvaged from his ship as a gift for my *Siren*. I took on some of his crew, and we sailed the seas until my boatswain, a man named Beauchamp, turned most of my crew against me."

Josephine stared at him when she heard his harsh tone.

"Why did they mutiny? Were you a harsh captain?"

His brown eyes still held shadows as he gazed at her, his face solemn.

"My charter gave equal shares to all men, even me. But our take had been poor the last few months, and Beauchamp convinced them I had lied to them about our fair portions and got them thirsting for blood. The men still loyal to me were slaughtered as we escaped the *Siren*. Only Ronnie and I survived. That was mere hours before I met you. Abandoning my ship was the worst grief I have ever felt aside from the night Charity chose Griffin."

She replayed the night they'd met in her mind with fresh eyes, seeing now how terrible that night must have been for him. Betrayed, wounded, lost, and exhausted, he had sought refuge in the only place he'd ever been safe, his childhood home. But instead of finding his twin brother, he'd found her.

As if he could sense her thoughts, he kissed her. "I'm glad it was *you* who found me." Then he kissed her chin, the tip of her nose, and when she closed her eyes, he kissed her eyelids. "I'm a selfish man, lass. I don't let my treasure go so easily." He held her gaze meaningfully.

Her heart twinged with pitiful longing and the foolish hope that he meant it, that she was a treasure to him. If it was true, did that mean he meant to keep her? Would she have a life of freedom with him on his ship? She dared not ask, not yet. She wouldn't ask him until she was certain that he would say yes.

"Why don't you rest, lass? I need to speak to Ronnie." Gavin settled her under the covers, retrieved his clothing and dressed, and then stole one last lingering kiss before he left her alone. She pulled the sheets up over herself and stared at the cabin door as he closed it behind him.

Her pirate wanted time to savor her, but Josephine had a terrible feeling that they didn't have much time. It was almost as if she could feel some cosmic clock was counting down the minutes that remained of her freedom.

"You may want to wait, Gavin, but I don't," she whispered to the empty cabin.

CHAPTER 11

They had been at sea two full weeks before the first sign of trouble appeared. Josephine had grown almost lazy with the peaceful days of good wind and sailor duties and nights spent in Gavin's arms, where he showed her pleasure over and over until she fell headlong into a deep and restful seat.

On their fifteenth day of the voyage Josephine saw the storm. She was stationed on the lookout post atop the mainmast crossbeams, her favorite spot. With her eyes trained on the horizon, the skies, and the water, she saw the storm coming before anyone. The clouds, once soft and lazy, began to build into a tower behind the ship. The jagged edges of the wispy vapor formations were a clear sign of tossing air currents. She cupped her hands and yelled down a warning to a sailor below her on the shrouds.

"Storm off the port stern!"

The sailor heard her warning and bolted for the deck far below as he passed along the warning. By the time the rest of the crew was aware of the approaching danger, Josephine could hear Gavin bellowing commands.

"All hands, wear ship! Main clew garnets and buntlines, mizzen and brails!"

Every man rushed to take in the mizzen sail and the mainsail. Josephine descended the rigging to join the men on the shrouds below as they worked hand over hand to pull the mainsail into a rolled canvas so it wouldn't be battered against the mast if the wind reversed and blew directly at them rather than from behind.

"Man weather main, lee crossjack braces!" Another command echoed across the decks.

Ronnie held the helm, where he would ride out the storm because changing the helmsman in the midst of a storm was too risky. Men had been tossed over or crushed beneath a wildly spinning helm when it had been released to let another man take over.

Gavin shouted to secure the guns for bad weather. A group of men followed him down the companionway to the gun deck below, but Josephine feared the command would come too late. A sudden squall raced ahead of the approaching storm, and Josephine sprinted back up the rigging for safety. She wrapped her wrists around the shrouds and threaded her ankles through the lines, trying to hold herself to the stiff ropes as the squall hit.

The *Cornish Pixie* lurched to one side as the waves smacked her port side. The impact of the wall of water made the *Pixie* lurch like a man taking a blow to the jaw. The ship pitched, rolling wildly as the wind swirled through the forest of masts and rigging.

Bartholomew clung to the rigging near her. "Hold fast, lassie!" They were like a pair of spiders on quivering webs caught in a thunderstorm. The wind whipped her hair against her face in stinging lashes, forcing her to shut her eyes. The waves surged across the decks, and two sailors were swept off their feet. Fortunately, they crashed into the bulwark instead of going over the side. The men on watch struggled to stay behind the shield of the tarpaulin weather cloths. The moment the wave cleared the decks, the men below finished rigging the lifelines and battening down most of the hatches.

"Bartholomew, will you keep a lookout?" she yelled at her friend.

"Aye, lassie. I'll stay here. Jim is on the foreyard above us. You check on the cap'n and the guns."

Hands freezing from the cold rain, Josephine scrambled down the ratlines to the deck and rushed for the companionway where Gavin had gone. She chanced a glance at Ronnie at the helm. His head was thrown back, red hair blowing wildly, laughing like a madman as the ship dipped into the trough of a building wave.

She ducked below into the modest safety of the gun deck as Gavin and several of the crew fought to secure the guns. Her heart pounded at the deadly threat the massive guns posed. If even one cannon got loose and slid across the deck, it would crush any sailor in its path. It could also unbalance the weight of the ship, causing it to be unable to right itself. There was even a chance it could crash down through the hull. Two sailors held one of the loose guns and were jamming the muzzle up against the clamp above the gunport so that the barrel pointed up at a forty-five-degree angle.

One of the guns lurched forward on the deck a few feet, unseen by the crew, who were focused on the opposite side of the ship. She had no time to think beyond a flash of a mad idea. She raced one deck below to where some men were storing their hammocks.

"We need to choke the trucks on a loose cannon! I need hammocks!"

Two men grabbed their hammocks and raced up after her to help. Together, they caught the sliding gun halfway across the deck by using the hammocks like slings and started to drag it back to the wall where it belonged.

"Heave!" Josephine shouted at the men helping her. Her cry caught Gavin's attention, and he glanced her way. His eyes widened when he saw the massive gun that had been coming toward his exposed back and realized that Josephine had been the one to stop it.

He joined her, grabbing the hammocks' ends as he lent his strength to theirs. The gun groaned in protest as it was dragged sideways toward the ship's planking.

"Lash it alongside!" Gavin shouted at the other two men. They answered with nods and fresh cries of "Heave!" The gun was finally swung around and lashed forward and aft against the inside planking of the ship.

Josephine's legs shook as she collapsed onto the deck. She'd given all that she had to help pull that gun across the deck.

Gavin put an arm around her lower back and helped her back up onto her feet. "Is Ronnie still at the helm?"

"Yes," she gasped. They paused on the steps leading to

the weather deck, and Gavin pinned her against the bulkhead when the ship made a sudden roll. Their soaking bodies were pressed flush against each other, and his ragged breath mixed with hers. His eyes were dark and burning as he stared at her trembling lips.

"Stay down here. Don't come up on deck, you understand?"

"Gavin, I have to help—"

"You've done enough, and done it well. Now I want you safe."

He silenced her with a hard kiss, one that sent her head spinning and her legs quaking. When he tore his mouth away from hers, she saw his grim resolve.

"Stay below. That's an order. If you disobey, I'll have no choice but to whip you in front of my crew." The violence of his threat was so unexpected that she could only stare at him.

When he released her, he bolted up the steps as a clap of thunder broke through the wailing winds. She sank to the deck, leaning back against the bulkhead as she fought to steady herself. The storm was unlike anything she'd ever experienced before. She'd witnessed and lived through plenty of violent storms on land, but a storm like this took on new depths of terror because one couldn't escape it. The knowledge that at any moment the right wave could topple the *Pixie* or smash it to pieces filled her with raw terror. Everyone on board could perish, all of the eighty men, including her and Gavin.

For the first time in her life, Josephine understood the nature of fear as it crawled through the walls of her mind and sank its teeth and claws into her chest. She couldn't breathe. No air was moving in or out of her lungs. There was a buzzing in her skull like a hive of raging wasps.

"*Josie!*" A voice penetrated the fog of terror inside her, and she looked up to see the cook, Olive, holding out a hand to her.

"Come on, girl, *move*! The surgeon needs us." Olive pulled her to her feet, and they headed for the surgery.

Two sailors lay on a pair of surgery tables, and Dr. Gladstone was doing his best to keep one man lying flat. The man's leg was broken and jutted out at an awkward angle. The sailor screamed as Dr. Gladstone tried to calm him. The man on the other table had a broken arm, which he cradled with his hand, his face pale as he watched the doctor and the sailor with the broken leg struggling.

"Hold him down so I can get some laudanum," Gladstone ordered.

Olive and Josephine helped pin the man down on the table. Gladstone grabbed a dark-blue bottle of laudanum from a cabinet and tipped it into the sailor's mouth. The poor man coughed and swallowed, before drifting to sleep.

"I need to set the bone," Gladstone muttered, and Josephine winced as the sight of flesh and bone being moved back into place unsettled her stomach.

"Watch him, Mrs. Castleton," the doctor ordered. "Olive, I need you to help Thomas while I fix his arm."

Josephine sat down on a stool that was nailed to the deck and held on to the table with one arm as the ship swayed. The man on the table shifted in his sleep and Josephine lunged, grabbing his shoulder to keep him steady. The lamps above their heads swayed, and she stared up at the ceiling, her fear returning in full force. What was happening on the top deck?

Please let Gavin come out of this alive.

GAVIN THREW OUT AN ARM AND CAUGHT A SAILOR before he was washed overboard. The man grunted and they both slammed down onto the deck as the wave passed over them. He held his breath as the seawater briefly engulfed him and then sucked in great lungfuls of air once the deck cleared of water.

Above them, a dozen men were in the shrouds, lashed to the foreyard, where they were in some ways safer than anyone on the deck. This was one of the things he hated about sailing. Even the sturdiest frigates could roll in storms like these, and every man on board would be lost. It didn't matter how skilled a captain and crew were or how well the ship was built. Gavin had always hated storms, but with Josephine here he felt a new intensity to his old fears.

Gavin looked at Ronnie, who still manned the helm. A rope had been wrapped around him, securing him to it so he wouldn't lose his footing when the waves smashed over the deck.

"Storm's clearing!" Ronnie called out, and Gavin turned to see behind them as the distant clouds were in fact clearing, but so much could happen between where they were now and the clear blue skies coming up behind them as the storm overtook them and surged on ahead.

A tremendous roar came from all around. Gavin turned to see a massive wave heading toward the ship.

"Everyone get below!" he bellowed.

The crew on deck scrambled for safety. One of the older men, a sailor called Bartholomew, slipped as the wave came toward them. With a curse, Gavin dove for the man, slamming him down against the shelter of the railing. Water pounded them with such force that it knocked the breath from his lungs. Water drained around them, pouring in a deluge off the sides of the besieged vessel, but he and Bartholomew were still alive.

"Thank you, Cap'n," the old man sputtered and wiped seawater from his face.

"I want you inside," he growled. They started for the entrance to the lower decks, but Gavin realized too late they wouldn't make it. Everything slowed down as he and Bartholomew raced for the companionway steps. Suddenly Josephine appeared in the entrance leading belowdecks, her eyes widened as she saw what he had seen a few seconds before. A great wave arched up and over the ship.

"*Run*, damn you!" Gavin shouted at the older man in front of him as he pushed him into Josephine's waiting arms. A second later, the wave knocked Gavin clean off his feet . . . and then off the deck of the ship entirely.

The world spun around him as he plunged into the dark black waters. He kicked out, swimming frantically, but he couldn't tell which way the surface was. Not that it mattered. A man overboard in a storm was a man *lost*.

Still, it wasn't in him to give up. He kicked toward what he prayed was the surface. His head broke the water, and he spotted the *Pixie* not far off. He kicked hard, powering his arms and legs to reach the ship, but there was no hope. Wave after wave struck him hard. Finally, exhaustion and pain won out. He watched his slim chance of salvation sailing off without him. He had but one thought, one regret before he sank beneath the waves: he had never shown Josie what she meant to him.

THE INSTANT THE WAVE CARRIED GAVIN OFF THE SHIP, Josephine screamed his name.

"He saved me," Bartholomew muttered in shock as he huddled under the raised deck beside her. When Josephine took a step toward the deck outside, he caught her arm. "He's gone, lass. You can't save a man overboard. Not in a storm like this."

"Watch me!" Josephine snapped.

She grabbed the longest coil of rope she could find and wrapped one end around her waist, tying a secure knot like Bartholomew had taught her. Then she secured the other onto the center mast of the deck. She prayed the rope was long enough.

Without a backward glance, she ran for the railing and dived off the side as the ship rolled downward toward the water. Her calculated jump meant she had only a dozen feet before she dropped beneath the waves rather than twenty. Once she hit the water, she searched for Gavin. She crested with a wave and spotted him not too far off, just as he went under. She plunged below the surface, her fingers closing around his arm. She pulled him, all the while fighting toward the faint light of the surface. Her lungs burned like fire. Every muscle in her body screamed, demanding air. The *Pixie* drifted away from them, and the rope pulled taut against her waist, squeezing her stomach. She wanted to scream at the agony, but if she did, she would take in water.

She begged her body to not give up. *Just hold on* . . . A wave lifted them, and then sweet, glorious air filled her lungs. She shifted her grip on Gavin, but didn't let go of him. His head bobbed above the water as she dragged him behind her while the ship pulled them in its wake. The clouds above began to thin and the tumultuous waves died down. She prayed someone would soon realize that she and Gavin were still there in the water. A face suddenly appeared over the stern railing, and a cry went up. Whatever the sailor shouted was lost on the wind, but he pointed at her and Gavin as more faces appeared over the side to stare at them.

She wanted to weep with relief, but she knew she had to stay strong just a little bit longer. The rope around her stomach tightened again, this time as she moved forward. They were reeling her and Gavin in. When they reached the hull, she gripped the wooden treads against the ship.

"Can you climb, lassie?" Bartholomew yelled down at her.

"Yes, but Gavin can't. Send me another rope." The sailors dropped a line down the ship, which allowed her to tie the rope around Gavin's waist and upper body, forming a harness.

"Pull him up!" she called out to the sailors. A moment

later, Gavin's body was lifted from the water and began the ascent upward. Bone weary, she blew out a breath and started climbing the wooden treads on the side of the ship. Gavin was pulled up over the side long before she reached the top. When she did finally got back on board, she found the boatswain, Mr. Greenwell, bent over Gavin's prone form as he pressed down on his chest. Gavin coughed, and water flowed out of his mouth.

"That's it, Cap'n, breathe," Greenwell encouraged as he rolled Gavin onto his side while he expelled the last of the seawater from his lungs.

Josephine sank to her knees and stared at Gavin. He was alive. By some miracle, she'd saved him.

"That was a bloody brave thing to do, lassie," Bartholomew said as he crouched down by her. "You saved his life. We never would've been able to reach him in time. I hope your husband knows how much you love him."

It was on the tip of her tongue to say that she didn't love Gavin, but Bartholomew was right. She did. As mad as it was to love a man who might never love her back, she loved him with every fiber of her being.

"Three cheers for Mrs. Castleton!" Bartholomew shouted, and all of the men cheered.

Josephine tried to smile, but instead she slumped down onto the deck, her breathing ragged. The sailors around Gavin lifted him up and carried him down to Dr. Gladstone's surgery.

Bartholomew grasped Josie around her shoulders and lifted her up. "Come on, lass. Let's take you to your cabin."

"But Gavin . . ."

"He'll be fine," the salty old sea dog said. "You need to

sleep, lass. The good doctor will watch over the cap'n for you."

When they reached the captain's cabin, she stumbled inside and fell face-first onto the bed, too weary to do anything but sleep.

CHAPTER 12

A familiar voice dug into the fog of Gavin's mind as he struggled to wake up. "You have the devil's own luck, you do."

"Ronnie?" He put a hand to his head and groaned as a dull throb joined the haze filling his mind.

A cup was pressed to Gavin's parched lips. "Drink this," Dr. Gladstone said.

He drank the cold water and fumbled in his attempt to grasp the cup.

"Easy, Cap'n. You're in no condition to move," Ronnie said.

Gavin struggled to open his eyelids, but the world seemed to press down on him from all sides.

"What . . . What happened?" The words were barely audible even to his own ears.

"You went over the side. We thought you were lost, Gavin . . ." His friend's voice was rough with emotion. "I was lashed to the helm, trying to keep us steady, and I couldn't go after you." This spoke volumes as to Ronnie's concern, because he rarely called Gavin by his first name.

Finally, Gavin forced his eyelids up, and the world around him, blurry at first, slowly came into focus. He was in the surgery, and Dr. Gladstone was holding a cup of water near his mouth. He gratefully took another long drink before he turned to Ronnie on his other side.

"I remember washing overboard . . ." He shuddered as violent, rolling nausea tossed his stomach. "How did I end up here?"

Ronnie seemed to understand what he was really asking. How was he still alive?

"*She* saved you. I've never seen anything like it, Cap'n."

His mind and body were both numb with pain and exhaustion, and even this simple riddle was beyond him. "Who?"

"Your siren."

"My ship?" Had they managed to catch up with Beauchamp already? Why would he rescue him?

"No, your *real* siren, Cap'n. Your wife, I mean," Ronnie emphasized. It took a moment to remember who Ronnie meant. *Josephine*.

"Is she—?" He tensed with new terror at the thought that he might have lost her.

"She's fine, Cap'n. She's asleep in your bed at the moment."

Gavin sagged back on the surgery table. "How did she save me?"

Ronnie's eyes glinted with admiration.

"She was something to see, she was. Wrapped a rope around her waist and dove in after you. Christ knows how she found you. The men watching said you went under, but she managed to find you and grab hold of you. The waves batted you about like a cat with a mouse before the crew spotted your heads bobbing in the water. She held fast, your siren." Ronnie's voice glowed with pride.

"The men hauled you back on board after she made a harness from some rope to wrap around you."

"She did all that?" Gavin was stunned that she'd managed his rescue in the choppy waters of the storm. But he was also grateful and frankly in awe of Josephine.

"She did." Ronnie leaned down close to Gavin when Dr. Gladstone moved away to refill the cup with more water. "You know my thoughts on marriage, Cap'n, but if it was me, I would marry that girl before your brother catches up to us."

Gavin let his head fall back onto the small bundle of cloth that formed a pillow beneath him and stared up at the swinging lanterns. Josephine had saved him. Not only that, she'd risked her life to do it.

"How many men did we lose?" he asked his quartermaster, his thoughts clearing and focusing on his duties once more.

"Not one man, Cap'n. 'Tis a bloody miracle. We have two injured. Thankfully, the squall was brief and the men in the rigging lashed themselves down. We would've lost Bartholomew, but he says you saved him. That reminds me—he's waiting outside to speak with you, if'n you're up to it, that is."

Gavin was too weary to really talk, but he didn't want the guilt of sending an old man away. He nodded.

"Let him in, Doctor," Ronnie told Dr. Gladstone.

A moment later, the wizened old sailor Bartholomew entered, head bowed as he approached the surgery table. He appeared almost bashful.

"Cap'n. I'm right glad to see you awake. I wanted to thank you. You saved my life and nearly died for it. If it hadn't been for you and your wife, well . . . Thank you. I've been at sea almost all my life. Figured I die out here sooner or later, but you gave me more time. That means a lot to an old man like me." Bartholomew held out his hand and Gavin clasped it in his own, giving it a firm shake.

"Well, I'd best be getting back on deck. We've sails to mend." Bartholomew grinned and left.

"Who are the men who were injured?" Gavin glanced at the second table, where one man lay with his leg splinted. He breathed deep and slow, still under the influence of laudanum. But Gavin saw no other man in the room.

"The other fellow has a broken arm. He's bunking in his hammock right now. He'll be fine."

Gavin briefly closed his eyes, exhaustion creeping in. He had a vague memory of swallowing the entire sea and spitting it back up. Perhaps that was why it felt like the devil still sat on his chest.

"Ronnie, is Josephine . . . ? I need to . . ." But fatigue hit him even as he tried to sit up.

"Whatever it is, Cap'n, it'll keep, it'll keep. Rest now." Ronnie pressed a palm gently on Gavin's shoulder to ease him back down. "No sense in wooing a lassie when you can barely stand."

Gavin fell into darkness, but the dreams that followed were soft and golden, filling him with an ardent longing . . .

He chased a woman through a garden, the night air full of the heavy scent of flowers. He could see her, could almost catch her, if he ran just a bit faster . . . His hands closed on the back of her silk gown, halting her. She spun around and he saw that it was his beloved Charity, yet she wasn't his. Her face was more beautiful in the way a woman in the bloom of life looked as she drew close to motherhood. This was not the Charity he'd met at seventeen, but the woman who had married his twin brother and built a life with him. This Charity had never been his. Her eyes were luminous beneath the stars as she gazed up at him. She reached up and cupped his cheek.

"It's time," she whispered, her smile bittersweet.

"Time?" He didn't understand what she was saying.

Somewhere nearby a nightingale started to sing, and she glanced around at the sound before looking at him. "Time to let me go, Gavin."

Her words broke something inside him, and he clutched her tighter, suddenly afraid, his eyes clouded with tears. "No, I don't want to."

She caressed his cheek. "I had my life. Now it's time for you to live yours. I'm already gone . . . But she is the one fate always meant for you to find. Go to her."

Charity pointed to a silhouette of a person sitting on a bench he hadn't noticed before, a beautiful young woman. She looked lonely, and something about her called to his own lonely heart.

A wind stirred in the garden, and he felt that wind stealing Charity away even as he turned toward the other woman. Flower petals swirled around him, blinding him briefly of his view of the garden. Charity slipped free of his hold as the wind gently pushed him toward the other woman.

"I'm already gone . . ."

The words left a strange bittersweet hum in his chest as

he slowly opened his eyes. The surgery was quiet. No sign of Dr. Gladstone. The sailor on the other table was still asleep, and Gavin guessed that several hours had passed since he'd first awoken. He sat up and let his legs drape over the side of the surgery table. Dried tear tracks tugged at his skin as he rubbed his face with a weary palm.

He felt *empty*, as though a mighty wave had washed through his heart and soul, leaving nothing but a barren shore.

Had he truly dreamed of Charity? The memory of that dream was hazy now, and it stung his eyes merely trying to recall what he had seen. Yes, he had dreamt of her. She had told him to let go. Until that moment, he hadn't realized that he'd clung to her memory so fiercely. But now, without that old love to hold onto—or rather, without the memory of that love tethering him down—he felt lighter. A deep breath restored his clarity of thought.

The girl in the garden . . . Had Charity been right? Was Josephine the woman he was meant to love? The need to see Josephine, to touch her, suddenly overpowered him. He slid off the table and steadied himself as he got his bearings. Then he left the surgery and started toward his cabin.

As he passed sailors going about their duties, each man would stop, nod, or knuckle his forehead in a salute and murmur, "Cap'n." He responded each time with a small nod before continuing on. When he reached his cabin, his chest tightened with nervousness at the thought of seeing the woman who'd saved his life and quite possibly his heart.

He opened the door and glimpsed her on the bed. She was still in her soaked clothes, just like him, although he could tell the fabric of her shirt and trousers was likely becoming stiff with salt as they dried. He crossed the room and quietly eased down on the side of the bed. Her face was turned toward him, and her brow was furrowed, as if her dreams were troubling. A wealth of tenderness suddenly overflowed inside him. He bent down and pressed a kiss to her cheek, then stroked his fingertips over her brow until it smoothed and she relaxed.

"You saved me, lass, in more ways than you'll ever know," he whispered.

As if comforted by his voice, she shifted on the bed, moving closer to him. Even in her dreams, she seemed to seek him. Gavin didn't want to wait any longer. He felt ready to open himself to this woman and claim whatever future they could have. Even if it meant fighting his own brother to keep her.

JOSEPHINE MOANED AS HER SORE LIMBS WERE GENTLY bent and moved. She woke and blinked in confusion at the sight of Gavin bending over her. He paused in the process of removing her trousers. For a moment she was simply overjoyed that he was alive and well. She vaguely remembered someone escorting her to the cabin before she'd passed out. When his hands slid over the bare skin of her thighs, she realized he was taking her clothes off.

"I didn't wish to wake you," he apologized. "But these clothes are stiff with seawater, and you need to be out of them." The way he caressed her skin suggested that he wasn't entirely concerned about the seawater but was rather looking for an excuse to touch her, and she was more than content with that.

Something had changed between them—not that she could explain what exactly, only that she felt the difference in the air. It was no longer a time for waiting, a time for testing the control he'd said he'd struggled to have. This shift between them was pure, yet somehow far more dangerous than how things had been before. She knew now he would claim her the way she'd longed for since the night they met. She studied his features, noting how his mouth and eyes had softened, making him look years younger. He sat on the edge of the bed, gloriously naked. She took in the sight of him, every inch of tanned skin and corded muscle. He was beautiful, hard and lean. It made her ache deep inside to lie skin to skin with him and feel his body beside hers.

She felt strangely shy as she let him undress her. Neither of them spoke as he removed her stockings. He lifted her to sit, and her hair, now wavy with brine, fell over her shoulders. They were inches apart, staring into each other's faces, both waiting for the other to say something. Gavin's fingers skimmed along her belly, his thumbs caressing her as he pulled her shirt up and off, spilling her hair over her bare shoulders. Shyness and desire turned her skin pink. She was laid bare before him on the bed, yet she was too exhausted to move.

"You saved my life, lass." The words, although quiet, seemed to echo in the cabin. The rhythmic sway of the ship and the sound of waves against the hull made

Josephine feel like she was on an abandoned island with only him and the sea. It was a beautiful, *wonderful* feeling.

She slowly sat up, reaching out to place her palm against his back. "You saved Bartholomew." His muscles leapt beneath her touch as he let out a breath and released his tension.

"I told you not to come above deck," he reminded her. He did not look at her, but his tone held no bite to it.

Josephine had a sudden realization that whatever she said next would shape their future.

"I came on the ship with you because I *wanted* to be with you. I was not about to let the sea take you from me, not when I wanted you more than these waters ever could."

She leaned forward and kissed his bare shoulder, tasting the sea salt upon his skin. He let out another breath, a shudder rippling through his body and into hers. She curled her arms around his neck from behind, pressing her breasts against his back as she embraced him. He reached up, covering her hands with his.

"I don't deserve you, Josie. You are above me, beyond my *mortal* reach."

"You make me sound like an angel." She laughed softly, charmed by his words. "I'm certainly not that." She sobered and kissed his cheek. "Perhaps I'm an undine, a selkie, a siren. A creature of the water, but a creature that belongs to *you*, just as your ship does. *Claim me*, Gavin. I am yours."

He turned as she released him, but he didn't pull away. Rather, he claimed her with a kiss that held the fire of the very sun within it. She gasped as she tried to remember how to breathe, bathing in its glow. She lay back on the bed, pulling him down with her, their mouths fused in that endless kiss.

Her hips rose, her legs parting in a silent, ancient invitation as he settled over her. Her thighs tightened around his slender hips, and he stroked the outside of her knee with his palm as he continued to kiss her. Gavin rocked against her, and she lost herself in him, feeling as though they would sail upon the sea forever and she would never have to leave this cabin or him.

She dug her hands into his hair. He groaned as he adjusted his body and his hard manhood pressed at the entrance to the very core of her. She raised her hips, and the pressure of his entry made her gasp as he plunged into her. He nuzzled her cheek, whispering soft words that made her chest fill with warmth. As the pressure slowly eased, he began to move, letting her feel the true magic of lovemaking.

A wonderful sense of falling and then being caught up on the wind filled her as he moved. The gentle rhythm of his lovemaking began to increase, building toward a glorious intensity. Her passion and love were unfurling sails that caught and filled with the wind that was Gavin, and together they sailed upon the glass-like sea in a dream.

This was *heaven*, this sense of belonging not only to him but to herself. This was her choice, her body, her soul, and she chose Gavin and chose to love him. For the first time, she knew what freedom was. To let her heart and mind and body *choose* their destiny was like breaking the surface of the sea and breathing for the first time.

"Tell me what you're thinking," Gavin whispered as he

moved above her. She gazed into his brown eyes, which had once held such deep shadows. She saw no shadows now.

"I'm sailing," she confessed. Her words seem to need no further explanation as he captured her mouth in another searing kiss. This time, he moved harder, faster, as though a storm was chasing them and he fought to sail them safely toward a distant, glowing horizon. A burst of sudden exquisite pleasure overwhelmed her and she cried out in shock.

He roared her name and she clung to him, digging her nails into his back as they rode that last wave together, and then, slowly, the intense feeling faded, but the softer, quieter sense of pure joy that remained was just as powerful. He collapsed on top of her, but she didn't mind the weight of him. She stroked his hair, and this time she was the one to whisper soft, sweet words as he trembled in her arms.

"My *siren*," he breathed. He lifted his body off hers but didn't leave her. He settled onto his back and pulled her to lie against him, kissing the crown of her hair.

"My *pirate*," she replied with a drowsy smile upon her lips. Her body still ached, but in a far better way and for a far better reason than before.

She was almost asleep when he spoke again. "I have a home. A private place on an island that is hard to find. I want to take you there . . . Would you let me?"

"Of course," she replied at once. "What's it like?"

"I call it the Isle of Song. Thousands of tropical birds of every size and color fill the trees. I built a white house that faces the sea, and white sand lines the beaches. Fresh spring water forms streams across the center of the island,

and monkeys leap from branch to branch while you explore the jungle paths. It's a place of beauty and peace. It's been my sanctuary for the last few years."

She closed her eyes, picturing the beauty of this place, this Isle of Song. Just the two of them, alone with an island to explore. Her heart soared like a stormy petrel, riding the currents of the air.

Whatever came next, she belonged to Gavin and he to her. Neither of them had spoken yet of love, but she knew that day would come. For now, she knew what lay between them was real, true. They were no longer pretending to be a pirate and his stolen prize. They were two hearts bound by an emotion that ran deeper than any ocean and burned brighter than any rising sun.

She could face whatever came next, so long as Gavin was by her side. Storms might come, winds might rise, seas might darken, but she and Gavin would hold fast to each other.

CHAPTER 13

The Isle of Song was everything Josephine dreamed it would be. After a little more than four weeks at sea, the sight of the small island in the Atlantic was a welcome one. White sand surrounded the island, and at its center lay a jungle with leafy foliage and ancient trees.

Gavin stood at the helm, guiding the *Cornish Pixie* through the shallow waters along a path only he knew that kept the ship from catching on reefs or sandbars. The ship turned gently at his subtle guidance as it sailed safely past places that would have trapped other vessels. He slowed the *Pixie* down, and soon the anchor was dropped. Ronnie gave the order for two boats to be lowered so that some of the crew could accompany Gavin and Josephine ashore.

More than a dozen people flocked to the shallows as the boats slid onto the white sand of the beach. Men, women, and a few children, all of them dark-skinned, gathered to wave at them as they climbed out of their boats.

Men doffed their straw hats and women smiled in warm welcome.

"Gavin!" A young boy in rolled-up trousers and a white shirt rushed over and tackled Gavin in the waves.

"Sam, you devil! Been up to trouble while I've been away?" Gavin wrestled with the boy, who couldn't have been more than six, and lifted him up, carrying him under one arm like he was a sack of flour. Josephine covered her mouth to keep from laughing at the pair of them.

"Josephine, this is Sam," Gavin said, depositing the boy back on the sand in front of a beautiful dark-skinned woman who wore her hair tucked up in a scarf around her head.

"It's about time you brought a woman home, Gavin." The woman held out a hand to Josie as though she had known Josephine all her life. "Come, let me feed you. Ship food is nothing compared to island cooking." She studied Josephine's manly garb. "And I will find a dress for you to wear. My name is Jada, and this wild child is my son, Sam."

Gavin gave Josephine an encouraging nod before he faced his men and began giving instructions. Jada led Josephine toward a two-story white house.

Thick forests surrounded part of the home and a garden in the side yard was a garden full of vegetables rather than flowers. As they drew closer, she marveled at both the garden and the home itself. A porch wrapped around the other side of the building and was decorated with four comfortable-looking chairs that faced the sea. She could easily imagine sitting in one of those chairs and watching the sun set over the water. Large windows were open and white curtains billowed out with the sea breeze. The beautiful home felt light and airy.

"Will Gavin be joining us?"

"Come along, Miss Josephine. Your man will come soon enough. He has to see to his men and tell them the rules of this island."

Josephine couldn't help but blush at Gavin being called *her* man. While they'd been on the *Pixie*, the two of them had felt like they were in an intimate bubble. Now they were back in the world again. It felt different, somehow even more surreal than ever that she was *with* a man.

Jada led her inside the home, and Josephine's lips parted at the sight of the staircase leading up to the floor above. Even though the house was outwardly like many of the lovely houses she was used to back in Cornwall, the interior of the home was vastly different. Seascapes had been painted on the walls. It made this home feel like it was right on the edge of the water.

"Does it ever flood here?" She had heard Dominic spin tales of fierce hurricanes that could sweep entire villages off the map, killing everyone.

"No, this island is blessed." Jada chuckled. "We see the storms, but they always pass us by." Jada led her upstairs and opened a tall wardrobe in one of the bedrooms, where several dresses hung.

"Let's try this one," Jada said as she held up a light linen gown the color of pink coral, like the reefs surrounding the island.

Josephine was startled to realize that the gown Jada had given her did not take any sort of undergarments. No padding, hoops, or panniers were required to give the gown shape. Instead, it there was a single billowy petticoat under her dress. Josephine supposed that was to be expected, given the climate. It would simply be too hot to wear more than that beneath a dress most of the year.

She stood before the tall mirror in the corner of the large bedchamber and gazed upon her natural form, with her curves displayed gently rather than in the exaggerated fashions of London. The dress was short enough to show her ankles and let the breeze ruffle the skirts. She grinned and swayed her hips, making the skirts twirl around her legs.

"Much cooler, yes?" Jada chuckled and lightly squeezed Josephine's shoulders. "So, you are Gavin's lady?"

The hint of a question echoed in Jada's voice.

"Um . . . yes. I'm Gavin's wife."

Jada's eyes twinkled. "Newly married?" she guessed. "It is good to see that man finally settle down." Jada's smile faded. "But where's the *Siren*? That is not Gavin's ship anchored in the cove." She nodded at the open window, where they glimpsed the *Pixie* floating on the water.

"No, that's my brother's ship." She wasn't sure how much Gavin would want her to tell Jada. Did Jada already know that Gavin was a pirate? If not, Josephine did not want to be the one to tell her Gavin's secrets. "He gave us the ship as a wedding present."

"I see." Jada mused on that thoughtfully, then flashed her a bright smile. "Let's put some food in that belly of yours."

They wandered down to the kitchen on the ground floor, and Josephine noticed more men and women moving about the house, seeing to the various duties of cleaning.

She couldn't help but be curious as to their role here. Gavin hadn't mentioned anyone when he'd spoken to her about the island. Slavery was not something her family approved or condoned. As a woman, she often felt owned herself. The thought of owning another person simply felt wrong.

"You must be wondering if we are slaves. We are not. Gavin stopped a slave ship three years ago and freed everyone on board. My son Sam was only three years old and I was one of the lucky women who didn't have my child taken from me because of his age. Thirty of us chose to come here to this island with him. It is safer than the other islands, and we risk recapture if we go anywhere else. Here . . . it is only us. We have fields, we sow crops, the people here have their own houses. We live quiet but content lives." Jada's voice held such peace that Josephine envied her. What would it be like to feel so at peace with one's world?

Jada ushered Josephine to a seat at the table and then joined an older woman who was cooking in the kitchen. The two of them spoke softly to each other in a lyrical language before the older woman leaned over the stove and pointed at Josephine, whispering something. Jada nodded in reply. The woman's eyes widened, and she smiled shyly at Josephine.

Jada came over and introduced the woman. "This is Kai, our cook. I am Gavin's housekeeper. There are another six people who choose to live in this house and help Gavin with household duties since he is gone many months of the year. The rest of the island's residents work in the fields and gardens and live in a group of houses on the opposite side of the island. While Gavin is away, which is often, we all share the work of keeping the island supplied with food and the houses repaired. It keeps us busy, but we enjoy working and owning our own land and homes."

Josephine was impressed and glad to see that Jada and the others had escaped a life of slavery and now had lives all their own in this little bit of paradise. It was all she'd ever hoped for too.

"It's lovely to meet you, Kai." She smiled at the shy cook.

Jada chopped a pineapple into chunks and brought Josephine some of the fruit on a plate to eat while they waited for Kai to finish. Something delicious was cooking on a skillet, and when Kai removed the skillet from the stove, Josephine was treated to spicy grilled chicken. Wonderful new flavors exploded on her tongue.

She was licking her fingers clean, unashamed of her unladylike behavior, when Gavin stepped into the kitchen. He greeted Kai and Jada with a roguish grin. Kai said something to him in her language and tossed a towel at his face. He caught it and laughed, then kissed Jada's cheek in a brotherly way. She realized that *this* was Gavin's family now, one that he had made all on his own.

"And you," he said as he turned at last toward Josephine, that smile of his so bright that it nearly blinded her. She felt seen, *loved*, when he looked at her that way. In the last four weeks they'd sailed together, she and Gavin had grown close, not just physically, but emotionally. She hadn't imagined that it was possible to feel so connected to another person. She'd lived her entire life with her family, but she felt that she knew Gavin's heart and soul better than anyone else. She'd tried not to think about the future, about their lives diverging at some point. She only wanted to bask in the days she had left with him.

His once rare smiles were now becoming more frequent, and she'd grown addicted to how that made her feel. Like she could do *anything* in life.

"You've chosen your bride well," Jada said.

"I have, haven't I?" Gavin swept an examining look over Josephine. "Let me show you my island, Josie." He held out a hand, and she placed her palm in his. They left and started up a sandy path toward the jungle. She was grateful for the sandals Jada had given her.

She had asked Jada about the clothes she'd been given, wondering if Gavin had brought other women here. He hadn't. The dresses had been sewn by Jada and the other women on the island in hopes that someday Gavin would bring a bride home. They'd made clothing in all sizes, and leather sandals as well. Everything had been patiently waiting for someone to open that wardrobe and put them on.

"Your house is so beautiful, Gavin. It's so very different."

"Yes. No stuffy drawing rooms, no gloomy portraits. It's warm and welcoming, the way a home should be," he agreed. "When I built it, I wanted it to feel like it was *mine*." He said this with such simple honesty that she was moved to tears.

To hide her impending tears, she stood on her tiptoes and kissed his cheek. "I fell in love with you when I saw your *gloomy* portrait," she teased.

They halted on the beach path that led toward the jungle, and she wondered what she'd said to make him stop. And then she realized she had said *the words*.

"You love me, lass?" His face was so serious it seemed carved of stone.

"Yes," she replied. "I do. And I have no regrets in my admission. It's how I feel, and as long as I draw breath, I shall own my feelings. I'm proud of them, good or bad, because they are mine. You don't have to say anything."

"But I will." He cupped her face in his hands and gazed deep into her eyes. "I love you, lass." His voice was rough with emotion, but his lips curved slightly in a smile that threatened to break through the solemnity of the moment. "I want you to be my wife in truth." He smiled fully then, and it felt as though the sun itself burned inside her.

He stroked the backs of his knuckles over her cheek. "I heard once . . . if you say you marry someone three times, it becomes true."

She tried to ignore the flutter of excitement as he bent his head to kiss her.

"I *marry* you," he said, then kissed her again. "I *marry* you." He paused, nibbling at her earlobe before finally saying, "I *marry* you."

She threw her arms around his neck and covered his face with kisses before repeating the words back to him in such haste that he laughed with delight.

He kissed the tip of her nose. "Who knew you'd be so thrilled to have a second marriage proposal?"

"I'm thrilled because it is the *right* one, from the right man."

The words held no weight in a court of law or with any

church, but to Josephine they were real. Those words tied her soul to his forever.

"Let me show you our island." He took her hand and led her into the jungle.

GAVIN'S HEART FLUTTERED WITH EXCITEMENT. *Married*. It might be in name only, but it felt as though he was truly tied to Josephine. They would marry legally as soon as he could arrange it, but for now he was overjoyed simply *feeling* married to her. The old Gavin, the one who had fled to the seas and stopped believing in love, would have scoffed at the prospect of being married, but the month he'd spent with Josephine on board the *Pixie* had changed him forever. He no longer wanted to be alone, no longer wanted to mourn his once broken heart. Now he was moving toward a bright and beautiful future.

The path they took divided into several smaller paths throughout the forest. He led her down the central one toward the heart of the island. He pointed out yellow elder bushes with their clusters of flowers that resembled yellow daffodils, wild sage with its orange flowers, and the light-purple jacarandas that bloomed everywhere. The songs of tropical birds echoed through the canopy, and parrots of all sizes and colors flew from branch to branch ahead of them as they walked.

"Are all these birds from this part of the world?"

Josephine asked, taking in the multicolored flocks above them.

"Many aren't native. They flew off ships passing by and found this island," he explained.

"Their melodies are beautiful. I used to love the morning after a thunderstorm as a child. I would lie in bed and hear the birds chattering in excitement, and the sun always seemed to shine a little brighter after those storms."

As they walked, Gavin asked a great many questions about her life, and she did the same. He shared with her tales of his childhood and stories of his battles at sea. She drank in each detail.

"To think, you've known my brother Dominic longer than I have," she mused.

He paused on the path and stared at her. It was true. In a strange twist of fate, he'd known Dominic for a longer time than she had.

"You were a mere babe when he left, weren't you?"

She nodded. "I wish . . . I wish he'd known how much we missed him. It was like a piece of our hearts went missing with him when he vanished." Gavin saw a flash of unexpected emotion in her eyes. "I caught my mother talking to his portrait once. She thought no one was around. She said, 'I keep believing you're just on a simple journey and that one day you will come home and laugh it all off as a grand adventure. But what if you don't? What if you are truly gone and I never had the chance to say goodbye? Do you know that I loved you? Do you know how much I still do?'" The memory of this seemed to create such pain in Josephine that she choked down a sob.

Gavin pulled her into his arms and kissed her forehead,

then held her tight. He wished in that moment he could take all of her pain away.

"If this is a dream, I don't wish to wake," she whispered against his chest. "But I'm so afraid, Gavin."

"Afraid of what?"

"Of losing this, of losing *you*." Her words tore at his heart. "The future has never frightened me more than it does at this moment because I have so much to lose now."

"All dreamers must wake up sooner or later . . . But what if we wake to something even better than this?" he asked.

"You said you weren't romantic." She rubbed away her tears, and he couldn't help but smile at her.

"Any man in love becomes a romantic."

She lifted her head at his words. "You truly love me? That's twice now you've said it."

"I think it would be impossible *not* to love you," he said with such seriousness. "Perhaps I should show you, since you need some more *convincing*."

JOSEPHINE FOLLOWED GAVIN TO A DEEP POOL AT THE heart of the tiny island jungle, and she stared in awe at the bright-blue water. It was clear enough that she could see down to the bottom, perhaps twelve or fifteen feet deep.

"It's a freshwater spring," he explained and began removing his clothes.

She watched him, truly feeling he was hers, all hers.

Gavin had a strength in him that went far beyond his body, which was impressive. He moved with an easy grace, yet he bore the scars of a rough life lived on the high seas. She wanted to kiss each one. As he undressed, peeling away each bit of clothing with an almost deliberate slowness that both teased and tortured her, she bit her lip and held back a moan of longing at seeing his beautiful body.

Perhaps there was some sort of magic in the air of this island. It was Gavin's sanctuary, and now she felt it could easily be hers too, if they had this life together they both desperately wanted. She fisted her hands in her skirts as she watched with sensual hunger as he bared his legs and arms. Her fingers itched with the memory of lazy nights aboard the *Pixie*, where she had touched him with passion. He'd taken care to explore her body most of their nights in his bed, but now she wanted to explore him with the same freedom.

"Join me in the pool, *wife*," he called out with a flirtatious grin, then plunged into the water entirely naked.

She scrambled out of her clothes, trying not to think about how silly she looked, stripping down with such haste in front of him. She had never bathed quite so freely before. When she had bathed in a copper tub, she'd had a sheet draped over her for modesty, and when she'd swum in the sea or the lake, she'd always been in a chemise and petticoats. Now she was bare, naked, *free*. She dipped one toe into the water and sighed at the heavenly warmth of the pool. The water was surprisingly warm.

Gavin was treading water in the center of the pool, watching her, his eyes hot with desire.

"Jump in, lass!" He swam toward the back of the pool to give her room to leap in.

With a shriek, she leapt and plunged down into the brilliant water. When she reached the surface he was ready for her, catching her in his arms. She wrapped her arms around his neck while he guided them toward a rocky ledge that was deep enough in the water that when he sat on it and pulled her toward him, they remained chest-deep in the water. She straddled him as he sat, and their bodies rubbed teasingly against each other. He claimed her mouth, kissing her deeply. His lips tasted like the sea and were so wonderfully soft, while the rest of him was hard.

She fisted her hands in his hair so she could hold on to him as he moved his mouth lower down her body. He lifted her up in his arms until her breasts were level with his mouth and sucked at her nipples as though he was starving for her. The insistent tug of his mouth on her breasts sent sharp spikes of need through her.

As he drew one tip into his mouth, his palm cupped her other breast, his thumb and forefinger lightly pinching her nipple and tugging it, then gently kneading her breast. She rocked against him, almost mindless, desiring nothing more than to be taken. Her womb throbbed painfully for him.

"Please, Gavin. Please, stop teasing me."

He let go of her nipple and grinned. "Begging for me? I like that, wife. Now tell me what it is you want."

"I want you inside me." She blushed wildly at the admission.

"You wish to be *taken* by your husband?" His coarse words sent her desire shooting even higher. How did he know what to say to make this moment even more deliciously carnal?

"Say it, wife. *Beg* me." He kissed the spot between her collarbones, while one of his hands cupped her bottom and squeezed. She tightened her thighs around his hips.

"Please," she gasped. "Please take me, my husband."

He groaned at the word *husband* and lifted her up, settling her on the ledge. She braced her hands on the rocks at the edge of the pool. Gavin positioned himself behind her, his knees bracketing hers, and he gripped her shoulder with one hand while he used his other to guide himself into her. They both shared a groan as he sank deep.

"*Oh yes,*" she whimpered as his hips pressed into her bottom, sending him as deep as he could go.

She arched her back, and he moved one hand to her neck, fisting her hair, while the other hand cupped one of her breasts and gently squeezed it. He withdrew and thrust back in.

"Tell me you are *mine*."

"*Yours*." Josephine could only pant the word as she fell through a waterfall of pleasure into a sea of colored stars.

Gavin began to move faster and harder. He made her climax go on for what felt like forever before a second one chased it. She couldn't even scream. Her eyes rolled back in her head as the songs of the parrots above them serenaded her through peaks of pleasure while warm water cradled her body. The thrust of his hips made soft splashes, and she could only take what he offered and bathe in the beauty of what he made her feel. Josephine's body sang with pleasure. Her channel would be sore from his vigorous claiming, yet it was beautiful to be so wild and free, to let herself feel every second of her love for him.

When she thought she could bear no more, he withdrew from her and switched the positions of their bodies. Now he sat on the underwater rock ledge and she was straddling him. He impaled her on his cock, making her cry out at the sensitivity, and silenced her with a kiss before he raised her up and down on his body. He let her ride him while he sucked at one of her breasts again, letting her feel the blissful sensations of him inside her and the tug of his mouth at the same time.

A softer climax rolled through her, and she knew she was crying as tears dripped down her face to her chin. Gavin kissed away each tear and murmured soft words of comfort that she could not comprehend because she was too overwhelmed by her love for him.

Soon, she drifted to sleep in his arms, his shaft still deep inside her. When she woke much later on, she found herself dressed and being carried in his arms. He was walking back through the forest toward his home.

"Gavin?"

"Yes?" His low voice carried an indulgent tone she'd never heard before.

"I . . . I don't actually know what I was going to ask you," she admitted.

He chuckled. "It seems I wore you out, my darling. I want to sleep in our bed. I have plans to make this evening."

She didn't like the sound of that. "Plans?"

"Yes. I want to take the *Pixie* to Sugar Cove and find a vicar to marry us. I assume that's all right?"

"Yes," she said, a little surprised. "Shouldn't I go with you? Wouldn't that be easier?"

"No, I want you to stay here—for two reasons."

Now she was the one who chuckled. "You and your reasons. Very well, let's hear them."

"First, I wish to marry you here, on our island. And second, if I have the misfortune to run into your brother or mine, I don't want them to take you from me. If you're here, I stand a better chance of getting back to you without losing you. Not even Dominic knows I live on this island."

"Oh, well, that does make sense. When will you leave?"

"Tomorrow, if I can."

Disappointment pricked her heart. "So soon?"

"The sooner I leave, the sooner I can return to you."

They reached the house, and a smiling Jada met them at the door, holding it open for them.

"I hope you actually showed your wife the island," she teased.

Embarrassed, Josephine struggled to make Gavin put her down, but he ignored her attempts.

"Don't fight a man when he insists on carrying you," Jada said with a chuckle. "I'll send dinner up for you two. I imagine you still have *much* to discuss."

"We do?" Josephine asked as Gavin started up the stairs while he still held her in his arms.

"We certainly do, wife. Namely, how many times I can make you come apart in my arms."

She gasped. How could he talk so openly about something so scandalous?

"Mrs. Castleton, you saved me from a deadly squall—

tell me you are not so timid now?" He smiled at her teasingly just as they reached what she assumed was his bedchamber.

"It's just . . . Oh, never mind." She sighed as he deposited her on the bed.

It was a long while later when Jada brought them a tray of food and the two of them ate naked in bed. Josephine was enjoying this new side of Gavin, the teasing playfulness that was so gentle, combined with his fierce passion when he made love to her.

"Must you really leave tomorrow?" she asked as she lay atop him. Their bodies were still joined intimately, and neither of them moved. He stroked her hair back behind her ears and smiled softly.

"I must. We need a vicar for our marriage to be official."

"What happens after?" She nibbled her bottom lip with worry.

"After what?"

"After we're wed. What of the *Siren*? Aren't you worried about your ship?"

Gavin's eyes darkened for the first time in days as his contentment seemed to vanish.

"I am, but I want to marry you first. Once I'm certain you are my wife and not Griffin's, I will go after my ship and return the *Pixie* to your brother."

Another woman might have thought Gavin's comment about marrying her first was a matter of sibling rivalry, but Josephine knew it wasn't. He wanted her not because of her belonging, at least by contract, to Griffin, but because she *wanted* Gavin. Their mutual longing had deepened into true love, despite how quickly it had formed.

"I wish you didn't have to go," she mumbled.

He tipped her chin up so that she looked at him. "I will hurry back with the wind full in my sails."

His sweet promise hung in the air, while outside the birdsong faded into the gentle Caribbean night and the breeze and rolling of the waves became a pirate's lullaby.

GAVIN SLIPPED OUT OF BED JUST BEFORE DAWN AND paused to stare down at Josephine as she slept. Never could he have imagined the night he first met her that he would be here with her now and would see her as his other half.

The ocean could give a man her mysteries, but there was no greater or more wonderful mystery than the heart of a woman. He thought about Charity and Brianna, two women who were much like Josephine in some ways. He'd loved them both, despite how the relationships had ended. Now he saw those relationships not as failures but as practice. He hadn't been ready or worthy to love a woman like Josephine then. Now he knew what he wanted from life and what love truly meant. In just a month and a half, he'd found something more precious than silver or gold. He had Josephine's heart.

He bent and pressed a soft kiss to her brow, then quietly slipped from the room. Jada was waiting for him downstairs by the door. The pale morning skies lit her brown eyes. Those eyes of hers had seen all of his secrets, no matter how much he wished to hide them.

"You will give it up for her, won't you?" Jada spoke softly. She'd never judged him for his unlawful activities. Jada saw the best in people, which never ceased to amaze him, given that she'd been taken from her home in Africa, destined to be sold on an auction block before the *Siren* had intervened.

"Yes, I suppose I will," he agreed. He hadn't thought about it until now, but he would have to. A pirate's life was dangerous. He was a wanted man in many waters. It would be hard enough to stay out of the noose even *after* he left pirating behind him. He was thankful that the island provided enough to live on, and he did have some money set aside in a few banks on the other islands, as well as banks back in London. It was why he returned to England at least once a year, to add to his investments.

Jada nodded. "That is good. Love her and you will heal your soul."

He embraced Jada. "Take care of my lass until I return?"

She chuckled. "Of course. Go on, Ronnie is ready to leave."

Ronnie was waiting for him in the shallows with a few sailors who had a boat ready so they could return to the *Pixie*.

He climbed aboard, and the crew started to row. He turned back, staring at the island, at his home, picturing the woman he was leaving behind. It made him want to hurry all the more.

"This is the first time you've ever looked back," Ronnie mused.

Gavin realized with some surprise that his friend was right. Before, he'd looked ahead to the next adventure, where the wind would take him, but now he knew where he truly wanted to be. A life with Josie was the only adventure he wanted now.

"We'd best kidnap a vicar, and fast," Ronnie muttered. "I expect a wee babe will be here before Christmas."

Christ, he had not even thought of that. Josephine could be with child even now. He'd certainly made love to her enough times that it was a possibility.

"Oh, aye, you didn't think of that, did you?" Ronnie laughed. "You had better get married quickly, *Papa Gavin*."

He kicked Ronnie in the shin, and both men laughed as he took his position with the men and rowed. Even though it felt like he'd left his heart behind, the thought of having children with Josephine filled him with an incredible joy. This beautiful life he wanted with Josephine was within reach. All he had to do was beat Griffin to the altar.

CHAPTER 14

Gavin and Ronnie stared at the man lying face down in the mud of a pigsty.

"I suppose he'll have to do," Gavin said.

"Aye, he'll have to. Sheridan is the only vicar on the island. We can't risk going anywhere else."

They had stopped at Sugar Cove, a well-known pirate haven that the navy thankfully hadn't seemed to have set its sights on yet.

Gavin waved at the sleeping man. "Very well, get the man up." The two sailors who had accompanied him from the *Pixie* raised their buckets and tossed cold water on the man lying in the sty. He scrambled to his knees, blubbering, as the muddy water sluiced over his body.

"Oi!" the vicar roared, and Gavin was surprised to see the man was far younger than he'd expected and built more like a man who fought in boxing matches than a man of the cloth. He couldn't have been more than twenty-five or thirty years old.

"You *are* the vicar named Henry Sheridan, aren't you?" Gavin demanded.

"Among *other* things, yes." The man swiped the mud off his once fine coat and glanced around for something.

Gavin held up the bottle of rum that had lain just outside of the fence of the pigsty. "Looking for this?" The vicar reached for it, but Gavin turned the bottle upside down and poured the contents on the ground.

"You've just *wasted* the best spiced rum to be had on this side of the Atlantic." Sheridan shot Gavin a black look that promised retribution.

"Come with us and we'll pay you enough to buy all the rum in Jamaica. Until then, I need you sober."

"Sober?" The vicar slowly climbed out of the sty. "You're not offering me enough for *that*. What is this task you want me to do that requires the unfortunate state of sobriety?"

"I need a man of the cloth to wed me."

Sheridan snorted. "No offense, but you're not my type."

Ronnie shoved Sheridan hard from behind. "That's the cap'n. Show some respect."

"I've seen plenty of captains. It's a coin toss as to how many deserve respect."

"It's a highborn lady that I wish to wed," Gavin said, unfazed. "Are all of your licenses or whatever vicars require these days in order? I need this wedding to be aboveboard."

"Yes, unfortunately, all of my licenses are in order. I get offers every day to marry the bloody prostitutes to half the pirates on this bloody rock some fool decided to call an island," the vicar replied sourly.

"Good. Then come with us." Gavin led the way back through the pirate haven. Dozens of men drank or fought in the street, while prostitutes offered their favors by displaying themselves in colorful but ratty gowns. The vicar paused a moment to let a group of men carrying a drunk man pass them as they tossed the man through an open window into a tavern rather than out of it.

"Huh. Usually they toss a man out of a tavern, not into it," he said dryly, and they continued on their way. Shouts exploded from inside the room following the sound of knocked-over tankards clattering onto the floor.

"May I ask how a man of the cloth ended up in a place like this?" Gavin inquired.

"I used to be a captain in the navy."

"A bloody navy man," Ronnie hissed from behind them.

"Obviously, I'm not any longer," Sheridan spat. "I pursued a career in the church after I resigned my commission. As a second son, you don't have many options when it comes to making your own way."

"I can understand leaving the navy, but you don't seem like a man destined for the cloth."

"'Tis a long story and I'm not interested in telling it."

"Fair enough." Gavin was not a man to pry into others' secrets. Sheridan was a handsome enough fellow, built like any navy man. He still looked more like a captain than a man of the cloth. It must have been something truly desperate to drive him this low.

They had nearly reached the wharf when Gavin saw a familiar face among the men by the docks. Dominic Greyville was there, speaking to the harbormaster. The man shook his head and shrugged at whatever Dominic had asked.

"Blast."

Gavin motioned for the men with him to duck behind the wall of the nearby tavern. He had paid the harbor-master off when they'd arrived at Sugar Cove for his silence on any movements they made. It was a longstanding arrangement that the harbormaster wouldn't want to ruin since he was well paid. Gavin had the *Pixie* circling the island rather than making berth in the port. He was no fool. He wouldn't dare put the *Pixie* in the harbor, not when there was a chance of Dominic recognizing his own ship if he visited here.

"What is it, cap'n?" one of the men asked in a worried voice.

Gavin cursed silently. He'd tried to avoid telling the *Pixie*'s crew that he was a pirate who'd stolen the ship. Thinking quickly, he spun a tale to the two men who'd accompanied him and Ronnie.

"Er . . . it's an old friend, one I owe money to. He's not someone I want to see right now, and I feared he'd be here —that's why I had the *Pixie* circle the island."

"Oh, right." The sailor nodded as if that all made perfect, believable sense.

"Is that Dominic?" Ronnie whispered from behind him.

"Aye," Gavin whispered back.

"Who's Dominic?" the vicar asked in a low voice.

"My betrothed's elder brother," Gavin replied.

The vicar chuckled and then stifled the sound. "No, really, who is he?"

"*My betrothed's elder brother*," Gavin repeated, sending the vicar his grimmest look.

Unfazed by the pirate's tone, the vicar simply scowled back at him. "Good Lord, I'm in some sort of Shakespearian farce, aren't I?"

"We had best get back to the boat before he spots us," Ronnie suggested.

"Agreed." Gavin gestured for his small group to head back to where they'd hidden their small boat. It was a miracle that they reached the rocky outcropping on the far side of the island half an hour later without being spotted. The boat was still waiting for them where they'd hidden it, and once they were rolling out to sea, the *Pixie* appeared around the edge of the island as if conjured by Cornish magic.

Once everyone including the vicar were aboard and the boat was stowed, the *Pixie* shot out for the open sea, the wind in her sails. Gavin stood at the stern and watched Sugar Cove fade into the horizon. But he did not breathe a sigh of relief just yet. So long as Dominic hunted them, he could not rest, until Josephine was his wife. Even then, Dominic still might try to kill him. Greyville was a good man to have as an ally, but a deadly opponent as one's enemy.

GRIFFIN STARED AT THE OPEN SEA, HIS HEART UNSETTLED. They had stopped at a place called Sugar Cove and sought news of Gavin or the *Cornish Pixie*. It had been a dead end. Everyone on board was restless. He feared that the chances of finding Josephine in time to save her from whatever his brother intended to do with her grew smaller every day. He knew Gavin wouldn't hurt her, but he feared he would seduce her and make her fall in love with him before abandoning her. The coldness inside his brother's heart worried him beyond words.

The previous night at dinner, he and Nicholas Flynn had listened as Dominic and Brianna discussed their theories as to where Gavin could be. Brianna had pointed out that Gavin had knowledge of the small islands in the West Indies and could hide in any number of places. There were rumors that he had a place tucked away somewhere in the vicinity where he kept plunder from all his captured prizes. But Brianna could only guess at its location. Dominic suggested they reach out to the rest of the pirate Brethren and see what they knew of the pirate king's location. Surely someone had seen him. That was assuming, of course, that any of the pirates would betray Gavin's location, which wasn't entirely likely.

Now Griffin could only stare at the sea and worry. A sense of doom seemed to be creeping toward them, and he could not shake the feeling something terrible was going to happen.

Vesper came to his side at the bow of the ship, and their arms touched. Her golden hair was loose about her shoulders, and given the sunrise topping the horizon, he guessed she must have woken and come straight up on deck. The sight of her stilled that dreadful tension in him and gave him an immense sense of peace.

"You've barely eaten or slept in days," she said.

"Is it foolish to say I have a bad feeling? I do not wish to curse our voyage, but I fear we're doomed in our mission to rescue Josephine. Lady Camden agrees with me. She says she feels an ill wind in the air."

"No, I feel it as well," she admitted.

They stood in silence for a long while, and after a moment Griffin clasped her hand in his. He'd dared to steal a few kisses from her after dinner each night, but whenever he did, it felt like a betrayal. Josephine had no real desire to marry him, and the marriage contract had been signed by her father, not her. Still, he was doing wrong by her. He wanted Vesper with every fiber of his being. Could he ruin his duty and honor to be with the woman he truly loved? The answer was simple. *Yes*.

"Vesper . . . If I break my marriage contract before we find Josephine, it will bring shame upon my name."

She sucked in a breath beside him but didn't speak, so he continued.

"If I were to do that and then asked you to marry me, would the shame of that be too much?" He looked away from her, afraid of what she might say.

Vesper cupped his cheek, turning his face toward her. "You know I have my own shame."

"That is why I worry. I do not wish to add to it."

She smiled. "When people love each other, we share our burdens. It is nothing to carry yours."

"Then you would marry me?" he asked again, this time pressing the important question more clearly.

She smiled, and tears shimmered in her eyes. "Yes."

He pulled her into his arms, kissing her. No words were

needed to show how relieved he felt, but a warning cry soon broke them apart.

"Sail dead ahead!" the lookout on the foreyard above yelled.

Griffin and Vesper turned in the direction the man pointed. A sail was now visible on the horizon.

The next hour was fraught with worry as Brianna's ship closed in on the other vessel. Dominic prowled the deck like a wolf scenting prey. Lord Camden and Adrian seemed torn between watching him and the ship as they approached.

"It's not the *Pixie*!" Dominic growled as he put a spyglass to his eye.

"It's not?" Camden asked.

Brianna took the spyglass and studied the vessel. "He's right. It's not the *Pixie*, but I do recognize it. It's Encino's ship."

"Who is Encino?" Adrian asked.

Brianna and Dominic shared knowing looks as everyone gathered on the deck.

"Encino is a member of the Brethren," Dominic said.

"Pirate," Adrian added helpfully in a murmur to Griffin. Camden shot a glare at his younger son.

"He is one of the captains of our pirate court," Brianna said and moved closer to her husband. "Or was. He would never let a vessel like this catch up to him, not without raising a signal flag. Something's wrong."

Everyone gazed at the ship as they slowly caught up with her. Encino's ship's sails were full, but the ship was empty. Not a single sailor stood on deck or hung in the rigging. The wheel at the helm slowly spun back and forth as the ship glided aimlessly wherever the wind pushed it.

"Nick, Father, you come with me," Dominic said.

Griffin stepped forward beside Lord Camden and Nicholas. "I'm coming as well."

Dominic seemed ready to argue, then changed his mind. "Do not forget your promise to me."

"I haven't," Griffin replied.

The men boarded a boat and rowed to the drifting vessel. Adrian kept watch from the railing, along with Vesper, Roberta, and Lucia. The three women who'd dared to brave the long voyage with Griffin and the others, gazed at them with worry. Everyone knew this was dangerous. Brianna stayed at the wheel of the *Sea Serpent*, ready to steer it away at the first sign of danger. Griffin followed Dominic up the side of the ship, catching hold of the wooden planks that formed a ladder.

"Be ready. This could be a trap," Dominic whispered as they stepped up on deck. Then he cupped his hands. "Encino! It's Dominic Grey," he bellowed. No call answered.

"Griffin, you're with me. Nick, you and Father stay together. We'll search the ship from top to bottom."

Griffin and Dominic moved belowdecks. It wasn't long until they found the crew. Bodies littered the gun deck. Throats had been slit, and most had other wounds or gunshots. Griffin paled. He'd never seen death on this scale before. He placed his palm on the sword that hung at his hip, needing the comfort of steel at that moment.

"Watch your back," Dominic murmured as he led Griffin deeper into the ship. They reached what Griffin guessed was the captain's cabin. The door swung ajar as the ship rocked on the waves. It didn't bode well for whoever might be inside. Dominic pressed a palm flat and pushed the door open.

The cabin was in disarray. A single lamp swung above the table in the center of the captain's cabin, even though the sun shone clearly through the windows. Griffin guessed that whoever had committed these crimes had wanted this discovery to be visible even in the dark. A man's body lay on the table, his chest bare and his body carved deep with cuts.

Dominic approached and touched his shoulder. "Encino."

The man gasped, giving Griffin a shock. He'd thought the fellow to be dead, but that fate could not be far off now.

"Dominic . . . ," the captain groaned.

"I'm here, old friend. Who did this to you?"

Griffin peered down at the gravely wounded man. Encino's dark eyes drifted from Dominic to Griffin.

"You . . . He's coming for you, Castleton."

"Who?" Griffin demanded.

"Beau . . . champ . . ." The name escaped Encino's lips as his gaze slowly turned distant and the light faded from his eyes.

"Beauchamp . . . That name . . . I know it," Griffin said.

"He was one of Gavin's crew," Dominic said. "I met him once."

"That's the man who my brother said led the mutiny against him," Griffin said. The captain had mistaken him for his brother.

They both stared at the dead man for a long moment.

"We have to get off the ship," Dominic said. "Beauchamp could be following at a distance. I noticed he spiked the cannons so they cannot be fired. The line from the wheel was cut so the ship can't be steered. Anyone who boards this vessel would easily be trapped. All of the cargo was removed . . . I think Beauchamp set a trap for anyone who came to see this ship."

Dominic strode to the door, and Griffin was on his heels. There was no talk of burying the dead at sea. There simply wasn't time to even collect the bodies and give them a quick ceremony. Every life aboard Brianna's ship, including Vesper's, was in grave danger.

JOSEPHINE STOOD KNEE-DEEP IN THE SHALLOWS OF THE waves with Sam. They both held spears, watching for fish. She had left her dress in the wardrobe today and was in her borrowed clothes from Dominic's ship, which Jada had been kind enough to wash for her.

"Wait," Sam counseled as a silvery fish slowly swam around their feet.

"When?" Josephine whispered, even though the fish could not hear her.

He held his spear ready. "Not yet . . . Now!"

Josephine plunged her spear deep into the water, impaling the fish. With a hoot of triumph, she raised the spear up. Sunlight sparkled off the fish's silvery scales.

Sam grinned. "We'll cook it tonight. I'll show you how to remove its scales. We just need to—" His next words died as he stared off at something beyond her.

"Sam? What is it?" She turned toward the horizon and saw a ship sailing for the cove. It dropped anchor just outside the area only Gavin knew how to sail past.

"That's not the *Pixie*," she muttered to herself as she raised a hand over her eyes to shield her gaze from the sun as she studied the ship.

Sam whooped and waved at the vessel. "It's the *Siren*!"

"The *Siren*?" A sudden feeling of dread bottomed out in her stomach. If Gavin had recovered his ship, it would have been easy for him to guide it into the cove. But the ship stayed safely away from the maze of reefs, which meant Gavin was not at the helm.

"Sam!" She snatched the boy by the shoulders and shook him. "Listen to me. That's not Gavin. You must go! Tell everyone to hide. Oh God . . ." Was there even a place in this little spot of paradise to hide from such evil?

She glanced back at the ship and saw they were in the midst of lowering a small boat into the water.

"Josie . . . ," Sam began uncertainly, his dark eyes wide with terror.

"Go, Sam!" She hurried him toward the shore. At the sight of the sails, some of the island's residents had left their fields and homes to come greet the newcomers. Josephine screamed for them to run. They had only a few minutes before the mutineers would reach land.

Jada met them halfway to the shore. When she spotted the ship and then saw Josephine's face, she seemed to know at once that this wasn't Gavin.

"We have to hide. That man tried to kill Gavin, and he'll kill anyone in his path," Josephine explained as they raced toward the house.

Jada ran across the front porch of the house and toward a silver bell that hung from one overhead beam. Grasping the brown rope with a metal ball that hung from beneath it, she rang the bell hard. The sound echoed far and wide across the island.

"This will warn the others. We must go to the caves." Jada grasped Sam's and Josephine's hands in each of hers.

"The caves?"

"Gavin always feared something might happen to us while he was away, so he set up a shelter in the caves for us in case of storm or attack."

"But won't Beauchamp and his men know about it?"

Jada shook her head. "'Tis the only place on the island that Gavin's crew never knew about, except for Ronnie."

"Can everyone fit in these caves?" Josephine feared for all the men and women who lived here. She could not bear the thought of anything happening to them.

"We can fit. The caves run deep into the center of the island but never flood when it rains." Jada led the way, meeting others from the fields and the village along the way, stopping to explain what was happening as quickly as they could.

When they reached the cave entrance, Josephine was stunned to see that they were at the very spring water pool that she and Gavin had gone swimming in. Men and women were diving deep into the pool. Josephine saw a man dive in and swim straight down, and then he swam along the bottom before he disappeared suddenly from view.

"You can swim, yes?" Jada asked.

"I can."

"The cave entrance is underwater. Don't worry, it's not far. It opens up to caves with plenty of air." Jada urged several women to go ahead of them. Then she glanced around and her eyes widened.

"Sam? Sam!" Jada screamed her son's name. The little boy had been with them for most of the way . . . but somehow in the chaos they'd lost him.

The number of people who were taking turns diving into the pool was growing smaller. Jada tried to push her toward the pool.

"Go, Josie. Swim to the cave. I will join you once I find my son."

"You might need help. I'm not going to leave you." Josephine wasn't about to let Jada face down a dozen murderous pirates alone.

The two of them rushed down the jungle path, back toward the house. They reached the place where the jungle ended and the field leading to the shore and the house began, and Josephine saw Sam struggling in the arms of a pirate. They were too late. The boy was being carried away over the man's shoulder. Jada started to leave the cover of the foliage, but Josephine stopped her.

"You have to stay here. I'll go after him."

"They will kill you." Jada gasped, her face stained with tears. "It should be me. I'm his mother. I must go, not you."

"They have no reason not to kill you, but if I tell them

I'm Gavin's wife, I'll be more valuable to them alive than dead when Gavin arrives."

Jada frantically shook her head. "Or they may kill you the moment you tell them."

"I'm willing to take that risk to save Sam." Josephine cupped the woman's face until she was sure that Jada was focused on her and not the vanishing sight of her son.

"Someone has to tell Gavin what happened and help the other residents of the island. Do you understand? It must be you who stays," she told her friend.

"But . . . my son . . ."

"I will rescue him . . . and if I can't rescue him, I will defend him with my life," Josephine vowed, and she meant it. She would kill or die to protect the boy.

"Now, go! You must hide before they see you!" She shoved Jada back into the forest and crept toward the house, taking care not to leave a trail that would lead them back to Jada or the path to the pool.

She climbed through a window on the ground floor of Gavin's house and reached the drawing room. There, she saw two pirates searching the house. Their backs were to her, but it wouldn't take long for them to find her. She rushed toward the fireplace where a pair of blades hung crossed above the mantel as decoration. She prayed the steel was still sharp enough to kill. The moment she freed one of the swords, she heard the pirates shouting at her from the entrance to the drawing room.

She whirled from the hearth and cut down the first man who advanced on her. Blood sprayed across the walls and her face as the blade sank into his neck and shoulder.

He howled and gurgled before he stumbled back, clutching at the fatal wound.

The other pirate stared at her in shock for a brief instant before he raised his own cutlass and rushed at her. But years of training with her father and Adrian had given her some skill, and the pirate's assumptions about her because she was a woman proved a fatal mistake. The fight was over almost before it had begun. Only later would she dare to think about the lives that she'd just taken.

She rushed into the yard and chased the pirate carrying Sam toward the water. The landing boat waited for him there to take them to the *Siren*.

"You!" she bellowed at the man carrying Sam, who still struggled in his grasp. The brutish pirate holding the boy sneered at her.

She pointed her sword at him as she advanced. "Put the boy down."

Sam was dropped into the surf. He coughed as a wave smashed into him. The pirate advanced on Josephine. Despite the fear coursing through her, her steps and her grip on her weapon were steady.

"Leave this island and never come back," Josie said, her voice cold.

"Or what?" a voice said from behind her.

There was the crack of a pistol shot, followed by a searing pain exploding in her upper right arm. Sam screamed her name, but she didn't dare look at him. She turned and faced the man who still held a pistol pointed at her.

"You used your one shot," she said, her voice raspy. "You won't get another."

"Maybe not. But he will." The pirate nodded to a third pirate who now joined them, pistol drawn and ready. The pirate who had dropped Sam picked him up again, and the third pirate held the muzzle of his pistol at Sam's temple.

"Toss your sword down. *Now*," the first pirate ordered. "Or either your or the boy's brains will splatter this beach, and the other's body will feed the sharks in the bay."

Josephine's shoulders slumped as she threw her blade to the ground. It sank halfway into the white sand. This was not a fight she could win. She was already growing weak with pain and blood loss.

"Who are you?" the man demanded.

Now was the moment to gamble whether as Gavin's woman she would be worth more alive or dead.

"I'm Gavin's wife."

"Are you now? How *very* interesting." The man smiled, and the chill in his eyes told her that this must be Beauchamp.

"Take her," Beauchamp ordered. "The boy too. If she thinks to fight us, we'll remind her of all the *bad* things that can happen to a child at sea."

Josephine gasped as the massive pirate who'd first taken Sam suddenly grabbed her from behind, his arm wrapping around her neck and choking the air from her body as she was dragged toward the distant waiting boat.

"Now I have the one thing I need to kill a ghost."

CHAPTER 15

Something was wrong. Gavin sensed it the moment he smelled smoke upon the wind.

Something is burning.

They were perhaps an hour from the Isle of Song when he spied smoke on the horizon.

"Cap'n?" Ronnie stood at his side and handed him a spyglass.

"I don't like this, Ronnie," Gavin muttered. "It's too early in the year to be burning the sugarcane fields."

"Aye." His quartermaster folded his arms and stared at the horizon where the smoke now billowed in the sky.

The column of smoke grew larger as they drew closer toward Gavin's island. Gavin took the helm and guided the *Pixie* into the cove. The sight that met his eyes was one he would never have imagined. His beautiful home was nothing but blackened timbers and ash that drifted upon the wind like fiery snow.

"Christ . . . What happened?" the vicar asked as he

joined Gavin at the helm. Gavin said nothing. The sight had struck him dumb, something out of a nightmare.

"Drop anchor!" Ronnie gave the order, and Gavin didn't wait for a boat to be lowered.

He climbed down the side of the ship and plunged into the water so he could swim to the shore. No one greeted him with laughter or smiles. His Isle of Song was silent. Even the birds dared not sing.

He ran to the house, dripping wet, and stepped onto the once grassy lawn that had led to his beautiful home. The charred grass crunched beneath his boots. The second story of his home had collapsed. Only the ground floor remained, though all of the rooms had been gutted.

Gavin cupped his hands and bellowed, "Josie! Jada! Sam! Kai!" He shouted the names until his voice grew hoarse.

Just as he'd given up hope, a feminine figure stepped out of the woods. Jada, eyes wide with terror and hope. She wailed and ran toward him but collapsed onto the ground before she reached him, her body quaking with sobs. He knelt beside her, and she let out a scream.

"Jada, it's me. What happened?" he asked as he wrapped his arms around her, absorbing her shaking. Slowly, the woman in his arms calmed, and her breathing deepened as her terror passed.

"Gav—Gavin?" She uttered his name with such broken hopelessness that he truly feared what she would say next.

"Where are Josie and Sam? What happened?"

"The *Siren* returned."

The horror of what had transpired on his island locked into place.

Beauchamp had done this. Unable to kill him directly,

he'd destroyed Gavin's home, leaving it to be an open wound in case Gavin hadn't died when he'd fled the *Siren* during the mutiny. He realized in that instant that anyone he'd ever trusted or allied himself with in the past was now in danger. Beauchamp would kill anyone who might challenge his right to the *Siren*. Had Beauchamp come here looking for the gold he thought Gavin had hidden away? Why hadn't Beauchamp come here sooner?

"We thought you had come back, but Josie said we had to run and hide." Jada wiped at tears streaking down her face.

Gavin's body tensed at Josephine's name. "Where is she?"

"*Gone.*" Jada moaned the word. "They took Sam. She went after him. She said they would not kill her if they knew she was your wife." Jada spoke a little haltingly as she fought off fresh sorrow.

Now Beauchamp would know that Gavin was alive. He must have come to the island searching for the treasure he thought to be hidden here, but Beauchamp had found Josephine instead. *Dear God*...

"She made me stay behind so you would know what happened. I hid the others in the caves."

Thank God for the caves. He'd only ever shown Ronnie and those who lived on the island the system of underground caves he'd discovered under the central pond. He had intended it to be a haven in case a hurricane ever came their way or if they were discovered by the navy, but he had never allowed the rest of his crew to know about it precisely because of dangers like this.

"How long have they been gone?"

"Half a day," Jada said. "They set fire to the house as they left . . ." She burst into tears again, covering her face with her hands.

"I will get your son back, Jada. I promise." Even as he said the words, he feared it might not be a promise he could keep.

He helped her stand. "Come on. We need to tell Ronnie and the others what happened."

As they reached the burned-down home, they saw that Ronnie and a number of sailors from the *Pixie* had made their way ashore, including the vicar. Sheridan's expression hardened as he saw Jada weeping.

"How bad is it, Cap'n?" Ronnie asked.

"Beauchamp took Josie and Jada's son. Everyone else is alive and hidden."

Ronnie fingered the blade at his hip, his eyes dark with rage and his face as red as his hair. "We'll kill him this time, right, Cap'n?"

Of that, Gavin had no doubt. He wished he could kill Beauchamp a thousand times over for what had been done today.

Bartholomew spoke up. "Cap'n?"

"What is it?" Gavin asked, trying to keep the harshness from his voice, but knowing he failed.

"We . . . That is to say, the men of the *Pixie* . . . We know you weren't supposed to be our true cap'n . . . what with you being a pirate and all . . ." The sailor stared at his feet, almost shyly.

"You knew he wasn't your cap'n?" Ronnie broke in.

"Aye. You see, we all used to be pirates. Some of us sailed with Dominic Grey, the others with various crews.

Most of the lads recognized you as the captain of the *Lady Siren*. Dominic would have told us if he'd hired you, but the way we left, all secret like, from St. Ives Bay, we figured you weren't supposed to be on our ship. But we liked you anyway, and we thought your wife was a real fine lady. So we decided to let you stay our cap'n. Anyway, what I'm trying to say is . . . you need a ship and crew to fetch your wife back. We're *your* men now. We want to help you save Miss Josephine."

"Wife?" the vicar broke in. "I thought you weren't married yet?"

"At this point, it's merely a matter of legalities, Sheridan," Gavin said.

"Ah, I see. Well, I was a good shot once, and an even better swordsman. I'd hate to see this evil deed go unpunished." Sheridan flexed his arms as he bent and picked up a sword that was half buried in the sand at his feet.

Gavin recognized the blade's hilt. It was from above the fireplace in the drawing room. How the devil had it ended up on the beach?

"Where do you think Beauchamp would go, Cap'n?" Ronnie asked. "They could be headed in any direction."

That was indeed the problem. Gavin could only hazard a guess, but there was just one real possibility.

"The Black Isle," Gavin said aloud. It was the only place left that he had a tie to in the West Indies. He had been elected the leader of the pirate Brethren, and the Black Isle was his ruling seat. A bitter laugh escaped his lips. Some king he had turned out to be. Mutinied in the first year and his wife kidnapped by his enemy . . . He was not worthy of the title of king of anything.

Beauchamp would go to the Black Isle and try to establish a legitimate claim as the captain of the *Siren* . . . and he'd kill anyone who got in his way.

"Er . . . Cap'n, we have a problem," Ronnie suddenly announced and pointed toward the cove.

A ship larger than the *Pixie* had sailed to the edge of the cove and dropped anchor, blocking the *Pixie*'s way to the open sea. It was the *Sea Serpent*, which belonged to Brianna. Gavin scowled as a longboat was rowed toward them. Even at this distance, he recognized Dominic, Griffin, and two other men, who, given their looks, were most likely Josephine's father and twin brother.

"Blast and hell," he muttered. He had no time for this. Time was the only thing that stood between him and Josephine's death at the hands of Beauchamp, assuming she was not dead already.

"Hmmm," the vicar mused as he came up beside Gavin. "That wouldn't happen to be your betrothed's family arriving? And your brother?"

"Aye, it would unfortunately seem so," Gavin growled.

He had told Sheridan about his and Josephine's situation during the voyage back to the island. The vicar had proven himself a trustworthy man who didn't judge Gavin for the choices he'd made, or the questionable beginning of his courtship with Josephine. Gavin stood on the dry sand just past the reach of the water as he waited for the longboat to glide onto the shore. Griffin, Dominic, and Josephine's father were the first ones to climb out of the boat.

"Dominic, we don't have time to—" Gavin began, but without warning, Dominic threw a hard punch that sent him stumbling back. He would have fallen had Ronnie not caught him. Dominic shook his bruised knuckles and looked ready to strike again, but Josephine's father placed a hand on his arm to still him.

"Where is my daughter, pirate?" Lord Camden demanded. His look of hatred hit Gavin harder than Dominic's fist had.

Gavin rubbed at his jaw. "Taken. My former boatswain —the one who organized a mutiny and stole my ship—he took her. He also kidnapped my housekeeper's young son." He nodded toward where Jada still sat on the sand, staring emotionlessly at the rolling waves.

Dominic turned to the burned embers of Gavin's home. "Where the bloody hell were you? Why didn't you protect them?"

"I thought I *was* protecting them. I thought Josephine would be safe here." Now he could see how foolish it had been to think this place was safe. Beauchamp had been to this island before, and it would only be natural to look here for Gavin or the gold the man believed he had hidden from the crew.

"Why did you leave her alone?" Griffin asked. "Why not take her with you?"

"Because I was off fetching a bloody vicar and I didn't want you lot catching me and taking her away."

"A *vicar*?" Dominic growled. "*Why* would you need a vicar?"

At this Sheridan snorted. "Well, it's either for a marriage or a baptism, and I'm rather guessing you'd prefer a marriage."

Dominic looked torn between wanting to throttle the vicar and Gavin.

"Well, which is it?" Camden demanded.

"He's here for Josephine and me," Gavin snapped. "I love the bloody woman and want to marry her."

He met his brother's gaze, and Griffin's eyes widened at the statement.

Camden and Dominic both lunged for Gavin, but Griffin threw himself in their way, holding up a hand to stay them.

"Please, Camden, let us hear my brother out before we decide to hang him from the yardarm." Griffin then turned back to face Gavin. "You were truly going to marry Josephine? Does she *want* to marry you? What concerns me most is Josephine's wishes. Is this something she agreed to, or are you forcing her?" Griffin asked.

"Yes, that's a good question," Camden cut in dryly, his eyes promising violence. "Answer carefully, because your life depends on it."

"I would never force her. She is more than willing to be my wife."

Sheridan stepped forward. "I would never marry them if he tried to force her," he added.

Was that a flicker of relief Gavin saw in his twin's face, or had he simply imagined it?

"So you planned to marry her; that's a problem we will deal with later. We need to discuss where the bloody hell my child is." Camden stared at the burning wreck of Gavin's once beautiful home. "Did the man who killed that Encino fellow take my daughter?"

Gavin tensed at hearing his friend's name. "Encino is dead?"

"Beauchamp slaughtered his crew and tortured Encino. He died just moments after we found him and his ship two days ago. We worried about an ambush, but none happened. Then we spotted the smoke from your island and feared the worst," Griffin said.

"Where would he take my daughter?" Camden asked.

"I'm guessing the Black Isle. He wishes to legitimize his place as captain of the *Siren*. Now that he knows I've returned, he'll want me dead, and knows I'll come after her."

"Why did Beauchamp do this?" Dominic demanded.

"Is it about the treasure?" Griffin asked. "Gavin, you told me he mutinied because he believed you had treasure hidden somewhere."

Gavin glanced back at his ruined home. "Yes, though it couldn't be further from the truth. The last few months had been lean, and he believed I was holding back on the shares of our plunder from prize ships. All of my coin went into my ship and my house. This island was my real treasure. That damned fool could never understand that."

Griffin stepped forward and placed a hand on Gavin's shoulder, looking at the remains of Gavin's home. "I imagine it was quite a lovely house."

"It was," he admitted. "And Josie and I . . . We were going to be free here." His throat tightened, and then he curled his hands into fists. "I will cut out Beauchamp's black heart and feed it to him when I find him."

"You can have whatever is left of him when I'm done," Camden said darkly. "No one hurts my child. *No one*."

On this matter, they were all in agreement. Beauchamp was a dead man. Soon he would have no tales to tell, and he would learn what happens when a man steals a pirate king's greatest treasure.

JOSEPHINE BECAME AWARE OF THE PAIN IN HER HEAD first, and then the pain in her arm grew infinitely beyond that. Something sharp pricked her wounded flesh. She tried to pull away.

"Hold still, girl," a man muttered.

She blinked and raised her head, trying to see where she was. She looked to be in a dim room. Lanterns swayed overhead, and the tangy, acrid smell of alcohol wafted off an elderly man's breath as he leaned over her to peer down at her right arm. Thick spectacles were perched on the tip of his nose.

"Where am I?" She struggled to remember what had happened. She recalled fighting pirates on the beach, and Sam. *Oh Lord, Sam!*

She tried to sit up, but the elderly man tutted at her and pointed to the leather straps across her waist and chest that kept her secured to the table.

"You're on the *Lady Siren*, girl. Now hush and keep still." The man resumed stitching up her arm.

"The boy . . . Sam . . . Is he all right?" She tried to ignore the pain of the needle pulling at her flesh. At least this form of torture was supposed to be helping her—it just didn't feel like it.

"Yes, for now," the doctor said in a lowered voice. "You'd better do what Captain Beauchamp says. He will kill the boy if you don't." The doctor's pale-gray eyes softened as he patted her shoulder in sympathy. "Now try to rest. I've got to stitch this up or ill humors will set in."

"The captain," she scoffed. "The man is a mutineer. *A thief.*"

During the voyage with Gavin, she had learned all about Beauchamp. He was a greedy man and was always ready to cause trouble. That wasn't uncommon, of course, but it rarely resulted in mutiny. It had shocked Josephine to learn that Gavin's crew had so quickly believed he'd kept more than his fair share of treasure. But people were always willing to believe the worst about someone, it seemed.

"You'd best hold your tongue," the doctor warned. "The captain will cut it out of you, mark my words. Better to do what he asks and make no complaint. He told me to fix you up and deliver you to his quarters, and that is what I will do. You are to dine with him this evening."

Josephine held her tongue, not because of his warning but to give herself time to think. She needed to find Sam, and the two of them had to get off the ship somehow. Until then, she would play the part men always expected of her. A silent woman was a woman with time to think and plan. Beauchamp was a dead man—he simply didn't know it yet. She'd already killed two men, and their deaths had left no mark upon her soul. His would be no different.

When the doctor finished stitching her up, he removed

the leather straps and helped her stand before he escorted her from the surgery to the captain's cabin. A tall, brutish pirate who didn't speak pushed her inside and pointed at a gown lying on the bed. Then he slammed the door in her face, and she heard a lock slide into place. She was alone and safe, at least for the moment.

She gingerly touched her bandaged arm. The wound was deeper than a graze, but it didn't seem to have hit her bone. It was a small blessing, but it still hurt like the devil had jabbed a fire poker through her. She surveyed the cabin, seeking out possible weapons. There were none. A large figurehead of a mermaid stood against the wall in one corner, and the bed was messily made. Nothing in the room looked like it would make a decent weapon. Even the table in the center of the room had nothing with any substantial weight to it.

With a frustrated growl, she turned back to the bed. A fancy gown lay across the coverlet. The dress was a deep red with hints of orange, like the color of autumn leaves. It appeared to be clean, possibly never even worn. There were undergarments laid out, along with stays and pannier hoops. Despite the gown's beauty, she had no desire to wear it.

However, knowing that Beauchamp could come in at any moment, she stripped out of her clothes and changed into the gown. She had no desire to be forced to dress in front of him.

The bodice laced up the front over her stays, and the stomacher folded over her breasts and waist, hiding the laces from view. Three layers of fine lace bedecked the neckline and the ends of the sleeves at her elbows. A jewelry box on the bed held a necklace that contained a piece of black Chinese jade carved in the shape of a skull.

"Charming," she muttered.

Silver had been molded into crossbones beneath the skull. It was a necklace fit for a pirate's mistress, she supposed. It was clear Beauchamp had chosen all of these pieces himself. Her stomach roiled with nausea as she put the necklace on. Her hair was unbound, and she took care to brush it into something more pleasing than the frizzy mess it had been. If she looked presentable, it might keep Beauchamp in a better mood, which would buy her and Sam more time.

She had just finished dressing when the door to the cabin opened. The man who'd shot her on the beach stood there, his covetous gaze roving over her. *Beauchamp*.

Behind him, the tall, silent pirate with evil eyes who'd taken Sam held a large tray with two plates of food and a bottle of wine.

Beauchamp gave her a mocking courtly bow. "Ah, my lovely guest." The brute next to him set the tray down on the table and then, with a look at Josephine that gave her chills, backed out of the room.

"Don't mind Billy—he's anxious to have his turn with you . . . once I'm done, of course." Beauchamp laughed and then waved toward the food on the table. "Sit, eat. I'll not have you starve. I like my women plump."

Josephine sat, ignoring the urge to attack him when he called her his woman. She studied the chicken on her plate.

"I have no silverware," she said. When she glanced toward him, she realized that neither did he.

He chuckled. "After the way you handled that sword on

the beach, I wasn't about to give you so much as a butter knife." He picked up his chicken by the bone and bit into it. Josephine reluctantly did the same. She was hungry, and eating would keep up her strength.

"So tell me, how did you end up as Gavin's woman? I can't imagine him agreeing to take a wife, not given his free ways and his *many* conquests of the female persuasion."

Beauchamp was trying to hurt her, make her doubt Gavin's affections, but it didn't work. She and Gavin had been honest with each other about their pasts. He'd told her about the few women he'd been with in his life, including Brianna Holland, but he'd said he rarely went to bed with women when he brought his ship into port. She had no reason to doubt him.

"Let me ask *you* something. Why are you so determined to kill Gavin?" she asked, changing the subject. She wanted to get Beauchamp talking. The more he did, the more she would learn about the danger they were in and how she and Sam might survive it.

"Kill him? I aim to erase him from existence. Him and everything he's touched."

"What did he do to earn such enmity?"

Beauchamp slammed a fist down on the table. "Because he betrayed me. He betrayed his crew. And a man like that doesn't deserve to live."

Knowing it was risky given his temper, she pressed him further. "How did he betray you and the crew?"

He seemed to calm a little, as if remembering he was playing the part of a host, not a deranged madman.

"He's been hiding his treasure, keeping more than his

fair share, which is against our articles," Beauchamp said simply.

"What proof do you have of that?" Josephine finished her chicken and then took a sip of the Madeira wine. She was desperately thirsty, but at least her hunger had been appeased. She was already feeling less light-headed.

"A man knows when someone is keeping secrets, and Gavin is full of them. His little toad, Ronnie, was helping him to hide how much gold we collected from the prize ships."

"Ronnie? How so?"

"The quartermaster on any ship is in charge of counting the money, ain't he? What better way to steal from the rest of us? The pair of them, working together, hiding everything," Beauchamp sneered. "He took us all for fools."

Josephine glimpsed a touch of gold madness in someone's eyes for perhaps the first time in her life. Beauchamp was mad with delusions about treasure. Perhaps she could use that to her advantage.

She pushed her empty plate away. "I would like to see Sam now."

"No," Beauchamp replied without emotion.

"Please." She gritted out the word as politely as she could.

"No," he replied again, sipping his wine.

"Why not?" Josephine curled her hands into fists underneath the table.

"Because you haven't earned any privileges. We have three days till we reach the Black Isle. I'm sure in that time you can find a way to *tempt* me into letting you see the boy."

He stood and walked around the table toward her. She was on her feet in an instant, backing away from him. He stalked her like prey. She searched the room for anything that could be used to hold him at bay and grabbed the chair she'd been sitting on. But the moment she raised it, her wounded arm seared with pain. She cried out, and the chair clattered to the deck.

Beauchamp lunged and grabbed her by the throat, slamming her back against the cabin wall. He stared at her mouth, then down her body at her breasts, his icy gaze burning through her as she tried to pry his hands off her.

"What makes you special, eh? You're no different than any other woman who spreads her legs for a man. Has he convinced himself he's in *love* with you?" Beauchamp laughed. "If you're so important to him, perhaps I ought to carve your heart out and give it to him when he comes after you." He tilted his head, as if considering the violent threat. "Or perhaps when he gives himself up to save you, I'll rape and torture you in front of him unless he tells me where the gold is."

"If you harm me, you will lose out on a mountain of gold." Josephine gasped for breath as she still struggled to escape his chokehold.

"Gavin's gold? I will have that soon enough."

"You fool . . . Gavin has no gold. All that he had he spent on his home and the homes on that island you took me from. You asked why I was special? My father is a wealthy earl. My elder brother is a wealthy man in his own right. And the man Gavin stole me from who I was supposed to marry is also wealthy. They are all chasing Gavin to find me and will pay mightily to have me safely returned to them. But they won't pay for a violated or dead woman."

His fingers tightened on her throat again. "How do I know you aren't lying?"

"I have no reason to lie. How do you think that Gavin managed to chase you so quickly after you mutinied and forced him from his own ship? He stole one of my brother's vessels and a crew. My family has money. He kidnapped me and took that ship, knowing he could ransom me as well as the ship's return to my family." She had to think fast and pray Beauchamp would believe her tale.

"Let me and the boy go unharmed and you will be able to collect a king's ransom for us."

Beauchamp considered this, then released her. She rubbed her throat, trying to recover her breath.

"A king's ransom," he murmured, greed glowing in his eyes. He turned toward her and struck her hard across the face before she could react. She stumbled, colliding with the table, but didn't fall.

"You're a strong one, aren't you?" he muttered, then bellowed for Billy to come in.

"Take the girl to the hold and toss her in the cell with the boy. She is not to be touched by you or any of the crew. I will hear of it if she is harmed. She is worth a fortune in trade, and you and the others can have every whore in Sugar Cove with the money we'll get for her."

Billy narrowed his eyes at Josephine. He grunted and grabbed her by the hair, dragging her out of the captain's cabin. She stumbled behind him as he forced her down the corridor. The man clearly had an unusual definition of *harm*.

They reached the hold, and she saw Sam in a cell behind iron bars. He watched with wide, terrified eyes as the pirate shoved her into his cell. Her scalp screamed at having her hair pulled, but she didn't make a sound until she and Sam were alone.

"Are you all right?" she asked the child.

"Y—yes," the boy said, his lips quivering.

"My brave Sam. Come here." She held out her uninjured arm, and the boy cuddled up to her like a frightened puppy. He would never admit to being afraid, but she would still comfort him as best she could.

"Are we going to die?" he asked in a small voice.

She squeezed his shoulders. "Do you think Gavin would allow that to happen?"

"No," Sam snorted confidently. "He'll kill these bloody pirates."

"Yes, he will. He'll come for us. We just have to keep calm."

Sam let out a shaky sigh. "I'm glad you're here, Josie."

"Me too, Sam. Me too." She stroked his hair and held him in the darkness of the hold. She had bought them some time, but she wasn't sure how long she could keep Beauchamp and his men at bay.

Gavin . . . Hurry . . .

CHAPTER 16

The Black Isle was three days away, and every minute of that short voyage was torture for Gavin. He barely slept or ate and snapped at anyone who dared question him. He had but one driving purpose that kept him on his feet. He had to save Josephine and Sam. It was his fault they were in danger.

All of the women who had traveled from England on the *Sea Serpent* had chosen to remain on the Isle of Song, except for Brianna who needed to be ready to captain the Serpent if they encountered danger. No one could match her in quick wit and sailing ability and that would be important if they faced Beauchamp in a sea battle. Gavin had felt a twist in his gut as he'd watched her kiss the forehead of her sleeping infant son as she said goodbye. There was every chance she and Nicholas would perish in the coming fight, and that thought churned through Gavin with a ferocity he'd never experienced, not before he'd met Josephine. He kept thinking of the possibility of children with her and the thought of their baby alone in the world chilled him to the core of his soul.

Adrian had remained behind on the island as well, and had been given command of the *Pixie* and a decent crew to sail the ship. Griffin had expected Dominic to stay behind, but when the man had pulled him aside, he'd said that he was needed every man able to fight that they could spare. Adrian and the Pixie's crew he'd been given would provide everyone on the island a means of escape should they be attacked again. Gavin knew all of this heartbreak, all of the danger was because of him and choices he'd made.

"Gavin."

He jerked at the sound of his brother's voice, then glanced at Griffin as he stepped up next to him and caught his arm.

"Is that it?" Griffin asked, pointing toward the mist-shrouded island that slowly materialized on the horizon.

The twist in his gut tightened. "Yes," he growled.

Another man might flinch, but his brother merely tightened his hold on his arm. "We will save them both. But," he continued, a dip in his voice, "if you aren't careful, you could get them or yourself killed."

Griffin's care infiltrated Gavin's skin, sinking beneath his bones to awaken some of the affection he'd long buried.

"That's what this Beauchamp fellow wants, isn't it? He wants you to react rashly." Griffin continued, each word deliberate and measured. "If you are unbalanced, it will give him an advantage we cannot afford."

"We will save Josephine and Sam. But if *you* aren't careful, you could get them killed, or yourself killed. That's what this Beauchamp fellow wants. If you are unbalanced, he has the advantage."

Griffin was right. Gavin drew in a deep breath and stared at the distant shape of the dark island. The skies were black and the scent of approaching storms filled the air. Whatever sea winds swept across this part of the ocean also stirred up frequent storms around the Black Isle. Soon a blanket of mist would shroud their ship just as it cloaked the island. Dominic and Lord Camden joined them at the railing.

"What's our plan when we reach the island?" Dominic asked. "You know Beauchamp better than any of us."

Gavin continued to stare at the isle. "Brianna and Nicholas need to keep most of the crew here. If we need to beat a hasty retreat, I want the *Serpent* ready to sail."

"Fair enough," Dominic agreed. "And the rest of us?"

"We hunt Beauchamp and his men down and kill every last one of them. No mercy," Gavin said, his voice hard enough that it hid his fear for Josephine and Sam.

As the *Serpent* sailed into the mist and drew closer to the pirate haven that also housed the Brethren's shadow court, a hush descended on the *Serpent*'s crew. Orders were given as hastily and quietly as possible. Each creak of wood, every splashing wave could signal their arrival to their enemies. When they entered the cove, they glimpsed only one ship floating there. *His ship.* But seeing the *Siren* didn't bring a rush of joy with it. It was too still, too eerily quiet in the pale, cold sunlight that bathed the Black Isle when the mists cleared. Three other ships in the cove had been sunk, their wreckage nearly swallowed by the sea. Only the tips of their masts stuck up from the water.

"I've never been to a pirate haven before, but I imagine those ships shouldn't be sunk like that, should they?" Griffin asked.

Gavin stared at the remnants of the ships. There was no sign of dead bodies or the crews that would have been left to tend to the ships while the others were ashore. What the devil had Beauchamp done? Had he sailed into the harbor and opened fire on the ships docked here? That was what it looked like.

"No, they shouldn't be. Someone attacked these ships."

The *Siren* appeared entirely devoid of life, which meant Beauchamp and his men were somewhere on the island . . . possibly lying in wait.

"Send a small armed crew to the *Siren*. Search it for men."

Lord Camden scowled. "Do you think they want to draw us into a trap?"

"Most likely," Gavin said. He checked his pair of pistols and the sharp blade that was tucked through the belt around his waist. "Be ready."

As the landing party boarded the longboat, Gavin pulled Brianna aside. Her sharp eyes saw straight into his soul, the way they always had. The years between them and their friendship had created trust and had been transformed into an understanding between peers.

"Be ready," he whispered. "I don't trust any of this."

"Aye, we will be." Brianna nodded solemnly, a fierceness to the tilt of her chin. "Gavin," she added as he turned away from her. Her eyes softened on his face, and then she pressed a kiss to his cheek. It was a soft, quick kiss between old friends. "Be safe. Bring Josephine back."

It made him so very grateful to have these people who were willing to risk their lives and their families for the sake of the woman he loved and a small boy.

"You risked everything to be here, to help me, but if something goes wrong, you and Nicholas must leave the island. Your son needs you." He held on to her shoulders, his gaze locked to hers.

She swallowed hard and nodded, pulling herself away from him.

"Thank you." The words came out ragged as he fought off another wave of emotion.

"Go. Save Josie and the boy," Brianna urged and returned to the helm to take charge of her ship. Nicholas gave Gavin a nod of silent farewell before Gavin jumped in the longboat as it was lowered into the water.

They wrapped cloth around the oarlocks to muffle the sound of their rowing as much as possible. Everyone almost held their breath and tried to soften their grunts as they rowed. Damp cool air settled around them, addinf to the nervousness each man felt the closer they got to shore. Once they reached land and stepped onto the beach, they kept a wary eye out for Beauchamp and his men. The heavy jungle that covered much of the island was unusually silent. No calls of birds, no howling monkeys. The island felt . . . *dead*, and a chill raked down Gavin's spine. No one said anything as they used their blades to hack their way through the underbrush to reach the heart of the island.

At the center of the Black Isle two rows of houses formed a small street where the pirates gathered during the large meetings of the captains, or where pirate crews came to rest between long voyages. But now the little village was silent. There were no pirates celebrating the capture of their latest prizes. The small group of men and women who lived permanently on this island were nowhere to be seen. The tavern workers, the innkeepers, even the prostitutes who dwelled here were absent.

"Something isn't right. This island shouldn't be . . . empty. There were at least three ships sunk in the cove. Where the devil are the crews for those vessels?" Dominic muttered and glanced at Gavin, who shrugged. He didn't know the answer either.

"Perhaps they are hiding? Check the tavern," Gavin suggested.

Dominic crept up to the tavern door and eased it open. He halted abruptly, his body going very still. Then he slowly backed away from the open door, his face pale as he turned toward the group. Gavin had never seen his friend so shaken before.

"I found the villagers . . . and most of the crews from those ships. They're scattered all over the tavern. Even the children . . ." He choked hollowly on the last word.

"Children?" the vicar, Henry Sheridan, repeated, his look of horror making everyone else flinch.

The children . . . there were always a few children running about the island, usually the offspring of pirates and prostitutes and the occasional lad wanting to become a powder monkey on a ship. They'd always been safe here, looked after by the townsfolk . . . A metallic taste filled Gavin's mouth, and his stomach clenched as he fought off the need to empty his stomach.

Lord Camden opened the door to an inn across the street and slowly backed up. Just beyond him, Gavin glimpsed bloody corpses strewn all over the floor inside the dwelling.

"I believe these are more of the missing sailors from those ships," Camden said quietly. Then he closed the door and turned away from the house of death. Beauchamp had broken the rules of this island. He'd broken every code the Brethren had made together.

When Gavin recovered himself, he exchanged a look with his twin. "If we find them, you help get Josie and the boy out. Kill anyone who stands in your way, but Beauchamp is mine."

They moved beyond the little village that had been so clouded with death and worked their way to the towering cliffs at the far side of the island. As they reached the thinning boundary of the jungle, Gavin spied exactly what he'd feared.

A dozen pirates waited for them at the edge of the cliff. One man held Sam by the throat, pointing the muzzle of a gun at the boy's head. None of the men were Beauchamp, however, and there was no sign of Josephine. A black pit formed in his gut. Why wasn't she here, and where was the bastard who'd taken her?

Gavin held up a hand, signaling his party to halt before they left the cover of the jungle and exposed their location to the pirates.

"Where's Josephine?" Griffin asked in a whisper.

"I don't know. Everyone, be ready. I'll go out first. The rest of you remain hidden." Gavin left the shelter of the trees. The moment he emerged into view, the men by the cliff tensed and faced him.

"Well, well, if it isn't our old cap'n," the man holding

the gun sneered. "You just cost me a small wager with the new cap'n. I thought you'd have been smart and stayed home."

"Sorry to disappoint you, Blackspot." The man's nickname came from his reputation of delivering black spots to doomed men. Gavin had never liked the man, but Beauchamp had vouched for him when he'd first signed Gavin's charter. It wasn't always easy to get the crew you wanted, and often captains were forced to make do with whoever they could find. Gavin now saw that Beauchamp had taken advantage of that fact and filled the ranks of Gavin's crew with men who could easily be turned against him.

"Where's my wife, Blackspot?" Gavin demanded.

"Ah-ah! Not one step closer, cap'n. We wouldn't want anything to happen to the boy here, would we?"

Sam struggled, hands bound behind his back, face marred with bruises. Gavin tightened his hold on his pistol.

Blackspot nodded his head at Gavin's belt. "Lay your weapons down. *All* of them."

Gavin hesitated for a second before he crouched, dropped two pistols and his sword to the ground, then stood back.

"I've done what you asked. Release the boy."

"Oh, I'll release him," Blackspot crowed with a cruel laugh. He shoved the little boy off the side of the cliff. Sam's faint scream was erased by the wind.

"No!" Gavin roared and dove for his weapons.

The fight broke out instantly as his men from the trees rushed forward to aid him. Sheridan stopped by Gavin and gripped his shoulder as he fired over Gavin's head at one of the pirates, killing one with a well-aimed shot. "I'll get the boy. You take care of these men."

"The fall could kill you," Gavin warned. "There are rocks directly below and a riptide."

Sheridan laughed. "If the admiral of the fleet couldn't kill me, this won't." The vicar ran for the cliff and dove over the edge, no hesitation.

"Gavin! Behind you!"

Dominic's warning had Gavin turning just in time to parry Blackspot's a lethal strike.

Gavin swiped the sword aside and ducked as Blackspot's blade arced back over his head. He punched the pirate's stomach, and Blackspot grunted hard as a woosh of air escaped him. Blackspot glowered as he raised his sword for a thrust, only for a blade to punch through his chest from behind. Dominic grabbed the man's shoulder and shoved his sword deeper. Blackspot looked down in surprise, then stared at Gavin as his strength left him and he sank to his knees.

Gavin grabbed the man by the shirt and shook him. "Where's my wife, you scurrilous cur?"

Blackspot laughed through bloodied teeth. "You're . . . too . . . late."

"What does he mean? Too late for what?" Dominic shook Blackspot's shoulder. "Where the devil is my sister, you bastard?"

A distant sound of cannons echoed through the quiet jungle.

"Told . . . you." Blackspot laughed, coughing up blood, and his body went limp in Gavin's hold. Dominic's face paled as he looked to Gavin.

"Brianna," they said in unison.

They had to go, but first Gavin sprinted to the edge of the cliff and looked down. Two figures were swimming toward the rocky coastline below. "Sheridan has the boy. We'll come back for them."

Gavin faced the clearing and saw that all the pirates were dead and a few of his own sailors lay dead or dying. The gruesome sight and the cost of lives were a heavy toll on his soul. He wanted to stop and retrieve their wounded men and return them to the ship, but there wasn't time. Griffin stood there watching him, breathing hard, his face splattered with blood.

"I'll stay with 'em, cap'n," one of the uninjured sailors from the *Pixie* volunteered. "I know a little about tending to the wounded."

"Thank you," Gavin said and clapped the man on the shoulder. "We'll be back for you. Tell Sheridan that as well." Every head turned at the sound of cannons firing again.

"Back to the ship!" Gavin shouted.

JOSEPHINE WAS SHOVED AGAINST THE FOREMAST OF THE *Siren* by one of Beauchamp's men. Wind whipped through the unfurling sails above her head as the pirate circled her and the mast with rope. She pulled at the ropes, but the pirate backhanded her the moment she tried. The pain made her dizzy as she slumped against her bindings.

She didn't dare look toward Beauchamp, who was prowling the deck. It had become frighteningly clear in the last few days how much he suffered from gold madness. It consumed him to the point that he'd ordered his men to fire on the other pirate ships in the cove . . . and to slaughter the crews and the villagers. That would haunt her the most . . . hearing the screams of innocent people being murdered by a madman. She was terrified for Sam since he'd been left on shore with a small group of pirates.

Most of Beauchamp's crew hid nearby in the woods with a quick route back to the cove, while a small group of men had taken Sam away as bait. Beauchamp had fully expected these men to be slaughtered by Gavin, but he'd told her that it was a reasonable price to pay for the ransom he could collect for her. Then Beauchamp had given the signal and his men had slunk back aboard the *Siren* like rats climbing mooring lines. They'd only been spotted once they'd reached the deck and weighed anchor.

The ship that had come into the cove hadn't been the *Cornish Pixie*, like she'd expected. It was a larger ship, one that had a dragon for a figurehead. She recognized it as Brianna's ship that she'd seen from the docks in St. Ives Bay in Cornwall. If the *Serpent* was here . . . it meant her family might have come for her. Was Gavin with them? She could only pray he was. How else would her family know where to find them?

Brianna's ship had opened fire, but the *Siren* was closer to the cove's entrance and at just the right angle for most of the shots to fall short of the *Siren*'s stern. The bright flashes of cannon fire broke through the mists while their percussive booms ricocheted off the dense jungle hills that wrapped around the cove. Josephine wanted to cover her ears, but her hands were trapped.

The *Siren* had fled the cove, despite the *Sea Serpent*'s cannons firing at her. The last few hours had felt like an eternity, and now everything had become a blur of furious fighting and terror.

The pirate who was tying her to the mast tugged hard on the rope, which pressed hard against her ribs, causing her to scream.

"Shut yer mouth!" The man struck her hard enough this time that black dots clouded her vision. The mist surrounding the ship began to clear as the *Siren* caught a strong wind in her sails and began to fly out to sea, leaving the island behind.

Beauchamp stood on the stern, watching the island grow smaller and smaller before he turned with an evil grin on his face. His plan was working. He'd told her the previous night what he intended to do. He'd made her dine with him while he bragged about his grand, devious plan: to use the boy to keep Gavin on the island while Beauchamp escaped by sea and took her far away. Then he could arrange a ransom from her family for her safe return at his leisure. Her plan to distract him with more gold had worked a little too well, unfortunately.

She bit her lip to hold in a sob as the pain from her bruised ribs and the blow to her face made her ill. Beauchamp walked down the deck toward her, with that evil grin still stretching his lips. He'd wanted her tied to the mast where the crew of the *Serpent* could see her. It would make them hesitate to fire upon the upper decks or the masts.

"They won't catch us. Castleton will have gone to the far end of the island looking for you, and he won't be able to reach the ship in time, not once we're out to open sea. No one can catch the *Siren* on open water."

No one but the *Serpent*, she thought silently. Gavin had told her about Brianna's ship, how it had once belonged to Thomas Buck, her adopted father and the previous Shadow King of the West Indies. Gavin had once said that a fast ship could still be beaten if the ship chasing it had a better captain and the right wind. And according to him, Brianna was one of the best captains alive. It had filled Josephine with pride to think that a woman pirate was one of the best captains on the high seas.

She'll catch you, Beauchamp. She's fast enough.

From her position on the deck facing the island, Josephine focused on the distant shape of the *Serpent* as it appeared. It helped distract her from the pain in her ribs and her shortness of breath.

"Cap'n! Sail!" the lookout cried.

Beauchamp paced the deck, flummoxed by this turn of events. "Jettison the cargo!" he ordered. The crew rushed to throw what wasn't necessary over the side of the ship to increase their speed. Josephine feared that it would give the *Siren* the advantage in the race across the water.

Beauchamp then pointed to her. "Billy! Pour the oil!"

The large mute pirate named Billy grabbed an unlit oil lamp and approached Josephine. He poured the oil in a large circle around her and the foremast. Then he stared at her with a dark toothy grin before he walked away. She looked down at the circle of oil around her and then up at Beauchamp. The madman must plan to burn her alive if he thought he couldn't outrun the *Serpent*. She struggled even harder against the ropes, but she'd been bound too tight to even move. Her hands already felt numb.

"Run out the guns!" The cry was relayed across the deck, and sailors rushed to prepare the guns.

The pirates on the *Siren* scrambled across the decks and up the rigging to unfurl the sails, but it was no use. The weather had suddenly turned against Beauchamp. Despite the pain she was in, Josephine managed a smile. It was as she'd always believed: the sea and the wind were female, and they wanted revenge.

The *Sea Serpent* now chased them across the open water. Josephine knew that Brianna would be at the helm. The ship was barely even touching the water as it flew toward them like a peregrine falcon diving toward its prey. Even though her life was in terrible danger, Josephine cheered on the *Serpent*.

When the other ship caught up with them, the deck of the *Siren* filled with pirates ready for a fight. A gunner shouted commands to ready the guns in response to the other ship. Josephine stared in horror at the black barrels of the *Serpent*'s guns, which were now aimed at the *Siren* . . . and her.

The *Siren* unleashed a salvo of fire at the same moment as the *Serpent*. Grapeshot ammunition tore through the bodies of men at the stern, far away from her on the fore-mast. Screams mixed with shouts as the gunner ordered the next round readied. Josephine tried to see through the thick smoke to the other ship. Was Gavin there? Had he made it back to the ship before the *Serpent* gave chase?

The ships were close now, *too* close, in fact. With a

chilling rush, Josephine watched as the *Serpent* crashed into the *Siren*. Both vessels groaned on impact, though neither hull broke. Through the haze of smoke, she saw men swinging on ropes through the vaporous clouds and dropping onto the deck of the *Siren*. She shouted Gavin's name, hoping he could hear her.

"Leave none alive!" Beauchamp screamed, drawing his sword. Then she watched in terror as Beauchamp came toward her instead of joining the fray. He grabbed one of the lit oil lamps and smashed it at her feet. Josephine screamed as a circle of flames roared up around her, sealing her off behind a wall of heat.

GAVIN AND GRIFFIN LANDED SIDE BY SIDE ON THE DECK of the *Siren*, along with the rest of the boarding party. The brothers had pistols and swords at the ready. Griffin took in the blood and death that now surrounded them and gave Gavin a nod.

"You lead, I'll follow." It had been something they had done as boys. Gavin had always led in mock battles with the other children, and Griffin had always followed. Not because Gavin was more assertive or brash, but because his brother understood the value of support. Together, they had been unbeatable.

They moved with panther-like grace across the decks, slaughtering any who stood between them and Josephine.

When the smoke had cleared from the cannon fire, Gavin had glimpsed her figure tied to the foremast.

"Find Josephine! I'll guard your back," Griffin told Gavin as he faced the opposite direction, holding off a new wave of attackers.

Gavin spied Beauchamp just as the pirate stopped in front of Josephine. Too late, Gavin realized what the bastard intended to do as he smashed the burning oil lamp at Josephine's feet. A circle of flames wrapped around her, and he heard her scream his name. Gavin let out a howl of rage.

He charged across the deck, pistols raised as he fired at his enemy. The shot missed Beauchamp's head by an inch and buried itself in the wood. Beauchamp raced up the companionway to a higher deck, laughing madly as he went.

"Choose, Castleton! Your woman or me!" Then he vanished behind a wall of battling pirates and sailors from the *Serpent*.

"Go!" Griffin said, rushing for the fire. "I'll get her!"

Just as when they were kids, the twins were of one mind. Gavin was the sword, Griffin the shield. One brother could destroy the threat, the other could protect. They knew who was best suited to deal with Beauchamp, and that meant Griffin could focus on Josephine. Gavin hated to leave Josephine, it cut him deep, but only he could protect her by destroying the threat to her. Gavin chased the pirate up the steps, drawing his sword as he tossed aside his useless pistol.

"Face me, you bloody coward!" he challenged as Beauchamp ducked behind a massive pirate who wielded a pair of sabers. Gavin recognized the man, Billy, yet another sailor he'd taken onto his crew at Beauchamp's recommendation. With Billy in the way, Gavin couldn't reach his target. Beauchamp escaped.

Billy made a deep huffing sound and lunged for Gavin. Gavin threw up his sword, deflecting Billy's attack. He ducked as a blade swung over his head and dropped to one knee, spotting his opening to strike. He thrust up, sending his sword deep into Billy's chest.

Billy grunted, staggered, his fingers fumbling to grip the hilt of Gavin's sword as he tried to pull it out. Blood bubbled up around his mouth as his hands dropped from the handle. Gavin scrambled back as the big man fell, shaking the deck with his impact.

Gavin frantically searched for another weapon and found one of Billy's sabers abandoned on the deck. When he got to his feet he glanced toward the foremast, only to find it empty. There was no sign of Josephine. Where was she? Where was Griffin? He had to fight his way across the deck for a few minutes, killing any man that got in his path. Each second he had a chance, he searched for Josephine and Griffin.

There! Griffin had his back to the railing, but he was trapped, Josephine hanging limply in his arms.

Beauchamp had gotten around him in all the confusion and now had a pistol aimed at Griffin's chest, a triumphant sneer on his face.

No! Gavin vaulted over the railing of the upper deck and sprinted for the bow of the ship.

Griffin turned his back, shielding Josephine with his body. A moment later, a shot rang out. Griffin stumbled, then fell forward with Josephine still in his arms. Neither moved as they collapsed to the deck.

The roar that escaped Gavin's mouth shook the entire ship. Beauchamp spun, his eyes wide as Gavin came down on him like a dark avenging angel.

"No . . . I killed you!" Beauchamp shouted, glancing back at Griffin's body, clearing confused.

"You cannot kill a man already dead!" Gavin slashed through a pirate standing in his way as he fought to reach Beauchamp.

None of the crew except for Ronnie knew he had a brother. In the heat of battle, he and Griffin must have looked completely identical to Beauchamp.

Beauchamp and Gavin met in a clash of steel, their blades singing a hymn of death as the pair dueled. Beauchamp was a strong and talented swordsman, but Gavin would not lose this fight. This man had taken everything from him, his woman, his brother, his home, his ship. And the price Beauchamp would pay would be his life.

Gavin leapt back as Beauchamp swung his sword low, aiming to slash Gavin's legs. He landed nimbly and thrust his blade, nipping Beauchamp's arm, but his foe escaped the deeper wound meant for him.

The two crews fought for their lives, but Gavin saw only one man, only one heart that needed to stop beating forever. He was tired of life taking away those he loved. Beauchamp pulled a pistol off a dead man and fired. The bullet ripped through Gavin's shoulder. He stumbled and grunted as the pain hit him like a falling mast. He caught hold of a nearby railing and forced himself to keep moving.

"You won't be able to do that again," Gavin warned as he advanced.

"One shot was all I needed," the bastard hissed, raising his sword. Gavin had but one instant to strike before he would lose his strength.

The ship grew eerily quiet. Beauchamp looked around and saw that most of his crew had fallen, and more and more eyes were turning toward him. Toward Gavin. Clearly recognizing this as his last stand, Beauchamp grinned, eager for this last moment of glory. Beauchamp launched himself at Gavin just as Gavin lunged forward. They collided, and Gavin sank his blade into the man's stomach, Beauchamp's blade only grazing him. A gunshot echoed across the deck like the crack of a whip. Beauchamp's eyes widened. They both fell to the deck, lying side by side as Gavin stared at the blood spreading around a bullet wound in Beauchamp's chest down to the blood spilling around Gavin's sword. The pirate's eyes were empty of life.

Confused, Gavin lifted his head and looked around.

Lord Camden stood just beyond them, half silhouetted by smoke and sunlight as he held a pistol aloft.

"No one hurts my child," Camden said in a voice that could freeze water.

Gavin groaned as his body surrendered to the pain in his shoulder and he collapsed on the deck, breathing hard. Camden approached and held out a hand to him and lifted him back onto his feet.

"Josie? My brother?"

Josephine's father didn't answer, but slung Gavin's good arm over his shoulder and helped him walk down the deck.

Gavin's eyes sought out the two still figures lying upon the deck. *No . . . Surely they couldn't be . . .*

The two people he loved most in this world weren't moving. This ship had cost him everything. He stumbled down the steps and ran toward the crowd gathering around their bodies. Griffin lay half sprawled over Josephine.

He had *shielded* Josephine with his body. Gavin had always been the sword and Griffin the shield. But it was the shield that had saved the woman Gavin loved, not the sword.

He fell to his knees next to them. Brianna was there, blood splattered across her chest, though none of it was her own. She held Josephine's hand and was leaning over her, checking her breathing. Josephine's face was covered with soot, but she looked as though she were sleeping.

"She's alive, Gavin, but I believe she's taken in too much smoke." Brianna's hand moved to Josephine's throat, checking her pulse. Her chest rose and fell evenly. Gavin fought to breathe through the fear that suddenly seized him as he turned toward his twin.

"Griffin . . ." He turned his brother over, seeing the spot where a bullet had passed through his abdomen. His brother was alive, but his breathing was shallow.

"Gavin . . . ," his brother whispered, his eyes fogged with pain. Griffin tried to raise a hand. Gavin grasped it and held it as he brushed the hair away from his brother's eyes. In that moment, he had a strange feeling that he was watching himself die as he gazed at his twin's face. Their pain had always been shared, just like their joy. Would they share the feeling of death?

"Owed you . . . a *life* . . . brother . . . ," Griffin rasped, then his eyes rolled back in his head and he passed out.

"Help him! Someone, *please*!" Gavin's voice broke in agony. A thousand images of them as boys flashed across his mind, and the gaping emptiness left by their years spent apart tore him open. He'd been such a damned fool to run away. *A coward.* If he'd stayed, everything would have been different. Everything . . .

"Someone help me move him back to the ship," Brianna said, and several men helped lift Griffin and carried him toward the *Serpent*.

"The *Siren* is sinking. We need to move, lad." Camden put a hand on Gavin's uninjured shoulder.

His ship was lost. The thing he had so foolishly believed was worth fighting and dying for was soon to be swallowed up by the sea. He couldn't even feel pain now. He could only feel emptiness. He could not mourn the *Siren* as the blue waters of the West Indies took her. He got to his feet as Camden lifted Josephine in his arms.

"Let me take her." He reached for Josephine but Camden hesitated in giving her to him.

"You're wounded, lad. You've lost a lot of blood. I will carry my child. We'll see to your arm, and then you may sit with her," Camden said. His tone was firm but gentle, and Gavin felt too bloody tired to argue with him. He wanted to hold her for a moment but Camden was right, he couldn't carry her to the other ship.

Camden navigated the gangplank between the two ships, and Gavin followed behind him. When he reached the *Sea Serpent*, Dominic took Josephine from his father.

"Let's get her settled below to rest," Dominic said.

"Then you need someone to look at your shoulder." His tone was surprisingly gentle for such a fierce pirate.

Because my brother is dying . . .

A great and terrible hollowness filled him like a black night sky devoid of stars. Blood dripped down his arm and he stumbled when he tried to descend the companionway as he followed Dominic.

"Here, lad." Camden helped him the way a father would an injured child. "This way . . . Easy now . . ."

The pain and the loss had numbed his whole body as he struggled to walk toward the surgery. If he lost his brother or Josephine, it would surely kill him.

CHAPTER 17

Josephine felt like she was underwater, a dark and terrible weight pressing down on her from all sides. She fought to breathe, and the first thing that she became aware of was the warmth of a hand holding hers. The grip on her hand tightened as she struggled to open her eyes. She craved to see only one person, but the man watching her wasn't him.

"Where's Gavin?" Her voice was a bare rasp. Each word scraped against her throat.

Her father stroked her hair back from her face, his eyes soft. "He's with his brother."

"Brother?" Griffin . . . Griffin was here. Her father was here. But how? At first, it all tumbled about in her head before she finally remembered . . .

Griffin cutting her free of the foremast while she was barely alive. Smoke and heat had nearly overwhelmed her. Then, as they had escaped the fire, she had seen Beauchamp charge them. She saw a pistol raised and the flare of a spark as Griffin turned. Then . . . nothing.

"Is Griffin . . . ?" Her lips trembled. She couldn't finish her question.

Camden looked away. "He's nearly gone, my child. It won't be long now."

The pain of those words pierced deep and tore at her heart so deeply it felt like she was dying. Griffin had given his life to save her. Gavin had lost his twin because of her. What if she had lost Adrian because of something Gavin had done? Would she have been able to forgive him?

"Can I see him?" she asked her father.

"I suppose, if you feel you can walk. You inhaled a lot of smoke, and the doctor believes you should rest."

Her father helped her to sit up. She sat for a moment, getting her bearings in the small cabin. She still felt short of breath, and it hurt to breathe.

"What about everyone else?"

"There were some losses among the crew, but not as many as we'd feared. Your brother, Brianna, and Nicholas are fine. There were a few minor injuries here and there. Gavin took a bullet to the shoulder, but the surgeon says it will heal with time." Her father reached out to touch her arm, but she flinched.

"What happened to you, my child?" he asked.

"I was trying to save Sam. And . . ." The moment came flooding back to her. "Oh my God, Sam!"

"The young boy? He is all right." His reassurance lifted a great weight off of her.

"Tell me Beauchamp and his men are dead." She needed to hear the words.

Her father met her gaze as she stood. "He is. I shot him

myself. His crew are dead, save for a handful who surrendered. The *Siren* is at the bottom of the sea."

The weight returned to press against her chest. Gavin had lost his ship and his brother because of her. Perhaps that was truly unforgivable.

Her father escorted her to another cabin and knocked softly on the door. When no one answered, he tried the handle and the door opened. Griffin lay still upon the bed, his chest slowly rising and falling. Gavin sat on a chair beside him, his hand clasped around Griffin's bare arm. Griffin had been stripped to the waist and his abdomen bandaged with strips of cloth.

"Thank you, Papa. I'll be all right." She embraced her father and then joined Gavin at his brother's bedside.

His vigil was so deep that he was unaware of her approach. When she moved one of the chairs to sit by him, it scraped on the deck. He jerked and turned to her, his eyes full of tears.

She parted her lips, but no words came. She wasn't sure if any words were right for a moment like this. She placed the chair beside him, and for a moment he simply stared at her. She reached out and put her arm around his shoulders. He started to shake and his head bowed. His hair fell to shield his face as he pressed his fingers to his eyes and wept.

Josephine held on to him, a lifeline in the storm, and said nothing at all. Her touch would say what words could not.

Time passed, and eventually Gavin stopped shaking. His grief softened into lighter, uneven breaths as he tried to calm himself. They both watched Griffin's pale face as he slept. Then, without warning, Griffin's lips parted and a whisper escaped.

"Vesper." The name drifted in the airy silence.

"Vesper?" Josephine said aloud and reached for Griffin's hand. Had she misheard him?

Griffin's muscles tensed slightly. "Vesper," he said again. "Tell her . . ."

Gavin glanced between her and his brother, seeming confused. "That's your maid, isn't it? She was on the ship with Griffin and the others."

Josephine's eyes began to water. "She came? But Vesper is afraid of water." Did her maid, her *friend*, love her so much that she had crossed an entire ocean to find her? She would have spent more than a month with Griffin on the same ship. Perhaps they had spent time together talking and . . .

"Tell her . . . ," Gavin said softly. "Tell her what?"

Suddenly, she understood. "He *loves* her," she whispered. "He loves Vesper."

It made sense. Vesper was quiet, generous, and kind. She was very much like Griffin in temperament, just as Josephine was more like Gavin.

Josephine had a sudden burst of hope. "Is she on the ship?"

Gavin shook his head. "No. Vesper and the rest of your family are on the Isle of Song. We left them there with the *Pixie* and some of the crew, should the need arise to escape."

Josephine gently grasped Griffin's hand. "Griffin, Vesper is close. You must hold on for her."

Griffin's lashes fluttered and Vesper's name escaped his lips again, but he did not fully wake.

"We cannot give up." She rested her head against Gavin's shoulder. It was so clear to her that life was a tapestry of a thousand strands woven together. Had this been their fate all along? To end up here, fighting to keep Griffin alive?

Gavin drew in a breath. "You're right. He wouldn't give up on me. I cannot give up on him."

"How far are we from the Isle of Song?" she asked.

"With good winds? Two days."

Two days. If they got him to Vesper, it might give him the strength to fight, to stay here with the woman he adored. Her father would argue that love had little to do with the healing of a physical wound, but Josephine believed deeply in the power of love. After everything she and Gavin had been through, she believed in love above everything else.

Gavin set his brother's arm down gently, then cupped Josephine's face. She knew she looked dreadful. Her face still hurt from the blows she had taken, her hair was a tangled mess, and she ached all over. She was no pirate's pretty prize now.

His brown eyes warmed as he seemed to drink in the sight of her. "You are the *most* beautiful thing I've ever seen." He lowered his head, and their lips met in a soft kiss that seemed to go on for hours.

"I must look absolutely frightful, and I feel even worse," she said, but he had relit a glow within her that Beauchamp had nearly extinguished. Gavin's words and that single kiss full of all the love that existed between them, a kiss that held a thousand beautiful unsaid words within it, had brought her back to life.

"I'm sorry I wasn't there when you woke," he said. "I couldn't bear to leave him. I . . ."

She pressed her fingers to his lips.

"This is where you should be. And it is where *I* should be as well. Right now, he needs both of us."

They kept their vigil at Griffin's bedside, and Josephine sent a prayer upon the sea breeze. She prayed for the sea to carry them swiftly and for the wind to fill their sails so they could reach the Isle of Song as quickly as possible.

Save him . . . save him.

TWO DAYS LATER

Vesper was keeping herself busy, helping another woman cook in one of the small island homes, when a cry sounded through the village. A sail had been sighted. Hope flaring within her, Vesper hung her apron up on a hook before following the villagers to the shoreline.

There was a mix of hope and fear among everyone. Hope that it was Gavin and the others returning, fear that it was Beauchamp coming to finish what he'd started. But it seemed the ship had been recognized as the *Sea Serpent*, because the islanders soon started to wave and cheer.

She smiled as she saw a small boat lowered, rolling toward shore. Josephine was at the bow. Vesper rushed into the shallows, uncaring that her gown got wet. All that mattered was that Josephine was alive. Josephine hiked up her skirts and jumped down into the surf and threw her arms around Vesper in a tight embrace.

"My lady, you're all right!"

"I am. I can't believe you came all the way here for me," Josephine said.

"I'd do anything for you, my lady. Anything."

"And I'd do anything for *you*, Vesper." Josephine seemed to be on the verge of tears. Vesper could only imagine the ordeal she had been through to get here.

Vesper turned to the rest of the boat's passengers, searching for the face she longed to see most aside from Josephine's. Griffin was not among the passengers in the first landing party. She smiled a little. Knowing him, he would have let the others come to shore first .Lord Camden, Dominic, and a little boy leapt out, along with a tall, rather attractive dark-haired man with brown eyes who watched over the child with a fatherly protectiveness that Vesper didn't miss. His uniform, while faded, was clearly a naval uniform. It was not, however, a new uniform. Working as a lady's maid the last few years, she'd become adept at recognizing old clothes that someone was doing their best to keep well mended.

Jada, one of the women from the island, rushed over to the little boy, the one who had been kidnapped along with Josephine. Jada shouted his name, and the little boy threw himself against his mother, hugging her around the waist. The dark-haired man followed closely behind, keeping an eye on the boy. Sam pointed at the man and chattered excitedly about how this man who apparently was a vicar, had saved him.

"My name is Jada." She held out her hand to the man, who gently took it and kissed her fingers with respect.

"Henry Sheridan," he replied.

"I cannot thank you enough, Mr. Sheridan."

"Please, it's just Henry." Sheridan's face turned a little red as he stared at Jada's beautiful face.

Vesper tore her eyes away from the lovely scene. It only made her think more about who she wanted to be with right now.

"Where's Grif—Lord Castleton?" she asked Josephine. "Was he needed on the ship?"

The concern on Josephine's face now grew to a deep agony. "Griffin is . . ." Her friend apparently couldn't bring herself to say the words.

"No . . ." Griffin couldn't be dead. *He couldn't.* It wasn't right. He was the one person who had seen the *real* her. The one person she'd dared to believe truly loved her.

Josephine gripped her shoulders. "Breathe, Vesper."

Vesper struggled to draw air into her lungs, and her legs became unsteady.

"He's alive, but he needs you. Please, come with me." Josephine grasped her hand, and they waded back into the shallows. Lord Camden helped Vesper and Josephine aboard the longboat and then the sailors rowed them back to the ship.

Once the sailors helped Vesper and Josephine on board, they bowed their heads respectfully to Vesper. The pit in her stomach deepened. It was clear they did not expect Griffin to survive.

"He's this way." Josephine led her to one of the cabins below.

She found Griffin lying on a bed, his chest bandaged. A man sat beside him, one hand on Griffin's arm. The man in the chair turned at their approach, and Vesper gasped. He looked so like Griffin that for a moment she nearly ran to him.

Josephine introduced them. "Vesper, this is Gavin. Griffin's brother."

"He's been asking for you," Gavin said, his voice thick with emotion. He got up and stepped back to allow her to sit next to her love.

"He has?"

"Yes," Josephine said. "I'd hoped . . . I know it sounds foolish, but I hoped that if he heard your voice and felt your touch . . ."

Vesper's eyes blurred with tears, and she took Griffin's hand and pressed it to her cheek.

"I'm here, Griffin. *I'm here.*" Her voice trembled as she spoke. "You promised me that we would be together. Do you remember? You cannot break that promise. I won't let you." She pressed her lips into his palm in a kiss and closed her eyes as she focused on him hearing her. "*Please* fight for me."

"Vesper . . ." Griffin's lips shaped her name, and a sliver of hope sprang free in her chest.

"Yes. I'm here. Come back to me."

GRIFFIN HAD NEVER UNDERSTOOD THE SEA, OR THE WAY it called to some souls and not others. He had always loved the solid earth beneath his feet. But now he was drifting, rocking in an endless dark sea he couldn't escape. The ocean called for him to *let go* and sink beneath the surface into gentle nothingness. Surrendering would be easy.

Yet each time he tried to let go, something kept his head above the water. *Green eyes, soft honey-blonde hair, a warm laugh, an even warmer heart* . . . These images and sensations teased him, haunted him, made him unable to relinquish himself to the sea. The siren's call of the water began to fade as a voice on the wind whispered to him.

"Come back to me, Griffin . . ."

An island appeared in the distance. The horizon behind it was bathed in a brilliant golden glow. But every stroke in the water hurt, every inch he swam more agonizing than the last. Yet the harder it became, the more he wanted to *feel* that pain instead of escaping it.

"Fight for me . . ."

He was so bloody tired, but he couldn't give up. Not with that voice begging him to fight. The shore was closer now. So close. He was almost there...then it all faded away into nothing . . .

His eyes opened. Muted light filtered into the room where he lay. He blinked and licked his dry lips. A woman sat in a chair beside his bed, her body bent over the bed as she slept with one hand lightly wrapped around his. The visions of the ocean and island faded, and he began to remember the battle on the *Siren*.

He had taken a bullet to the back to protect Josephine. The evidence of that wound was found in the weight of the bandages wrapped around his chest. The woman beside him was not Josephine, but Vesper. *Vesper*. The sight of her there at his side filled him with a joy that, for a moment, robbed him of his speech.

Finally, he spoke her name and she stirred. When she lifted her head, her green eyes were wide with hope and love.

"Griffin?"

He smiled wearily. "I came back." It was all he could say in the moment, but she seemed to understand what he meant. Those three words echoed as strongly as the three words he should have said instead. *"I love you."*

She wiped away tears and smiled at him. "You're free."

"Free?" he asked.

She nodded. "Josephine and your brother wish to marry. That means you are free."

Wonders would not cease today, he thought, and a flood of joy surged like a wave through his chest.

"How long have I been . . . here?" he asked.

"It's been two weeks," she said. "We couldn't bring you ashore, not in your condition. I've been feeding you soup and water."

She had? He hadn't even been aware of that.

A knock at the door interrupted them, and Gavin stepped through the open doorway.

"I thought I heard voices," his brother said, his face etched with lines of worry.

"I will let you talk." Vesper stood, pressed a kiss to Griffin's lips, and slipped from the room.

Gavin sat down beside the bed after she left, and for a

long moment the two of them were silent. Finally, his brother spoke.

"You *saved* her."

There was only one "her" Gavin could mean. The ship, the sea, they no longer held Gavin's heart the same way. It was a woman he loved most now.

"Of course I did," Griffin replied. He ached for a glass of water, but there were things that needed to be said between them first.

"When we arrived on that island and saw your home burning and Josephine gone, I knew there was only one way I could help you. I would do *anything* for you, Gavin. We're *brothers*." He said this with such pride and joy that it felt like it had been before Charity had come into their lives. Before he had broken his brother's heart by loving the same woman.

"When Beauchamp raised that pistol, I knew there was really only one choice I could make. Josephine is the very heart beating inside you. I couldn't let you be robbed of love a second time."

Gavin's eyes grew bright and he blinked rapidly. "She's my every dream."

Griffin smiled. Despite the pain in his body, he felt *gloriously* alive.

"You renounce your claim on her, then?" Gavin asked. "And you'll tear up that bloody marriage contract?"

Griffin wished he had the strength to laugh. "I had already decided to break off the engagement, so long as Josephine didn't wish to marry me. I spoke to Camden about it before we found your island. He agreed, on one condition."

Gavin frowned at the word. "What *condition*?"

"Haven't a clue. All he said was that he would need to talk to you about it."

Gavin settled back against his chair, but Griffin could tell his brother was thinking deeply.

"Will you be here . . . for the wedding? Will you stand up with me?" Gavin asked, his voice soft and almost shy.

Griffin lifted his hand from the bed and Gavin clasped it in his own.

"There's no place I'd rather be than at your side."

Gavin opened his mouth, then closed it again and smiled instead. After a long moment, he stood and called for Vesper. She came back in and rushed to Griffin's side. She gave no extra look toward Gavin as they passed each other. That was when Griffin knew with certainty that whatever had gone wrong before when the stars guided their fate seven years ago had now been repaired.

Vesper was his and his alone while Josephine had always been meant for his brother. Griffin sighed and closed his eyes. For a brief moment, he swore he saw a woman in a silvery gown standing in the doorway, smiling sadly at him before she vanished into a stray beam of sunlight. That couldn't have been Charity . . . she was gone. He was simply imagining things. Vesper closed her hand around his, kissing the backs of his knuckles, and he smiled at her.

"We are free," he said.

Her lips warmed him with a promise of a lifetime of joy. "Yes, we are."

UP ON DECK, GAVIN SAW JOSEPHINE SPEAKING TO HER father as the two faced the open sea. When she noticed him, she broke away from Lord Camden and rushed over, and he clasped her to him tightly. He couldn't seem to hold her long enough or kiss her long enough. Losing her once had made him afraid to ever miss a single moment with her again. Of course, having Lord Camden watching over Josephine had kept Gavin on his best behavior. There was nothing like seeing Josephine's father shoot a pirate in the back for hurting his child. One could only imagine what he'd do to Gavin. He hadn't been allowed to sleep in the same cabin with her, and he'd missed the comfort of her lying beside him every night.

"Is everything all right?"

"Yes," he promised. "Griffin woke up. His fever finally broke. The doctor says otherwise, but I believe it was Vesper's love that brought him back, just as you said it would. It's a damned miracle."

The surgeon believed that no organs had been pierced by the bullet. Nevertheless, the bullet had done much damage to his muscles. They had stitched up his wounds and prayed for the best. It would still take a long time for him to heal.

"Josie. He's agreed to break the marriage contract."

She glanced across the deck at her father. "I suspected that he might."

Gavin cleared his throat. "Then you will marry me?"

She looked up at him, a sudden light in her eyes. "Well, you did go to all the trouble of fetching a vicar and rescuing me. I rather suppose I must."

He knew she was teasing, but he still felt a flutter of nerves inside him.

He cupped her face in his hands. "My whole life I've been drifting at sea, chasing the horizon and letting the wind push me farther and farther away from shore. It wasn't until I met you that I realized how lost I was and how much I wanted to come home." His breath caught as he suddenly found it hard to speak. "*You* are my home."

Love transformed her face with a look of awe, and he wondered what she saw in him at that moment. He was a pirate, a man scarred inside and out. She reached up and her fingers curled around his wrists.

"Marry me," she whispered. "Marry me, marry me." It was an echo of their vows on the Isle of Song.

"I will marry you today. I will marry you tomorrow. I will marry you every day for the rest of our lives."

She stood up on her toes and pressed her lips to his. He closed his eyes, feeling the wind rise up around them just as it rippled through the canvas of the sails. But this time the breeze would not push him away. He was *here*, anchored by his love for her. Griffin had been right.

As Josephine kissed him, he felt the pure strength of her love like bright summer morning sunlight after a dark storm had ravaged the night. She'd found him in the midst of a storm, hadn't she? That night long ago when he'd fallen into her arms and she had brought the dawn.

Their mouths broke apart, and he was breathing fast with excitement.

"A man like me doesn't deserve to be this happy," he confessed as he smoothed his thumbs over her cheeks and nuzzled her nose.

"Well, you do still have to speak to my father," she replied with a little laugh, and he kissed her again.

"Bloody hell, I do, don't I? It would be far easier if we simply ran off to Sugar Cove and let the vicar marry us there." He groaned. "Stay here." He crossed the deck to where Lord Camden still stood. The man had one hand on the railing and was watching the water ripple with light.

"Lord Camden . . ." He honestly had no idea how to begin this conversation. "I apologize for taking your daughter the way that I did, but I won't apologize for wanting to claim her."

Camden smiled sadly. "You're wrong, my boy. She claimed *you*. That's the first lesson in marriage you have to learn. No man can own a woman. There are those who foolishly think they can treat women like butterflies trapped in a jar, but that jar in time will suffocate a wild, beautiful creature. Set a woman free and if she truly loves you, she will claim you as hers. Do you understand?"

"I believe I do," Gavin said.

He finally faced Gavin. "I have two sons, both of them fine, good men. I see myself in them. But my little Josie was always something *more*. Daughters are like that. You try to shield them from the evils of the world, to protect them. The hardest thing in life is to let them go."

He looked once more out onto the water. "She was so small and perfect when I first held her in my arms. I didn't think it was possible to love something so new to this world in an instant, but I did. And I can't let her go to just *any* man." He tapped his fingers on the railing and then gripped the wood as he seemed to fight back a tide of emotions.

"She will marry you, regardless of what I say. But I want your word, Castleton. Give her the world, give her freedom, and give her yourself fully and completely. It's the only thing I can demand of you, but it's what matters most."

"She's the very beat within my heart," Gavin said, his throat tight. "She has me and all that I can give her for as long as life gives me breath. I promise you, she will always be free."

Camden slowly turned again and held out a hand. "Then we'd better find that bloody drunk vicar."

Gavin laughed as they shook hands. "The sooner the better."

CHAPTER 18

One month later

Birds sang all across the island as Josephine and Gavin made their wedding vows in front of her entire family, Brianna, Nicholas, Griffin, Vesper, Reverend Sheridan, and the islanders. She wore the pale-blue gown her mother had intended for her wedding to Griffin. The last time she'd worn this dress, she'd been another woman in another life. She was glad that it hadn't been ruined when Gavin had taken her from Cornwall.

And much like herself, the dress had changed since then. Now, the ice-blue gown that was festooned with pearls, billowed around her in the sea breeze and made her feel like Venus walking out of the sea.

How far she'd come since that night Gavin had snuck into her bedchamber and whisked her away. That life, that path not taken, that had been the dream. This was her reality.

"All dreamers must wake up sooner or later . . . But what if we wake to something even better than this?"

She'd been so afraid to believe him when he'd said that, but Gavin had been right all along.

This certainly was better than anything she could have dreamed. Everyone she loved was here on this little island, and she was moving toward a future of her own choosing. Not her family's, not society's, but hers.

Before she started down the aisle, her father leaned down and kissed her cheek.

"I could part with you to no one else." His words were choked with emotion, and his eyes brimmed with tears as she embraced him. Her father had always been a proud and stubborn man, but she'd never once doubted that he wanted her to be happy.

"I will always be your daughter, Papa. *Always*," she whispered.

He held her just a little bit tighter. "I don't know how your mother and I will get on without you." Then he let her go and stepped back. He wiped his eyes, and her mother came forward to take his arm and kissed his cheek. Josephine now turned to Gavin. To the future.

Griffin stood by Gavin's side, leaning on a cane for support. He flashed her a smile filled with brotherly affection. He and Vesper had married the day before, which had resulted in a number of the islanders requesting that the vicar marry them as well, even those who had been together for many years. By the end, Henry Sheridan was grousing that he had married half the island and had only been paid for one ceremony.

Josephine and Gavin had waited a full month to wed. They'd wanted Griffin to be well enough to stand for the ceremony. More important, Gavin had wanted to have a home to present to Josephine as an official wedding present.

In just thirty days, they had managed to start the rebuilding of the house that had been destroyed in the fire. With Dominic's blessing, Adrian had taken charge of the *Pixie*, with Ronnie acting as his first mate. They'd brought timber from the bigger islands and hired an architect from Port Royal at her father's insistence to have the building plans drawn up. The first floor of the home was rebuilt under a new design that featured a bedchamber for her and Gavin on the ground floor.

During those busy days of rebuilding, Josephine's family had settled into some of the empty cottages in the village that had been built in case Gavin brought anyone new to the island. It had been a mercy that Beauchamp's men had only burned Gavin's home, and not the village.

Everyone had worked together to rebuild the life that had been on this island and put the past behind them. Josephine had worked tirelessly to help Jada and the other women cook for the laborers before she fell into bed each night in exhaustion. Her father had insisted she sleep in her bed alone, even though he was well aware she was no longer a virgin. She missed Gavin lying beside her, but she knew the wait would be worth it.

Now the time had come for them to officially begin their lives together in this tiny paradise.

They repeated their vows in front of Henry Sheridan, their heads bowed as they were joined in matrimony. At the end, Gavin stole a kiss as the sun set on the horizon beyond them and the world fell into a twilight hush. Josephine curled her arms around his neck and held on as that kiss seemed to carry her away. It felt like they were flying across the water together at the bow of a ship, chasing the dying light. Kissing Gavin would always be like that, like sailing toward an endless glow, sailing into eternity. His warm mouth moved over hers, and she parted her lips so he could deepen the kiss.

"*Ahem*." The vicar cleared his throat. "Plenty of time for that later, when your father-in-law has had a bit more rum."

Blushing, Josephine broke away from Gavin. It was the first time she saw Gavin appear even a little bit bashful. Her father glared at Gavin for daring to have such an open display in front of their guests.

Gavin clasped Josephine's hands in his. "Sorry, vicar. Even a pirate gets carried away on his wedding day."

His strong grip made her feel safe and sure and reminded her how *completely* in love with him. If someone had tried to explain this feeling to her in England, she wouldn't have been able to imagine it. It was all-encompassing, to love someone with her whole heart. But rather than fear such an overwhelming thing, she felt only excitement and joy.

Yet it wasn't simply love for her husband that gave her wings to fly. It was a newfound love for herself, faults and all, and not feeling like she had to apologize for being who she was. She'd had moments where she failed, moments where she'd doubted herself, and yet she'd also proven that she was brave, that she was strong. Loving herself gave her the strength and courage to love someone like Gavin. It made this moment all the sweeter.

She wished she could go back in time and find the girl she had once been and tell her not to lose hope, that all she'd ever dreamed of would someday be within her reach if she stayed strong.

Gavin pulled her into his arms, holding her as the people gathered on the beach clapped and cheered. She couldn't imagine feeling happier than she did at this moment. More than one sailor whistled, and Gavin's body shook with delighted laughter.

"Come along, wife." Gavin led her back through the crowd. They first stopped by her mother, who held her in a long hug and then looked to Gavin.

"Welcome to our family," she said. Gavin's cheeks turned a ruddy shade.

Dominic and Roberta approached them next. Dominic held out a hand.

"I suppose it's all right to have another pirate in the family," Dominic said.

"We might have to amend that to 'retired' pirate," Gavin said with a glance at Josephine. "I was thinking, if you need another captain for your trade fleet, I would happily take a position, provided Josephine can come with me."

Dominic's smile was wide. "I think we can find a ship for you."

Roberta laughed as she embraced Josephine. The redhead who'd won over her older brother murmured in her ear, "It seems you finally have your very own pirate."

Josephine chuckled. "I do, don't I?"

Adrian and Gavin shook hands, he asked for a moment alone with his twin. He caught one of her hands in his, helping her down the sandy path to the shore until they were far enough away from the others to speak with some privacy. Adrian's face was filled with both joy and sorrow. He cleared his throat.

"It's going to be different, isn't it? When you were going to marry Griffin, it all felt as if nothing would change. You would be close by. But this is *different.* You love Gavin, don't you?"

She nodded. "Desperately."

"I can feel it." He touched his chest. "*Here.* Knowing how happy you are makes it easier to let you go."

She wiped away a tear on her cheek. "I am, but I will miss you." For so long, it'd been just the two of them against the world. But as with all things, time brought change, and this was one thing that they hadn't been ready for.

"You know," he said with a wry grin, "I kept my promise to you."

"What promise?"

"The one I made before you left. I said you would marry Castleton, sail the seas, and have the life you always dreamed of. I never said it would be Griffin. After all, Gavin is in fact the Earl of Castleton since he isn't dead and the title will revert back to him. I simply didn't say which Castleton you'd marry."

Josephine laughed at her brother's cleverness.

But her laughter died as a new realization made her pause. She hadn't once given a thought to the fact that she was married to the *older* of the Castleton brothers. Gavin had lived seven years without that part of his life and likely no longer thought of it either. Would they have to return to England to let him resume his life as the earl and handle the estate?

"What's wrong?" her brother asked.

"I'd actually managed to forget that he is the earl and not Griffin." She stared down at the white sand, her hopes fading so quickly.

Adrian lifted her chin. "Talk to him. I imagine he hasn't thought about it either. Perhaps there is a solution. His brother and Vesper will be returning to England. If it was me, I'd have Griffin handle all the immediate affairs of the estate, leaving you and Gavin here. No one said you had to live in England. He will be the earl wherever he lives. It's not uncommon for titled lords to let others help them with their land and property while they live elsewhere. I'm sure Gavin would much prefer that sort of arrangement."

"You are quite brilliant." She threw her arms around his neck, hugging him.

"I always was the smart one—*ow*!" He winced when she punched his shoulder. "Go back to your husband, feisty wench!"

They both burst into laughter.

When they walked back up the beach, Gavin was waiting for them. He held out his arms to Josephine, and she buried her face against his chest.

"Everything all right?" he asked in a soft voice.

"Of course. I was just speaking to my brother about... well the fact that you are now the Earl. Griffin assumed the title after your father passed and you were presumed dead. But now that can all change. I was afraid of what that means for us. Adrian suggested that you resume the title, but have Griffin remain at the house in Cornwall with Vesper and run the estate for you. That would leave you and I free to be here."

Gavin was silent a long moment. "I hadn't honestly thought of that. I've been a pirate so long, living this wild life that I hadn't given a thought to it. I believe your brother is right. Griffin and Vesper could stay at the house in England and you and I can remain here and we could visit once or twice a year to see how things are. I'm sure your brothers will also make journeys frequently. Is that a life you could be content with?"

"Content? No...blessed I believe is the word I would use," she said. "I will miss seeing my family as often as I was expecting, but this life...this place here with you and Jada and the others...it's the home I truly want."

"Good." He seemed to relax at her words. "Are you ready to retire for the night?"

"Yes." They quietly slipped away from the crowd and walked to their new home. Everything inside smelled new. The wood gleamed and the furnishings, while still sparse, would do well enough for now. They had a large bed in their shared bedchamber, and a gossamer-thin nightgown was laid out upon the blue coverlet.

Gavin chuckled as he lifted up the shimmering cloth, his hands visible through the fabric, which left very little to the imagination. "It's lovely, but you won't be needing it tonight."

She held still as he slowly unlaced her gown. She trembled as his fingers touched her skin, feeling so much like the first time they had been together. Soon she was bare, and his hands explored her body, cupping her breasts and her bottom, curving around her hips and shoulders until she could have melted into him. Then he turned her in his arms and kissed her. There was something wonderfully wicked about kissing a clothed pirate while she was completely naked.

"I can feel you smiling against my lips," he said with a chuckle. "What on earth are you thinking about?"

She curled her arms around his neck and nuzzled her nose along his jaw. "I was thinking of how wicked you made me, to enjoy moments like this."

"How wicked *I* made you? Darling, you were born wicked. I am quite glad because we can be wicked together." He moved his hand down to her bottom, then he slid his fingers between her thighs, teasing her until she wriggled in his arms. She so wanted him to be inside her, to make love to her.

"No more teasing." She tugged on the strands of his hair as she kissed his chin, followed by his mouth. "*Please*, Gavin. I need you."

"And I you. Lie back." She sat on the edge of the bed and then lay back, bending her knees up a little. He grasped her waist and pulled her toward him so that he could reach her easily. She liked how he handled her, not roughly, but with confidence and desire.

Gavin bent over her and his mouth began to worship her breasts with flicks of his tongue, then he sucked on the peaks until they were tender. His lips moved down to her belly, then to her mound, before he reached the most sensitive part of her. The part that ached for him. She was already close to coming apart as he worked his tongue along her wet folds, but he stopped just before she climaxed. Josephine whimpered a protest, but her frustration eased when she realized he'd only stopped so he could remove his clothes.

She raised her head up to admire the view of her naked husband as he returned. The man had muscles everywhere. Even his hands and feet were beautiful and strong. She wasn't a tiny creature, but seeing him like this made her feel petite and feminine. He climbed on the bed and crawled over her, caging her body with his. But he did not enter her yet—he simply kissed her, stroked her tongue with his, and made her feel loved.

"As a pirate, my mind was always focused on finding treasure or capturing the next great prize. I always thought I would find treasure as a pirate," he whispered as he finally entered her. She groaned and raised her hips, eagerly meeting him. The moment he was fully inside her, they both remained still, taking a moment to relish the connection. It was the closest she'd ever felt to anyone. He kissed her lips, then the tip of her nose and her forehead.

"Oh? And tell me . . . what was the greatest treasure you found?" Her voice became breathless as he raised his head. He moved inside her, gently at first, and then passion overtook them both as he made love to her with complete abandon. The pleasure tore through her like a tropical storm and only began to settle as she rolled him over to lie atop him, breathing hard. He brushed his fingers along her cheek, their gazes holding on to each other.

"I discovered something far better than silver or gold. I found *you*." The love in his eyes carried her worries away. They were sailing once more toward that bright, beautiful horizon, their ship coasting on the very clouds. She was the sea and Gavin the shore, always connected, never to be parted. Their love was as endless as the sands in the wake of moving tides.

And outside their window, the music of the birds of the Isle of Song carried across the waves and out to sea.

THREE WEEKS LATER

Adrian stood on the deck of the *Cornish Pixie*, hands gripping the spokes of the wheel at the helm. Above him in the twilight, the sails billowed out, catching the wind. The *Pixie* glided over the water, heading out to open sea, and leaving the Isle of Song behind her. He smiled as the sun began to rise over the ocean. Its rays bathed the brilliant blue water with splashes of gold.

"Nothing like it in the world, is there?" Ronnie asked as he came up to the wheel and stood beside Adrian.

"It's as close as one can come to flying," Adrian confessed.

He hadn't thought he could handle captaining a ship yet, but Dominic had trusted him to try. For the past couple of months, he and Ronnie had taken the *Pixie* between the Isle of Song and its neighboring islands for the supplies needed to rebuild Gavin and Josephine's home. Things had gone exceedingly well on the voyages, and his older brother had decided to officially make him captain of the *Pixie*. Adrian had felt bad for taking the ship that Gavin had sailed so well, but Dominic had assured him that there was another ship in his fleet sitting in Port Royal at the moment that would be delivered to the Isle of Song as a belated wedding present for Gavin and Josephine.

"Nervous about taking her out on more than just a quick supply run?" Ronnie asked.

Adrian was surprised at how perceptive his first mate could be. "A little."

Ronnie grinned. "Don't worry yourself. I'll teach you everything you need to know, laddie."

"Thank you." Adrian was surprised by the man's honesty. "Tell me, why didn't you ask to be captain instead? You have far more experience than I do."

Ronnie shrugged. "Not rightly sure. It just never called to me. I prefer to be a quartermaster. Er . . . first mate," he amended with a grin.

"Well, I'm damn glad to have you," Adrian admitted.

Adrian had raised his concerns with Dominic about being a suitable captain at his age, but Dominic had laughed. "I was a captain at your age. All you need is a proper first mate to teach you how to listen to your ship, read the water, and feel the wind." If that were true, Adrian felt he had been left in the best possible hands.

"Well, laddie, where are we off to?" Ronnie asked. "To taste the favors of those fine Spanish ladies in Cádiz? Or perhaps the Barbary Coast, where we can ride upon the backs of elephants?" Ronnie's eyes sparked with excitement. "What about the Spanish Main? We could hunt for treasure!"

"We're bound for the colonies. New York, to be exact," Adrian exclaimed with a laugh. "Dominic has rum and sugar to sell, and we've much to buy and bring back when we return."

"Where's your sense of adventure, laddie?" Ronnie jabbed Adrien playfully in the ribs. "You've pirating in your blood. Why not chase a bit of gold along the way, eh?"

Adrian pretended to give it a moment's thought. "Perhaps a *small* detour wouldn't harm anything, should an opportunity present itself."

His first mate clapped him on the shoulder. "There's my captain!" he said with pride. "To New York! And any adventure we find along the way!"

Ronnie bellowed orders to the crew as the wind changed slightly. Adrian held fast to the wheel, his eye upon the eastern horizon.

Adrian adjusted the wheel slightly as the crew worked the sails above him. Then, without quite meaning to, he started to sing an old sea ballad under his breath, one his father used to sing. The brilliant gold of the rising sun was such an exquisite, addictive color. Even the shape of it was like a Spanish doubloon.

At that moment, he understood why men like Dominic and Gavin had taken to the sea and chased gold.

Our names shall be blazed,
And spread in the sky.
Come all you brave boys,
Whose courage is bold.
Will you venture with me?
I'll glut you with gold . . .

EPILOGUE

1752 – Ten years later
Cádiz, Spain

The brothel was busy for the middle of the day. Sailors filled the common room and some even spilled out into the doorway into the bright sunshine. Ships had arrived earlier that morning bringing goods for trade which mean hundreds of sailors filled the port town looking for places to spend their coin. Alcohol and women were the two most sought after pleasures.

Normally, Adrian would not visit brothels, but he and Ronnie had passed by this one and saw the growing crowd. Torn between curiosity and worry for whatever was happening inside, they slipped through the crowds into the lamplit interior of the brothel. It was a large room full of couches and floor cushions which at the moment were empty of women who usually sat ready to entertain men for the right price.

Everyone's focus was drawn to a raised platform that would likely have the occasional dancer or singer. But there was no such dancer tonight. A grubby faced man in a fine waistcoat and trousers in rather gaudy colors, stood there speaking to the crowd. Adrian tensed as the words 'woman for sale' rippled through the ranks around him.

He stroked his jaw, glad for the short, well-trimmed beard that concealed many of his expressions, especially the frown he wore at the moment. He didn't like auctions like this at brothels. They made his stomach turn. In the last ten years since he'd taken command of his older brother's ship, the *Cornish Pixie*, he'd seen many things that left him feeling *helpless*. Women being sold in brothels filled him with rage.

"Easy, Adrian," Ronnie murmured from beside him. As always, his first mate could sense his tension, his need to intervene. "The brothel has a dozen guards watching for trouble. You remember what happened last time you tried to take a woman from a place like this—we barely made it out of port with the skin on our backs."

That was a memory Adrian could have done without. He'd tried to convince a woman to escape with him, but she'd been too afraid to leave and fought him. The guards had noticed the commotion and come after him and his men.

"I trust our men are nearly done loading the cargo?" Adrian asked, his voice tight.

"Aye, nearly done, cap'n." Ronnie crossed his arms and joined Adrian. Adrian recognized a dozen men in the crowd close by him. They were pirates. Men he'd crossed who'd tried to take their cargo on more than one voyage.

"What are they doing here, Ronnie? These bastards don't usually bother with *buying* women, they just pay for them here." Most pirates didn't want women onboard their ships, which made him fear what could be intended for whatever woman was about to be sold.

"It's because of her . . ." Ronnie pointed to a woman who stumbled as she took the few steps up to the wooden dais where the grubby man running the auction grabbed the rope that was tied around her throat..

Her long brown hair tumbled about her shoulders, loose and messy, and her ivory skin was marred with dirt. It wasn't unusual to see women being sold in brothels. Many pirate ships with less than honorable captains would attack private and merchant vessels and kidnap passengers, especially women. They usually didn't keep the women on board long. They either used them and killed them or sold them in faraway places for usually very bad reasons to very bad people. Adrian briefly shut his eyes, his fists clenched.

The man running the auction grabbed the young woman by her hair and dragged her a few steps closer to the end of the platform. She wore a filthy rag of a dress that was ripped at one sleeve to expose a bare shoulder, and the dress didn't cover her past her knees. Her shins were scraped and her knees bloody. Adrian turned his focus to her face. The girl was watching him, her cornflower-blue eyes striking him like lightning.

The auctioneer began to call out in the lingua franca so that most men present could understand him.

"Fine English lady. Not touched. Good teeth, strong

and wide hips." He smacked the girl's bottom with a rough hand and the young woman cried out, making the men watching her laugh.

"Ronnie . . . ," Adrian whispered.

"Aye?"

"Ready the ship to leave the port at once. Be ready to weigh anchor the moment I'm on deck."

His first mate cursed. "Ach, lad, what the devil do you mean to do?"

"I mean to intervene." Adrian rolled up his sleeves, his blood starting to pound.

A hand suddenly grabbed his shoulder, halting him when he would have charged forward.

"Think with your head, man. Don't start a fight."

"I can't stand here and let her be sold to someone that will use her and likely kill her."

His first mate met his gaze. "You have to, lad. You can't save her. We can't save everyone." Ronnie's bright-blue eyes were shadowed.

"Ready the ship, Ronnie. *Now*," Adrian ordered.

"Be wise, lad," Ronnie warned, but he sighed when he seemed to realize Adrian wasn't leaving the brothel. "Fine. I'll ready the ship," his first mate muttered and turned away to head back to the docks.

Adrian knew attempting to free this woman could get him killed, but he had to try. Those blue eyes hadn't begged him to help her—they'd challenged him to set her free. He was a Greyville through and through and never backed down from danger when someone needed help.

. . .

Thank you for reading Devil of the High Seas, book 3 in the Pirates of King's Landing! If you haven't read the first two books be sure to read them!

Check out Dominic and Roberta's story HERE!

Check out Nicholas and Brianna's story HERE!

If you are excited to read Adrian's romance, be sure to sign up for my newsletter and follow me on social media at the link below so you will know when it releases!

Visit www.laurensmithhbooks.com

ABOUT THE AUTHOR

Lauren Smith is an Oklahoma attorney by day, author by night who pens adventurous and edgy romance stories by the light of her smart phone flashlight app. She knew she was destined to be a romance writer when she attempted to re-write the entire *Titanic* movie just to save Jack from drowning. Connecting with readers by writing emotionally moving, realistic and sexy romances no matter what time period is her passion. She's won multiple awards in several romance subgenres including: New England Reader's Choice Awards, Greater Detroit BookSeller's Best Awards, and a Semi-Finalist award for the Mary Wollstonecraft Shelley Award.

To connect with Lauren, visit her at:
www.laurensmithbooks.com
lauren@Laurensmithbooks.com

Made in the USA
Middletown, DE
13 November 2023

42542926R00191